PRAISE FOR *THE KING TIDES*

"James Swain's *The King Tides* is a hundred percent adrenaline rush disguised as a detective novel. Its hero, an ex-detective named Jon Lancaster, is as adept at using the latest digital sleuthing software as he is shooting a gun. The pacing is terrific, the dialogue memorable, and the characters, including a tough-as-nails female FBI agent and some truly frightening serial killers, jump off the page. You will read this book in one sitting. It's that good."

—Michael Connelly, #1 *New York Times* bestselling author

"Lancaster is a terrific new character and Swain's writing is better than ever—together they're smart, tough, suspenseful, and rewarding."

—Lee Child, #1 *New York Times* bestselling author

"*The King Tides* takes off like a rocket and doesn't ease up until an edge-of-your-seat finale. Swain is a pro at creating memorable characters, but the duo of Jon Lancaster and Special Agent Beth Daniels might be my favorite yet—tough and confident, but utterly fresh and modern. More please!"

—Alafair Burke, *New York Times* bestselling author

"*The King Tides* is crime fiction of the finest vintage—fast and furious, with memorable characters and skillful plotting. Jon Lancaster is a great protagonist, and Jim Swain is a terrific writer. Don't miss this one."

—Michael Koryta, *New York Times* bestselling author

"Jon Lancaster is a former Navy SEAL and a retired cop, who works rescues of abducted children and is a kick-ass private investigator. Tough as nails, Jon doesn't take no for an answer when searching for missing kids. As a private investigator he doesn't have to abide by the same rules of law enforcement officers, giving the perpetrators no rights. Author James Swain has created a protagonist who is real enough to be your next-door neighbor. I have read, and loved, many of Swain's books over the years, but I think *The King Tides* is his best work yet. The story is action-packed, tough, and believable. I hope the Jon Lancaster adventures will become a series."

—Cheryl Kravetz, Murder on the Beach Bookstore, Delray Beach, Florida

NO GOOD DEED

ALSO BY JAMES SWAIN

Jon Lancaster & Beth Daniels Series

The King Tides

Billy Cunningham Series

Take Down

Bad Action

Super Con

Jack Carpenter Series

Midnight Rambler

The Night Stalker

The Night Monster

The Program

Tony Valentine Series

Grift Sense

Funny Money

Sucker Bet

Loaded Dice

Mr. Lucky

Deadman's Poker

Deadman's Bluff

Wild Card

Jackpot

Peter Warlock Series

Dark Magic

Shadow People

NO GOOD DEED

A THRILLER

JAMES SWAIN

THOMAS & MERCER

This is a work of fiction. Names, characters, organizations, places, events, and incidents are either products of the author's imagination or are used fictitiously. Any resemblance to actual persons, living or dead, or actual events is purely coincidental.

Published by Thomas & Mercer, Seattle

www.apub.com

ISBN-13: 9781542040488
ISBN-10: 1542040485

Cover design by Shasti O'Leary Soudant

Printed in the United States of America

First edition

NO GOOD DEED

PROLOGUE

The screaming child went ignored by the people in the parking lot as they unloaded their shopping carts and turned a blind eye to the boy's cries. A horrible crime was taking place in front of them, and they chose to ignore it.

The twisted man had his routine down pat. Inside the store, he'd surreptitiously punched the child in the stomach and knocked the air out of him. Then he dragged his victim out the door by the arm, just the way a parent of a misbehaving toddler might do. When the child regained his voice and started to scream, the man scolded him in a calm voice.

"That's enough out of you! Now be quiet, or you won't get any dessert tonight."

The child kept screaming and kicking the ground. The man came to his vehicle, a '71 black-over-white Cadillac with a dented bumper, and dug out his keys. He popped the trunk and lifted the child off the ground by the back of his shirt.

"If you don't shut up, I'll throw you in," the man threatened.

The trunk's interior was lined with carpet. On it lay a collection of rusted tools, including a shovel and a machete. Seeing them, the child stopped crying.

"That's a good boy," the man said.

The child was fixated on the machete. He had seen landscape crews in his neighborhood use them to prune trees. They were dangerous, and they scared him. "Please don't hurt me," the child whispered.

The man laughed under his breath. He didn't mean for the child to hear him, the sound born out of the sickest of impulses.

But the child did hear him, and screamed even louder.

PART ONE

The Fourth Day

CHAPTER 1

The dead woman in the crime scene photograph had gone down swinging. Her mouth was bloody from biting her attacker, and her knuckles were raw from the blows she'd inflicted. She was at an age when most people *didn't* fight back, but that wasn't the case here. She had put up a hell of a battle, and had the wounds to show for it.

Her name was Elsie Tanner, and she was seventy years old. Her granddaughter, Skye Tanner, was now missing, a victim of ruthless kidnappers. Based upon evidence found at the crime scene, Elsie had tried to save Skye, and paid the price. She could have run, but had fought back instead. That made her aces in Jon Lancaster's book.

He slipped the photograph back into the string envelope and secured it, then climbed out of his vehicle. The American Legion hall was serving as command center for the search for Skye, and was his first stop.

The hall was as quiet as a tomb. On the first few days of a search, the victim's memory was still fresh, and the energy level was high. There would be frequent police updates, TV trucks parked at the victim's home, and volunteers plastering phone poles with posters. No stone was left unturned.

That changed after three days. By the end of the third day, the energy had faded, and most of the volunteers had gone home, leaving the victim's friends and family to fill the void. The ranks of the police thinned, with officers pulled away to handle new cases. The media moved on as well, needing a new story to keep viewers tuned in.

Most people stopped caring after three days. Lancaster was different that way. It was on the fourth day of a search that he started caring. As a cop, he'd learned that if a person wasn't found in three days, something terrible had usually happened to them. The missing person needed help, and he was willing to give it to them.

The hall was prefab, with a pitched aluminum roof and a concrete floor. A bar took up the right wall. On the opposing wall, two women sat beneath a giant American flag, answering the phones. With any search, it was standard procedure to set up a hotline where tips could be called in. The women's task was to field these calls and, if the information was important, get the caller's name and number and pass it on to the police.

He was being stared at. Behind the table stood a nicely attired redhead with a cell phone glued to her ear. He'd been around enough newspaper reporters to peg her as one. He ignored her, and approached the bar.

The bartender nodded politely. He had sad eyes and hadn't shaved. Lancaster introduced himself as an agent of Team Adam and ordered two coffees. He asked the bartender what the ladies liked in their coffee. The bartender placed two steaming mugs on the bar, then handed him two creamers and several sugar packets.

"My name's Russ," the bartender said. "It ain't none of my business, but what's Team Adam? Can't say I've ever heard of it."

"It's a special arm of the National Center for Missing and Exploited Children," he explained. "We assist in missing kid cases when law enforcement hits a wall."

"Well, the police sure need your help here. Sheriff's office can't get out of its own damn way. An outsider did this, anyone can see that."

It was common for fingers to be pointed at the police when searches stalled. He'd read the sheriff's report and thought they were doing a good job.

"Did you know either of the victims?" he asked.

"Elsie was my friend," Russ said.

"I'm sorry for your loss."

Russ pulled out a metal flask and took a swig. He was boiling mad, and the booze soothed his nerves. He offered Lancaster the flask, but he declined.

"Elsie was a fixture in these parts, always helping people out," Russ said. "My trailer burned down, and Elsie let me stay with her until I got back on my feet. She was into rescuing dogs, kept them at her place. They had to farm them out to families when she got murdered."

"What can you tell me about the granddaughter?"

"Skye's a good kid. She moved in with Elsie because of trouble at home. She was a server at G. Peppers and helped out when the lodge had parties. People liked her."

"You said that an outsider was responsible. Why?"

"You're not from around here, are you?"

"Fort Lauderdale, born and raised."

"Keystone's different. We have the lowest crime rate in the state, hasn't been a murder or a kidnapping that I can remember. People watch each other's backs."

"You lived here a long time?"

"My whole life."

Lancaster placed a Team Adam business card with his private cell number on the bar. "Call me if you hear anything."

"Be happy to. Coffee's on the house."

"Much obliged. Who's the looker on the cell phone?"

"Be careful. Her name's Lauren Gamble. She's a reporter with the local rag."

"Trouble?"

"With a capital *T*. Rumor is, she's trying to break a big story so she can get a job in another city."

"I thought Tampa was a nice place to live."

"It is, if you don't have stars in your eyes."

Lancaster crossed the hall and placed the steaming mugs on the table along with the condiments and his business card. The card had a catchy hotline—1-800-THE MISSING—that never failed to get people's attention.

Their names were Barbara Aderhold and Dawn Thrasher, and they'd been working the phones for twenty-four hours straight. Exhaustion was starting to creep in, their voices cracking. They echoed Russ's sentiments about Elsie and Skye being good people, and shared his view that an outsider was to blame.

"How are folks dealing with this?" he asked.

"People are staying inside and keeping their doors locked," Aderhold said. "They're convinced that what happened to Skye is linked to the other disappearances around the state."

"There's no proof of that," he said.

"You wouldn't have known it by the number of police that showed up," Thrasher said, sipping her coffee. "There must have been fifty cops at Elsie's place after it happened. It was like an invasion."

"The FBI's also gotten involved," Aderhold added. "Their agents hauled in a bunch of my friends, and interviewed them at the Marriott on State Road 54. I hear the agent running things is a real bitch."

The FBI played rough and mean and had no qualms about trampling on people while carrying out their jobs. He took a slip of paper that contained Elsie Tanner's address out of his wallet and showed it to the two women.

"Can you tell me how to find Elsie's place? I'd like to go have a look around. My GPS was worthless once I got into Keystone."

"Elsie lived down on Woodstock. The marker is impossible to see at night," Aderhold said. "You might want to wait until tomorrow."

There was rain in the forecast, and whatever remained of the crime scene would be washed away if he waited until tomorrow. He thanked the women for their time and walked out of the hall.

- - -

Standing in the parking lot, he wrestled with his next step. He needed to visit Elsie Tanner's place to get a feel for what had happened. Every year, a half million kids went missing. The good news was, nearly all came home, safe and sound. But a tiny fraction were never heard from again. Up to now, Skye was part of that fraction, and if he was going to have a chance of saving her, he needed to look at the crime scene tonight.

The warmest summer in the state's history had ushered in the coldest winter in fifty years, and he shivered while going to his car. A woman's voice stopped him.

"I can help you."

A yellow security light illuminated the gravel lot. Gamble had followed him outside, and wore an eager look on her face.

"Do you have information to share?" he asked.

"I don't know any more than you do," she said. "I'm a reporter—"

"I know who you are. Your name's Lauren Gamble, and you're with the local newspaper. The bartender filled me in."

"So he did. I can take you to Elsie Tanner's home, if you'd like. I've been there twice. You won't find it yourself, even in daylight."

"That's very kind of you. What do you want in return?"

Her pretty face registered surprise. "Who said I wanted anything?"

"If you didn't, you'd be home having dinner. Now what do you want?"

"I'd like to interview you for the story I'm writing."

"Why? I don't know any more than you do."

She held her cell phone by her waist. Her eyes darted down to the screen and then back at him. He hated when people glanced at their cell phones during conversations, and he stifled the urge to rip it out of her hand and give it a toss.

"Checking for messages?" he asked.

"I was looking at a story I found about you on Google," she said. "You helped catch a pair of serial killers a few months ago, among other things. You're famous."

"I don't want to be the focus of your story. This isn't about me."

"But people need to know that you're helping."

"What good would that do?"

"You heard what those women said. Everyone is scared. Not just in Keystone, but around the state. Ten women vanished before Skye Tanner, and the police don't have a clue who's behind it. It will put people at ease knowing that a famous cop was hired to help solve this."

He felt a raindrop on his head. He needed to see the crime scene before it was washed away. He electronically opened the doors to his vehicle.

"I'll drive," he said.

"Do we have a deal?" she asked.

"Yes, but only if you agree not to print anything prematurely."

"You're saying that I can't run my story until you give me an okay."

"Correct."

"I can't do that. My publisher has final say."

"Then I can't help you. Good night."

He got into his car. The best relationships were mutually beneficial. Gamble needed him for her story so she could punch her ticket out of here, and he needed her to be his navigator. But he could always find another navigator, and Gamble would have a hard time finding another investigator who'd be willing to talk with her. As he threw his car into reverse, she rapped her knuckles on his window. He lowered it.

"You win," she said. "I won't run the story until you give me permission."

"I want that in writing."

"Will a text do?"

He nodded, and Gamble came around the vehicle and took the passenger seat. He gave her his cell phone number, and she sent him a text, promising that her story wouldn't run until he'd agreed the time was right. He pulled out of the lot, and she told him to turn right on Gunn Highway, which was Keystone's main artery.

"What's with the snorkeling gear?" she asked.

A mesh bag containing a mask, snorkel, and flippers lay across the back seat. Beside it, a duffel bag was stuffed with clothes.

"I was planning a trip to Key West," he said.

"But you came here instead," she said.

He nodded, and she finished her thought.

"That must suck, having to ruin your vacation for work," she said.

She was reading the situation wrong, and he decided to set her straight.

"Just so you know, no one told me to come here," he said.

"Then why are you here?" she asked.

"I volunteered."

CHAPTER 2

While he drove, Gamble gave him the lay of the land. Unlike the rest of Tampa, which had been ravaged by development for fifty years, Keystone's residents had thwarted the bulldozers by showing up at every rezoning, arguing how they wished to keep their rural lifestyle. Sometimes they brought lawyers, but mostly it was residents wearing yellow T-shirts, loudly telling the county commissioners how they felt.

"Why yellow?" he asked.

"It made them stand out," she said. "From what I heard, the commissioners got tired of dealing with them, and decided to let the residents write the laws. That's why Keystone is still rural, while everything around it is ugly strip malls and cookie-cutter houses. Take a left at the next traffic light."

"Was Elsie Tanner part of the group?"

"She was one of the ringleaders. I saw a tape of her giving a speech at a rezoning. You did not want to cross that woman."

He took a left onto an unlit two-lane road lined by a canopy of imposing oaks.

"She must have pissed off plenty of developers," he said. "Could one of them be behind her murder, and Skye's abduction?"

"I doubt it," Gamble said. "Developers are a funny group. Once Keystone got its way, the developers moved in because they knew the property values would hold."

"If you can't beat them, join them."

"Something like that. Take the next right."

He made the turn and drove past a farm ringed by an eight-foot-tall chain-link fence. The creatures residing behind it didn't look like any breed of horses that he'd ever seen before, nor did they resemble goats or sheep.

"What are those animals?"

"Those are alpaca. They're part of a ranch that's open to the public."

"Why the tall fence? Are the owners afraid they'll jump out?"

"The fence keeps away predators. Alpaca can't protect themselves. It's amazing they've survived as a species. Your next turn's on the left. May I ask you a question?"

"Go ahead."

"The first four abductions took place in Miami. The fifth and sixth took place in Collier County, outside of Naples, the seventh in Fort Lauderdale. The eighth, ninth, and tenth took place in Central Florida—one in Winter Park, one in Kissimmee, and one in Lakeland. The tenth happened in Jacksonville, and now Skye gets abducted. Do you think the kidnapper is driving around, randomly picking his victims?"

He shook his head and took a sharp left.

"Why not?"

"The victims are being moved to a place that the police can't locate. That would indicate their abductions are premeditated, and not random acts."

"Do you think the victims are alive?"

"I do. We have a dozen missing women and not a single body. If our assailant wanted these ladies dead, he'd kill them on the spot, like he did with Elsie Tanner. But he's not doing that. He, or they, have an ulterior motive."

"You think it could be a gang?"

"I'm not ruling it out. The abductions have taken place several hundred miles apart. That would be difficult for a single person to pull off."

"What would their motivation be?"

"I have no earthly idea."

"Have you ever dealt with a case like this before?"

No two abduction cases were alike, and he let the silence be his answer.

"Could a demonic cult be behind the abductions?" she asked.

He hit the brakes. There wasn't another vehicle in sight, and he turned to face her, freezing Gamble in her seat. "That's a stupid question. Cults leave clues as a way of claiming responsibility, and there's none of that here. Cut it out, or I'll take you back to the American Legion hall."

"The sheriff in Polk County said during a news conference that a group of devil worshippers might be behind these crimes. If you don't agree with the sheriff, then just say so."

He threw the car into drive and pointed it down the road.

"The sheriff of Polk County is an idiot," he said.

"May I quote you on that?"

"Be my guest."

"Slow down. It's up ahead."

A hundred yards down the road, she made him stop and retrace his steps. Using his headlights, she found the unmarked dirt driveway that led to Elsie Tanner's farm, and told him to drive down it. Elsie lived in the sticks, and he wondered how her abductor had managed to find her place without drawing unwanted attention to himself.

The driveway led to a clapboard house with a rusted tin roof. Light streamed through the front windows. He parked and stayed in the car.

"Did Elsie have a husband or a partner?" he asked.

"Not that I'm aware of," Gamble said.

"Well, there's someone home, and we're trespassing. Here's what I think we should do. Get out, but stay close to the car. If someone comes out, and starts acting funny, jump in the car. Understood?"

"Loud and clear."

They both got out. Lancaster made it a point to slam his door, so whoever was inside would know there were visitors. The porch light came on, and a short woman wearing coveralls stepped outside wielding a shotgun, its barrel pointed at the ground.

"Who the hell are you, and what do you want?" she demanded.

"Should we run?" Gamble whispered.

There was a difference between threatening someone and protecting yourself.

"Talk to her," he whispered back. "She's not going to hurt us."

"Hello. My name is Lauren Gamble, and I'm a reporter with the *Tampa Bay Times*. This man is Jon Lancaster, and he's a famous law enforcement agent. We're here because we're trying to find out who murdered Elsie Tanner and kidnapped her granddaughter. Would you mind if we had a look around?"

"You got credentials?" the woman asked.

They produced their business cards. The woman cautiously crossed the front yard. She was missing a front tooth, and her skin was bronzed by the sun. She took the cards and studied them. Looking at her male guest, she said, "Team Adam. Does that have something to do with the little boy that was murdered way back, Adam Walsh?"

"It was named after him."

"And you work with them."

"I offer my services when they're needed."

"There's been a few dozen detectives and FBI agents snooping around, trying to figure out who murdered my mother and stole my kid. What the hell do you bring to the party that they don't, Mr. Lancaster?"

"Are you Elsie's daughter?" he asked.

"Yes, I am," the woman said.

"I'm sorry for your loss. To answer your question, I'm a specialist in finding missing people. I worked missing persons cases as a cop, all of them successfully. Before that, I was a Navy SEAL, and participated in over a hundred and fifty missions whose purpose was to rescue people in distress."

She laughed in his face. "You were a SEAL? Well, I guess that makes me the fucking pope. Get out of here. You were no god damn SEAL."

Her words stung. He didn't have an athletic build, and his round belly suggested that he spent his off-hours lying on the couch guzzling beer. His appearance was the by-product of a condition called gastroschisis, which gave him a big stomach and made him look fat. The truth be known, he worked out every day, and could hold his own against the fiercest adversary.

"On the contrary, I was a SEAL," he said.

"Is that so? My cousin was a SEAL, and had a bone frog tattoo on his arm to prove it," the woman said. "He said that every SEAL got a bone frog tattoo to honor the SEALs who died in combat. Let's see your tattoo, Mr. Lancaster."

He undid the buttons on his shirt and parted the lapels. He had a single tattoo on his body, and it was of a large frog skeleton crawling up his right shoulder.

"Well, shut my mouth," the woman said. "Please accept my apologies. You don't look like you were a SEAL. I bet you hear that all the time."

"I'm used to it," he said, buttoning his shirt back up. "With your permission, I'd like to take a look around the property before it starts to rain."

"You're not going to find anything. It's been picked clean."

"I'd still like to have a look, so I can get a sense of what happened. I'm sorry, but I didn't catch your name."

"It's Carla Jean. My second husband and I are having issues. He and Skye don't get along, and Skye took my maiden name just to piss him off. I sent Skye to stay with my mom until we got things worked out. Then this happened." She shook her head and started to cry. "Fuck, there goes the waterworks again." She wiped away her grief and threw her shoulders back. "Can I offer you a glass of iced tea? It's all I've got."

"Iced tea would be fine. Thank you."

He arched an eyebrow. Gamble took the hint, and followed Carla Jean inside.

- - -

He traipsed across the property listening to the frogs. It was rectangular shaped, mostly pasture, the north side bordered by wetlands. Before the wetlands started, there was a large firepit. It was here that Elsie Tanner had died.

He stood with his belly pressing the crime scene tape and used the flashlight on his cell phone to light up the ground. Elsie had been cutting the grass when a stranger had driven onto the property, entered the house, and abducted Skye. It was believed the teenager had either been tied up or knocked out before being taken to the stranger's car. When Elsie had tried to stop him, she'd been beaten and dragged to the firepit.

Elsie's killer was a sadist. Not content to knock the old woman out, he'd broken her nose and jaw, then crushed in her head with a blunt object. Killers who used their hands had rage issues, and Elsie's killer had been filled with fury. The police report said the murder weapon hadn't been found, and the detective handling the investigation had speculated that the killer had taken it with him.

Lancaster found this aspect of the crime puzzling. The killer had made no effort to cover up his crime, so why take the murder weapon? It was possible that he'd purchased the murder weapon earlier, and didn't want it traced back to him, but that was only a guess.

It felt like a revenge killing. If that was the case, then hopefully the police would be able to find a person in Elsie's past who was carrying a grudge, and track them down.

He took another hike around the property. The main pasture was about four acres and ringed by three-board fencing. A John Deere mower sat in its center, waiting for an owner who would never return.

He sat down on the mower. The police report said that Elsie's cell phone was in her pocket when she died. Why hadn't she dialed 911 when the intruder entered her property? Had she panicked? Or was there another reason she hadn't made the call?

The mower was pointed at the house. He imagined Elsie seeing an unfamiliar vehicle come onto the property, and a strange man jump out and go inside. Surely it would have alarmed her, so why not call the police? Based upon what Gamble had told him, Elsie was a smart lady. Yet for some reason, she hadn't reacted.

It started to rain. First small drops, then larger ones that bounced off the mower and danced in the air. He stayed put, his thoughts consumed by this contradiction. Why hadn't Elsie called the police or a neighbor for help?

The light on the back porch flickered on, and Gamble came outside. Finding him in the darkness, she motioned that he was needed inside, and he climbed off the mower. He'd gotten to see the crime scene, but it hadn't provided any insight.

As he jogged toward the house, he gave the firepit a final glance, wondering if he'd ever know what had happened. A flash of white caught his eye. Behind the pit, a slip of paper impaled on a tree branch flapped in the wind. It looked like a receipt, and he realized that it was directly above where Elsie Tanner's body had been found.

CHAPTER 3

"What does it mean?" Gamble asked.

They sat in the American Legion lot as rain pounded his car. Pinched between his fingers was a sales receipt he'd rescued from the tree on Elsie Tanner's property. It was wet but still decipherable. He needed to turn the receipt over to the sheriff's office, and tell the detective running the investigation what he believed had actually happened the afternoon Elsie was murdered. The police had their facts mixed up, and he needed to gently straighten them out. He couldn't do that with a reporter hanging on his coattails, and it was time he and Gamble parted company.

"I'll let you know once I talk with the sheriff," he said.

She glared at him. "I thought we had an agreement."

"We do have an agreement."

"Then honor it. What does that receipt mean? I have a right to know."

He'd borrowed a stepladder from Elsie's garage in order to climb into the tree. Gamble had held the ladder so he wouldn't fall, and her pretty clothes had gotten soaked. She'd helped him, and she wasn't going to let him pretend that she hadn't.

"I think the police made a mistake. This receipt may confirm that," he said.

"You're saying they screwed up."

"Call it an error in judgment. The crime report states the kidnapper came onto the property and abducted Skye. Elsie jumped off her mower to confront him, and the kidnapper dragged her to the firepit and murdered her. That's the police's version, only there are problems with it."

"Do you mind if I take notes?"

"This is off the record."

She started to object, and he shut her down. "I could be wrong. If you publish it, and I *am* wrong, the investigation might get thrown into turmoil. Now, do you want to hear the rest?"

"Please."

"Here's what's wrong with the police version. First, Elsie didn't call 911, yet her cell phone was in her pocket. That would indicate that the kidnapper surprised her, and she didn't have time to make the call. Second, her farm isn't on Google Maps, yet the kidnapper knew where she lived. I think the kidnapper tailed Elsie when she was doing an errand, and followed her home."

"Which is how the sales receipt fits in. It fell out of her pocket when her assailant dragged her across the ground to the firepit."

"Correct. Now here's the third thing, and it's a big one. The police believe Skye was the target, but I don't believe that's the case. I think Elsie was the target, and Skye was collateral damage."

"Why do you think that?"

"The other ten victims are linked by age. They were either middle aged, or elderly. Skye is sixteen years old. She doesn't fit the profile of the other victims, but Elsie does. She was the one the kidnapper wanted."

Gamble spent a moment processing what he had just said.

"How does the sales receipt help you?" she asked.

"I think it may lead us to the killer."

"You've lost me."

He flipped on his car's overhead light and held the receipt so she could read it. It was from a GNC health and nutrition store in the Citrus Park Mall, which a search on Google had told him was six miles away. The receipt's time stamp showed that four days ago, at 3:56 p.m., a product called Dr. Joints Advanced had been purchased for sixty dollars.

"Here's what I believe happened. The afternoon that Elsie was killed, she went to the mall to buy supplements," he said. "I think the kidnapper was at the mall, and followed her home. He scouted the neighborhood to make sure it was safe, then came onto the property, and used a ruse to get Elsie off her mower. When he tried to abduct her, Elsie fought back, and he killed her. The receipt fell out of Elsie's pocket, and got blown into the tree. The kidnapper didn't want to leave empty handed, so he abducted Skye."

"How do you know the receipt wasn't just floating around the property?"

"The property was spotless."

She thought about it. "You're right, it was spotless. So was the inside of the house. How do you know Elsie bought the supplements, and not Skye?"

"I went on the GNC site, and read the product review for Dr. Joints Advanced. It's a supplement for older people suffering from joint pain. That tells me that Elsie made the purchase, and the receipt fell out of her pocket."

"Or it fell out of someone's trash can and got blown into the tree."

"A dollar says I'm right."

Gamble smiled. "Okay, let's say you're right, and that Elsie was at the Citrus Park Mall four days ago. There were probably hundreds of other shoppers there as well. How are you going to finger her killer?"

"I'll start at the GNC store, which should have surveillance cameras. I'll get the store to show me the videotape of Elsie buying the supplements. If the killer isn't on the tape, I'll pay a visit to mall security, review their surveillance tapes, and find Elsie leaving the mall. If I'm right, her killer was there, and followed her home."

"What if mall security erased the tapes?"

"I worked a mall robbery when I was a cop. Malls keep surveillance tapes for a year, in case they're sued. It's the only way they can get insured."

"And you figured all this out by that little piece of paper. I guess that's why they pay you the big bucks."

"No one's paying me anything," he reminded her.

"That's right, you volunteered. I was meaning to ask you why."

She was being a wiseass, and he did not respond.

"Not going to tell me, huh? I'll figure it out eventually. Guess you'd like me to get out of the car, so you can go see the sheriff," she said.

"If you don't mind," he said.

"The sheriff's office is on Gunn Highway, right next to the mall."

"Great. Thanks again for your help."

To his annoyance, Gamble did not get out.

"What about the clue I found in the kitchen?" she asked. "Are you going to share it with the sheriff as well?"

Hanging over the stove in Elsie's kitchen was a framed quote that read, "No Good Deed Goes Unpunished." Gamble had pointed the quote out to Lancaster before he'd gone tree climbing. He hadn't understood the significance, and had forgotten about it.

"Why do you think that quote's important?" he asked.

"There was a similar quote in the house of the Lakeland victim," she said.

"You went to the Lakeland victim's house?"

"My boss sent me. He thought it would add depth to the piece I'm writing. The missing Lakeland woman is a retired teacher named Amy Potter. Her husband invited me into the kitchen for coffee. There was a plaque by the refrigerator that said, 'Some of your greatest hurt will come from people you helped.' It struck me as odd, you know?"

He was suddenly glad Gamble had stayed in the car.

"You found a link between Amy Potter and Elsie Tanner," he said.

"It sure feels that way. But what does it mean?"

"I heard similar sentiments when I was a cop. You help people, but later regret it. Elsie Tanner and Amy Potter may have both helped people, and gotten burned."

"Is that significant?"

"It's a link, and needs to be explored. Are you up for it?"

"Me? I wouldn't know where to start."

Murder cases weren't solved in a day. It was all about digging, and grim resolve. Gamble's cell phone beeped in her purse. She pulled out the device and visually devoured the message. It seemed to rattle her, and she looked at him. "A nurse has gone missing in Gainesville. Her neighbor found her car running in the driveway. My boss wants me to drive up so I can file a story in the morning."

"Are you okay with that?"

"Not really. This is scary."

She shivered from an imaginary chill and started to get out. He stopped her.

"Do you own a gun?" he asked.

"It's back at my apartment."

"It's not doing you any good there."

"I know. My boss doesn't want us bringing guns to work, so I leave it at home."

"But you know how to use one."

"Absolutely. I got a concealed weapon permit when I moved into my apartment. I go to the pistol range twice a week."

He reached over and punched a combination into a lock in the glove compartment. It sprang open, revealing four semiautomatic handguns resting in a specially made rack.

"Take your pick," he said.

She examined each weapon before settling on the GLOCK and slipping it into her purse. It seemed to calm her down, and she flashed a brave smile.

"Thanks, partner," she said.

CHAPTER 4

The link between Amy Potter and Elsie Tanner may have been nothing, but it still needed to be explored. He let Google Maps guide him to the sheriff's office in Citrus Park, and parked in the lot beside the building. Then he called a fifteen-year-old girl named Nicki Pearl.

"Hey, Jon," she said cheerfully.

"I hope I'm not interrupting anything," he said.

"Nope, homework's all done."

"How would you like to do some snooping for me?"

"You bet I would."

Four months ago, Nicki's parents had hired him to figure out why strange men were stalking their daughter. During his investigation, he'd discovered that Nicki was taking a CSI course at school, and had a real passion for police work. After his job was finished, and Nicki was no longer in danger, he'd accepted an invitation to speak to her class about cases he'd worked back when he was a detective. He'd made it a point to emphasize to the class that while knocking on doors was important in solving cases, it was forensic work that often brought the bad guys to justice.

"Write down these two names. Amy Potter, Elsie Tanner," he said.

"Done. Who are they?" she asked.

"They're both victims of horrible crimes. Amy Potter was abducted in Lakeland, and Elsie Tanner was murdered outside of Tampa. A reporter found a link between them that needs to be checked out. It may be important."

"Cool. What's the link?"

"They both helped people, but got burned for it. I want you to do background searches of them on the internet. See if they're in some way connected."

"This sounds like fun."

"There's more. I also need you to visit the clerk of courts websites in Lakeland and Tampa, and do searches of their names. Maybe they were both involved in a lawsuit, and the person they sued is now paying them back."

"Which would explain the motive."

He smiled into the phone. During his talk, he'd emphasized the importance of learning a motive, since it often led to discovering a criminal's identity.

"Last thing," he said. "I need you to see if there are newspaper articles where Potter and Tanner are mentioned. I'll give you a tip that should help. Most newspapers archive past stories on their websites. These stories don't come up in a Google search. You have to visit the newspaper's site, and do a search on the internal search engine."

"That's stupid. Why don't they just post the links, instead of making people do the extra work?"

"I asked a reporter at the *Sun Sentinel* in Fort Lauderdale that question. She told me that when a person uses the site, they're exposed to advertising, and that's how the paper makes money."

"I still think it's stupid. I'll start tonight."

"Not before you get your parents' permission. Understood?"

"Sure, Jon. I'll ask them once I get off the phone."

"Good. Have you spoken to your aunt Beth lately?"

"Not in a while. She disappeared on us. Are you guys still dating?"

Nicki's aunt was Special Agent Beth Daniels with the FBI. He'd met Beth while protecting Nicki, and they'd ended up catching a pair of serial killers. A bond had formed that had led to several dates. The relationship had been going in the right direction, and they'd decided to spend a long weekend together hiking in the Smoky Mountains. On the first day, Beth had gotten a phone call from her boss, who'd assigned her to a new case. Beth had left that day, and he hadn't heard from her since.

"Status unknown. I haven't spoken to your aunt in a month," he said.

"She's like that. Don't take it personally."

It was amusing to get dating advice from a teenager, and he laughed silently into his cell phone.

"Would it be okay if I got my CSI class involved?" she asked. "My teacher gave us this cold case to work on as a project, only it's boring, and no one's into it. This case would be great, since it's happening right now."

Nicki's CSI classmates were sharp kids. After his talk, they'd asked questions about cutting-edge forensics such as scrape DNA and latent fingerprint detection, and obviously had done a lot of reading. Having them work on this would save time, and might very well lead to a breakthrough. The only problem was, if they discussed it on Facebook or Instagram, the police investigation could be jeopardized.

"I don't think that's a good idea," he said. "If one of them discusses the case outside of the classroom, or on social media, it would create real problems."

"What if I get them to sign a pledge?" she asked. "That's what the Secret Service agent who visited the class made us do. If we broke it, our teacher said she'd fail us."

"The whole class?"

"Uh-huh. We're all trying to keep our grade points up to get into college. Nobody wants to get an F, so we stayed quiet."

"Okay. Run it by your teacher. If she's willing to get the class to sign a pledge, then get them involved. If not, you'll have to play Sherlock Holmes by yourself. Sound fair?"

She giggled. "That sounds like a great idea."

He found Nicki—unlike most teenagers—easy to have a conversation with, and he would have kept talking to her, only the GNC store would be closing soon. He needed to go inside the sheriff's station, and convince whoever was on duty to visit the mall with him to review the store's surveillance tapes. If he was lucky, the face of Elsie's killer would pop up, and he'd be one step closer to rescuing Skye.

"I've got to run," he said. "Say hello to your folks."

CHAPTER 5

The sheriff's Patrol District III headquarters in Citrus Park was a squat brick building that backed up to dense wetlands. Entering the lobby, he combed his hair with his fingers so he looked presentable. A female deputy with a name tag that said Lacko sat behind a sheet of bulletproof glass at the reception area.

"Can I help you?" the deputy asked.

He took out his Team Adam business card and held it up to the glass. "I need to speak to whoever's working the Elsie Tanner investigation," he said.

She studied him. Not liking what she saw, she frowned.

"How do I know you didn't find that on the ground?" she asked.

Several clever answers came to mind. He buttoned his lip and pulled out his driver's license and also held it up to the glass. She did not back down.

"There's no one here. Come back tomorrow," she said.

"You're here by yourself?" he asked.

"Just me and T. J."

"T. J.?"

"Deputy Stahl. He runs the Special Investigations Division."

"Then let me speak to him. I visited Elsie's property, and found a piece of evidence that may be important." He removed the GNC sales receipt from his wallet and showed it to her. "It was stuck up in a tree."

"What did you do, climb up and get it?" she asked.

"That's right. I was afraid it would get ruined in the rain."

"Is that why you look like such a mess?"

"Yes, ma'am."

"That sounds crazy enough to be true. Give me the receipt and your driver's license and business card, and I'll go talk to T. J."

He passed the items through a slot in the glass. Lacko secured them with a paper clip and disappeared into the back of the station house. His earlier conversation with Gamble was bugging him, and he pulled out his cell phone and got on the internet.

Using Google, he found and quickly read a story about Amy Potter's kidnapping in Lakeland's only newspaper, the *Ledger*. The Polk County sheriff, a local character named Homer Morcroft, was quoted as saying that a demonic cult might be involved, yet he gave no evidence to back up the claim.

The quote bothered Lancaster. Saying that devil worshippers might be involved was like adding gasoline to a fire. On a hunch, he did a search of Morcroft, and discovered other outlandish quotes that he'd made over the years, along with press conferences posted on YouTube. Morcroft obviously enjoyed the spotlight, and seeing his name in the papers.

He looked up from his phone to find a man wearing jeans and a long-sleeve athletic shirt standing before him. He was built like a gymnast, with broad shoulders tapering down to a thin waist.

"I'm T. J.," he said, offering his hand. "It's an honor to meet you."

Lancaster's cheeks burned. Stahl had checked him out, and found stories on the internet about the cases he'd broken. He would have been happy if no one ever saw that stuff, but the internet was like an echo chamber, and nothing ever faded away.

"I'd like to talk to you about what happened at Elsie Tanner's place," Lancaster said. "I think I may have a new angle for you to consider."

"That sounds good to me. We can use all the help we can get." Stahl used a plastic key to get back into the station house, and they walked past a cubicle farm to a corner office. "You want some coffee? I just brewed a fresh pot."

Lancaster never said no to coffee. He took a chair in front of Stahl's desk and soon was sipping from a steaming cup. The desk was cluttered with family photos of Stahl's wife and freckle-faced son. In one photo, the boy was wearing a baseball uniform and holding a bat. It made Lancaster choke up, and he averted his gaze.

"So how does the sales receipt play into this?" Stahl asked, sitting across from him. "Lacko said you found it in a tree on Elsie Tanner's property."

"I believe it fell out of Elsie's pocket when she was dragged over to the firepit," he said. "The sales receipt establishes her at the GNC store in the Citrus Park Mall an hour before she was killed. I think her assailant was at the mall, and tailed her home."

"That explains how he found her place. That's been bothering us," Stahl said.

"I also believe Elsie was the intended target of the kidnapping. The kidnapper came onto her property, and talked her off her lawn mower. When he tried to abduct her, she resisted, so he killed her. Rather than leave empty handed, he grabbed Skye."

"Which explains why Elsie didn't call 911," Stahl said.

"Correct. Her kidnapper got the jump on her."

"What was his motive?"

"I don't know. She had a reputation for being a Good Samaritan, which may somehow play into this."

"I heard she was a do-gooder. You think she helped someone, and it came back to bite her?"

"Could be."

"If Elsie was at the GNC store, there would be a surveillance tape of her." Stahl paused. "And maybe one of her killer as well."

"That's what I'm hoping. If her killer didn't come into the store, he may have tailed her from the parking lot, and we can spot him on the mall's surveillance videos."

"I like it. The mall stays open until ten. Let me call the GNC store, and see if the manager will let us look at their tapes. We'll start there."

The key to any investigation was to keep it moving forward, and see where it led you. Stahl placed a call to the GNC store at the Citrus Park Mall, and was put on hold. Covering the mouthpiece with his hand, he said, "Did you run any of this information by the FBI? They're here, running their own investigation."

"No, I came straight here," Lancaster said.

"I'd like to keep it that way."

"You want me to stay away from the FBI?"

"If you don't mind. I had some good leads, and that bitchy agent in charge scared off my witnesses. She's a real horror show. You ever work with the FBI?"

"A few times. They're not the easiest bunch."

"That's an understatement." Stahl took a business card off his desk and passed it to him. "If you ever run across this little lady, run like hell. She's the worst."

He stared at the card and saw Beth's name in dull black lettering. Beth was a relentless investigator, and he could see her rubbing Stahl the wrong way. He saw no reason to tell Stahl they knew each other and spoil the party.

"Thanks for the warning," Lancaster said as he returned the card. "I was doing a little reading, and saw that the sheriff in Polk County is claiming that a group of Satan worshippers may be involved in these abductions. Why would he say that?"

"If I tell you, will you keep it a secret?"

"Of course."

"A schoolteacher was abducted in Lakeland last week. While the police were searching the property, they found the number 666 written in spray paint on the driveway. The husband claimed he had no idea how it got there."

"That's the number of the beast," Lancaster said.

"That's right. It's from chapter thirteen of the book of Revelation. 'Let the one with understanding reckon the meaning of the number of the beast, for it is the number of a man. His number is 666.'"

"Anyone could have painted that on the driveway."

"I know. It was a stupid thing for the sheriff to say."

The manager came on the line, and Stahl arranged for them to meet at the store before it closed. Ending the connection, he rose from his desk and strapped on his sidearm, which he covered with a baggy sweatshirt.

"Let's roll," Stahl said.

- - -

The Citrus Park Mall was a stone's throw from the station house. Stahl parked in a space near the entrance between Macy's and Sears and killed his engine. The deputy's negative comments about Beth were bothering Lancaster. Beth was a tough cookie, but her track record for catching criminals was stellar, and more than made up for her antics.

"Do you mind if I ask you a question?" Lancaster asked.

"Go ahead," Stahl said.

"I may run into Special Agent Daniels while I'm conducting my investigation. Would you mind telling me what she did to piss you off so badly?"

"Special Agent Daniels doesn't like District III, and we don't like her."

"Sounds like you have a history."

"That's one way to put it. A couple of years ago, a ten-year-old was found strangled in the woods not far from here. We had a suspect, a high school junior named Lenny DeVito, who had possession of the dead kid's bike. We got a sample of DeVito's DNA and sent it to the crime lab. If it matched the DNA on the kid's clothes, our case was solved.

"That same week, a local politician got shot to death answering his front door. The politician was fighting with his stepson over money, so the stepson gets hauled in, and his DNA also gets sent to the crime lab. Because the politician was connected, his stepson's DNA test was put in front of DeVito's test.

"That's when Daniels swooped in. Whenever a juvenile gets murdered, the FBI takes a look at the case. Daniels reviewed the evidence and decided that a psychopath killed the kid, and not Lenny DeVito. She ordered my boss to have DeVito's test done first. My boss doesn't like to be pushed around, so he said no.

"The next day, the paper ran a story saying the sheriff wasn't cooperating with the FBI, and how a rampaging killer may be on the loose. It made us look really bad."

"So Daniels leaked the story to the paper. How did it play out?"

"My boss caved, and had the crime lab run DeVito's test first. It was a match to the DNA found at the crime scene, just like we thought. DeVito was guilty."

"So Daniels was wrong."

"Dead wrong."

"Did the paper run a follow-up story, and clear the sheriff?"

"We're still waiting for that one."

"I'm guessing Daniels didn't apologize."

"When hell freezes over. Let's go."

Ersatz pop music serenaded them as they walked through the mall to the GNC store, where the manager waited for them by the checkout.

He had a shaved head and wore a tight-fitting polo shirt emblazoned with the store logo.

"We need to see your surveillance tapes from four days ago," Stahl said. "Are they located on premises, or do you work with an outside security company?"

"The surveillance tapes are on a computer in the back room," the manager said. "Can I ask what you're looking for? I might be able to help you."

"We think a lady named Elsie Tanner was in your store, buying supplements."

"That's the woman who was murdered," the manager said.

"That's right. Did you happen to see her?"

"I think so. She was a regular customer. Nice lady. I hope you solve this thing soon. We've hardly had any customers, and this is usually a busy time of year for us."

They went down an aisle stocked with vitamins and supplements that promised to make their users bigger and stronger. The back room was for storage and had cardboard boxes piled to the ceiling and a desk with a computer, which the manager booted up.

"What time of day would you like to see?" the manager asked.

Stahl showed him the sales receipt. "That time."

"Gotcha. I'll pull up the video taken on the camera at the checkout."

The manager worked the computer in slow motion. His forte was obviously sales, and Lancaster leaned against the wall to wait.

"What can you tell me about Elsie?" Stahl asked.

"She came in every few weeks, was always pleasant to deal with," the manager said. "Pretty smart too. She could talk about any subject."

"Did she ever mention any problems?"

"Not to me. Several of my customers knew her. She was well liked. Here's the tape you're looking for. Wait, I think that's Elsie. Have a look."

Most retail stores used security cameras to prevent theft, and these systems ranged from ultrasophisticated to cheesy. GNC's system was first rate, and the image on the screen was sharp. Elsie Tanner stood at checkout with a tub of supplements tucked under her arm. She paid with cash and made a point of counting out her change.

The manager chuckled under his breath. "Elsie was a stickler about her change. One time, the cashier shorted her a few pennies, and she raised a real ruckus."

Lancaster tuned the manager out and watched Elsie leave the store. If his hunch was correct, her killer had also been in the store, or in the mall, or in the parking lot, and had followed her home. If his hunch was wrong, and Elsie's assailant hadn't been in any of those places, then he was doing a fine job of wasting everyone's time.

Several seconds passed. A large man wearing a cowboy hat entered the picture. He sported a Fu Manchu mustache and thick sideburns, and was dressed in black like a gunslinger in a spaghetti western. He did not buy anything and also left the store.

"Who's that guy?" Stahl asked.

"Looks like Black Bart," the manager said.

"Come again?"

"A gentleman bandit from the Wild West named Charles Boles, used to leave poetry behind after his robberies," the manager explained. "I read a book about him in high school. That guy could be his twin brother."

"Let's take a look at him again."

The manager rewound the tape and found Black Bart. He was big and wide and had a pack of smokes tucked in his shirt pocket. Lancaster shot Stahl a glance. He wanted to ask the manager some questions, but didn't want to overstep.

"What are you thinking, Jon?" Stahl asked.

"Black Bart looks out of place," he said. "He didn't buy anything, and he smokes." The deputy shook his head, not making the connection.

It was the opening he needed, and to the manager, he said, "Do many of your customers smoke cigarettes?"

"Our customers don't smoke. They're health nuts," the manager said.

"What kind of person comes into your store?"

"We get a lot of athletes who are looking for an edge. And people who are health conscious. Those are our two main groups."

"Which group would Black Bart fall into?"

"Neither. He looks like a one-timer. One-timers never buy anything."

A smoker wearing cowboy clothes in a health and nutrition store with a woman who would get murdered an hour later. Either it was a coincidence, or they'd found their man.

"I need you to print copies of Black Bart's photo for us," he said.

The manager typed a command. A printer hidden by boxes started to whir.

"Does the mall monitor the parking lot?" he asked Stahl.

"Twenty-four seven," the deputy said. "The system is housed in the security offices. It's a pretty sophisticated operation."

"I need you to take me there," he said. "I want to see if Black Bart followed Elsie to the parking lot. If he did, there will be a film of it. If we're lucky, we might be able to read the license plate on his vehicle, and find out who he is."

The manager brought them the copies of Black Bart's photo.

"I hope you solve this," the manager said. "Elsie was good people."

CHAPTER 6

The mall was closing, the stores rolling down their security grilles. Together, they jogged to the security offices by the north entrance. The mall had a number of modern features to deal with terrorists and active shooters, including bomb-proof trash cans and bulletproof security cameras, and Lancaster hoped the surveillance videos of the parking lot weren't the usual *Twilight Zone* variety, but were instead high quality.

While he ran, he studied the photo clutched in his hand. Black Bart's legs were pencil thin, and grossly underdeveloped compared to the rest of his body. The man looked deformed, and would not be difficult to track down.

They were in luck. The security office remained open until the last employee went home. Two uniformed male guards sat in front of a wall of video monitors that rotated between surveillance cameras inside the mall and those out in the parking lot.

Stahl made the introductions. The guards were retired cops and very friendly. The thin one was named Woody, his partner Chase.

"You're working late tonight," Woody said.

"We caught a break in the Elsie Tanner case," Stahl said. "Elsie was at the GNC store four days ago, and a guy who was also in the store may have followed her outside and tailed her home. We need to see the surveillance tapes of Elsie going to her car. Hopefully, this guy will be on them, and we'll be able to make out the car he's driving."

"What's our suspect look like?" Woody asked.

Stahl handed him a photo of Black Bart. "Ever see this joker before?"

The guards studied the photo. They both shook their heads.

"That's some hat," Woody said. "Shouldn't be too hard to find him. What time did this take place?"

"Elsie made her purchase at the GNC store at 3:56, then left. Let's start there," Stahl said.

Woody and Chase began typing in commands. They were wizards on their keyboards, and surveillance videos from four days ago lit up the monitors. Not that long ago, mall security guards had been as skilled as school crossing guards. Times had changed; today, they were soldiers on the front line, and trained in everything from computer science to emergency preparedness.

"Found him," Woody said. "He's on monitor number one. Take a look."

The video was in the upper left-hand corner of the matrix. The camera was fixed, and recording the common area in front of the GNC store. The mall was busy, and they watched Elsie sift through the crowd with Black Bart trailing a few steps behind her. She crossed the common area and entered a Hallmark gift shop.

Black Bart sat down on a bench outside the store. He took out his pack of smokes and removed a cigarette, which he placed between his lips. He was about to light up when he seemed to remember where he was. He put the cigarette back into the pack and returned the pack and lighter to his pocket.

"That didn't look like a regular cigarette," Lancaster said. "Can you play it back again? I'd like to see what he was smoking."

The tape was rewound and played again. At the point where Black Bart placed the cigarette into his mouth, Woody froze the frame.

Lancaster leaned in for a better look. It was a normal cigarette, only it had been previously smoked, with a charred tip.

"That cigarette's been smoked before," Woody said. "Who the hell saves cigarettes, and smokes them again?"

"Guys in prison," Lancaster said.

Woody looked over his shoulder. So did Chase. Stahl eyed him as well.

"You think he's an ex-con?" Stahl asked.

Florida had over two million residents who'd done time in prison. It wasn't a stretch to think that Black Bart might be one of them.

"Probably," he said.

"How does that play into this?" Stahl asked.

"I don't know," he said.

Black Bart rose from the bench and went to a quiet spot to take an incoming call. He continued to watch the front of the Hallmark store while carrying on his conversation. He appeared agitated, and gestured angrily with his hand while speaking.

"Maybe it's his wife," Woody said.

"Or his girlfriend," Chase said.

"It's more likely his partner," Lancaster said.

The three men again gave him puzzled looks.

"Working off the assumption that this guy is planning to kidnap Elsie, he would let a call from a lady friend go to voice mail," he said. "Not so if the call was from his partner. He would take that call, because it was pertinent to what he was doing."

"What's the partner's role?" Stahl asked.

"His partner is probably the driver."

"Why do you think that?"

"His partner isn't inside the mall, because we haven't seen him on the video," he said. "That means he's probably circling the parking lot, waiting for Black Bart to call him." He paused. "These are just guesses. I could be wrong."

"It would explain a lot," Stahl said.

Lancaster looked at the deputy, not understanding.

"There are aspects of Skye's kidnapping that don't add up," Stahl said. "Skye worked out at CrossFit and was into mixed martial arts. We couldn't understand how the kidnapper subdued her so easily. According to a neighbor down the road, they heard Skye scream, but only once." He paused to let that sink in. "If there were two kidnappers, it would explain how they got Skye out of there so quickly."

The crime report had given the same account. Skye had emitted a single scream, then gone silent. He had read that line in the report twice. It was why he was here.

"He's finishing his call," Woody said.

On the monitor, Black Bart was wrapping up his call. He wore a frown, and was not pleased at how the conversation had gone.

Elsie emerged from the Hallmark store and headed down the mall. By changing camera feeds, Woody was able to follow her. She window-shopped at Banana Republic and queued up at Starbucks. Black Bart stood a safe distance away, watching her.

Coffee in hand, Elsie headed for the exit on the building's south side. Black Bart gave chase while making a call. His steps were quick, as if he were afraid of losing her. Elsie went outside, and Black Bart followed her.

The video stopped. Lancaster could feel his heart pounding in his chest.

"Let me retrieve the outside surveillance video," Woody said. "It's on a different platform, so this will take a second."

"Think he's calling his partner in the car?" Stahl asked.

"That's exactly what I'm thinking," Lancaster said.

"Got it. Here we go," Woody said.

The parking lot surveillance video began to play. The time stamp said 4:14. The sidewalk was wide and choking with people. Elsie sifted through the throng and made her way to her vehicle. Black Bart remained on the sidewalk, his cell phone pressed to his ear. His cowboy hat made him easy to spot in the crowd.

Elsie got into a Prius and backed out. The parking lot was full, and several drivers were vying to claim her spot. She left the lot at a crawl.

A midnight-black Chrysler 300 SRT pulled up to the sidewalk. The car was a favorite among criminals, with a cheap luxury feel, but dialed down enough to go unnoticed. It also had a Hemi V-8 engine that could produce over 470 horsepower.

The driver jumped out, and let Black Bart take the wheel. The driver ran around to the passenger side and hopped in. He looked to be in his midforties, and wore a baseball cap with the rim pulled down—an attempt to keep his face hidden.

It didn't work. Just as the passenger door closed, his face became visible. It lasted no more than a second. Just long enough for Lancaster to recognize him.

The Chrysler took off. The Prius was sitting at a traffic light, trying to leave. The Chrysler came up behind it. The light changed, and together they drove away.

"Let's see if we can get a read on the Chrysler's license," Stahl said.

Woody replayed the video. The back end of the Chrysler was never visible to the camera, and they could not make the plate.

"I need a copy of this video," Stahl said. "My boss needs to see this."

Woody made a copy and emailed it to the deputy. Stahl thanked the two guards for their help, and he and Lancaster left the mall. They didn't speak again until they were in the deputy's car.

"You got real quiet back there. Is something wrong?" Stahl asked.

He looked at the raindrops on the windshield and said nothing. Stahl had picked up on his anxiety, and stared at his passenger with murderous intensity.

"I said, is something wrong?"

He shook his head but avoided making eye contact. Telling Stahl the truth would only make the situation worse. He decided it was time to end the conversation.

"You need to share the video with the FBI," he said.

"Like hell I will," Stahl said, now on the defensive.

"That's a mistake. The FBI agents know what they're doing, even if they are jerks."

"I'll be the judge of that."

"It's withholding evidence."

"Screw you."

Stahl was steaming, and he drove Lancaster back to the District III parking lot without another word being spoken between the two men.

- - -

Lancaster's head felt ready to explode. Getting into his car, he drove up the street to a Key West–themed restaurant called Ballyhoo, and parked in the lot. The skies had opened, and the rain was coming down so hard that he couldn't hear himself think. Logan had been gone for twenty-five years, and yet it felt like he'd never left. Balling his hands into fists, he pounded the steering wheel.

"You stupid son of a bitch," he roared.

CHAPTER 7

He only stopped when his hands were sore.

He needed to track Logan down before the police found him. His brother was garbage, but that didn't mean he was going to throw him to the wolves.

He checked out the nearby hotels with his cell phone, and made a reservation at the Holiday Inn Express in nearby Oldsmar. Forty-five minutes later, he checked into his room, and placed a bag of takeout on the bed, then used the hotel Wi-Fi to get on the internet on his Team Adam laptop. He munched on flatbread while doing his search.

His first stop was the Florida Department of Corrections Offender Network website. Florida's prisons housed more than one hundred thousand inmates, and the FDC Offender Network was the easiest way to keep tabs on them. He typed in his brother's full name and ID number, which was Logan's birth date, shortened to six numbers. He clicked the "Submit" button, then leaned back in his chair to wait.

He tried to remember the last time he'd seen Logan. It was right before he'd gone into the military, twenty-two years ago. He'd borrowed his father's car and left at three in the morning so he could be there when the prison opened. Logan had been housed in Raiford with murderers and rapists, and the armed guards and oppressive razor wire fencing had scared the hell out of him.

He'd waited in the visitors' room for his brother. When Logan finally shuffled in, he'd been handcuffed and wearing leg shackles. His cocky attitude was gone, replaced by a withering sneer. Instead of saying hello, he'd grunted.

The reunion had gone downhill from there. Logan didn't show any interest in his enlistment, nor did he acknowledge the money their parents sent to his account at the prison canteen each month so he could purchase snacks and cigarettes. All Logan had wanted to talk about was the trial, and why Jon hadn't testified in his defense.

Thinking about the conversation made him uncomfortable. Logan had wanted him to lie, to say that he was at home with Jon watching TV during the robbery. But that wasn't true. Logan had come into the house and demanded that Jon get his father's handgun from the gun box. Then Logan had gone off with his friends and driven the getaway car for the heist. That was what Jon had told the police, and he wasn't going to change his story on the witness stand.

The visit had ended on a bad note. Logan had called him a fucking rat, and shuffled out of the room. It was all he could do not to cry.

Logan's file appeared on his laptop. It included his brother's headshot and details of incarceration, including date of parole, and the name of his parole officer, which he scribbled on a notepad. Prison had robbed Logan of his looks, and most of his hair. But the withering sneer was still there. Like the world owed him a favor.

Next stop on the site was the Supervised Population Information Search, also called SPIS. SPIS kept tabs on every inmate released on parole, of which there were many. He entered his brother's name, DC number, and the terms of the parole, which was probation felony supervision. Then he hit "Enter."

The information was slow to load. He finished the flatbread and washed it down with iced tea. Some things never changed. Logan had driven the car in the botched convenience store robbery that had gotten him sent to prison, and now he was driving for the guy who'd murdered

Elsie Tanner and kidnapped her granddaughter. Hadn't twenty-five years in the joint taught him anything?

The information appeared. Logan's parole officer was named Ricky Dixon, and he worked out of the Tampa office. He was making progress, and he closed his laptop, weighing his next step. He couldn't just call Dixon and ask him where Logan was living. He needed to be circumspect so as not to raise suspicion.

He'd kept in contact with dozens of law enforcement officers after retiring. Mike Andon with the Florida Department of Law Enforcement's missing persons division in Central Florida was a friend, and he gave him a call.

"Hey, Jon. It's been too long. How you been?" Andon answered.

"Keeping busy. How about you?" Lancaster replied.

"Just finished an undercover job. A Tampa real estate agent got tied to a cold case murder. I spent a week pretending to be a cleaning man, so I could go through his garbage. I found a soda can with his saliva, and we matched it to the old DNA."

"Did you bust him?"

"That happens bright and early tomorrow morning. Just so we can ruin his day. And all the days following. So what can I do for you?"

"I need you to call a parole officer named Ricky Dixon, and get the address for a parolee. Dixon works out of the parole office on North Florida Avenue in Tampa. I need you to leave my name out of this."

"Why's that?"

"Because the parolee is my brother, Logan Lancaster. Logan got paroled two months ago from Raiford. I need to talk with him."

"Is your brother in hot water?"

"Logan was spotted on a surveillance video at the Citrus Park Mall with a suspect in the murder of a lady named Elsie Tanner, and the kidnapping of her granddaughter. You probably saw it in the news."

"Your brother was involved in that? That's heavy, Jon."

"I know. Just so we're clear, I plan to turn Logan over to the sheriff after I talk with him. If Logan goes back to prison, so be it."

"No love lost, huh?"

"Logan got paroled two months ago, and never called me. We're not close."

"What story do I tell Ricky Dixon?"

He gave it some thought. He didn't want Andon to get any blowback. Logan was an accomplice to murder and kidnapping, and might not go willingly to see the sheriff. If Ricky Dixon heard about it, he might think Andon had played him.

"Tell Dixon that an agent with Team Adam contacted you, and said that Logan might have information about a kidnapping, and that you need Logan's address so the agent can talk to him," he said. "All of those statements are true. Just leave me out of it."

"How soon do you need this?"

"Tonight."

The line went silent. It was late, and Andon was probably ready to hit the sack after they hung up.

"I'll make it worth your while," he added. "A Hollywood studio is making a movie about me. I'll get you a part as an extra. What do you say?"

"You can really get me a part in a movie?" Andon asked, sounding starstruck.

"You bet I can."

"Can it be a speaking part? I just want a line or two."

"The studio sent me a shooting script the other day. There's a part for an undercover cop with a few lines. You'll be a natural."

"My kids are going to go nuts when I tell them," Andon said excitedly. "Let me track Ricky Dixon down and get your brother's address. Call you right back."

He bought a diet soda from a vending machine in an alcove outside his room. He was a producer on the movie being made about his life, and planned to leverage it to the hilt. Back in his room, he was channel surfing when Andon called back.

"You work fast," he said.

"Ricky Dixon is a lady, and she was more than happy to help," Andon said. "Your brother is staying at the Jayhawk Motel on Nebraska Avenue. It's not far from Dixon's office. She said a lot of parolees stay there when they first get out."

"Thanks, Mike."

"Just so you know, that's a scummy part of town. Half the homicides in Tampa took place there last year."

"Sounds like my kind of place. I appreciate the warning."

"When does the movie start shooting?"

"This summer. I'll email you all the details."

"Can't wait."

- - -

He went to his car while googling the Jayhawk Motel on his cell phone. The reviews were less than stellar. "Dirty rooms crackheads and whores." "Don't waste your money." "Wish I could give them no stars." He decided to take Andon's warning to heart, and popped his trunk. In the space for the spare tire was a plastic box lined with carpet that contained a tactical shotgun and several special handguns.

The latest addition was a GLOCK 17 9mm handgun. It was made of synthetic materials and nearly indestructible, and the seventeen-round magazine was also a plus. He got into his car, and slipped the GLOCK beneath his seat.

As he started the engine, he realized his hand was shaking. Logan had been a messed-up teenager, and he could only imagine his current state of mind. He asked Google for directions to the Jayhawk, and learned the trip would take thirty minutes.

An automated voice directed him to the expressway. Staring at the highway, he imagined seeing his brother again. They'd been best buddies as kids, and perhaps the euphoric recall would erase the ill feelings from later on.

He was kidding himself. Logan hated him for the betrayal, and Lancaster hated his brother for destroying their family. It wasn't going to be pleasant, and he didn't think it was unreasonable that they might end up wrestling on the floor.

So help me God, he thought.

CHAPTER 8

Nebraska Avenue had more slime than the beach at low tide, the street teeming with dealers and streetwalkers. The strip clubs were housed in windowless buildings that could have been bomb shelters, while the pawnshops were open all night.

Following Google's instructions, Lancaster turned into the parking lot for a joint called All Night Long. The Jayhawk Motel was nowhere to be found, and he realized he was lost.

A lady of negotiable affections sauntered over to his car, and he lowered his window.

"Hey, sugar."

"Good evening. I could use some help," he said.

"You came to the right place. What's your name?"

"Jon."

"How novel. I'm Chantelle. Nice to meet you."

"I'm looking for the Jayhawk. My GPS said it was around here."

"The Jayhawk's not far. Want me to hop in? I can show you the way."

"No thanks, officer. I just need directions."

Her playful manner evaporated. He'd worked stings as a cop, so he knew that she was wired, and that a surveillance camera was recording them from a van in the lot, the video to later be used in court after she busted him for attempted solicitation.

"I'm not a cop," she said stiffly.

"Oh yes, you are. Your smile gave you away."

She shook her head and played dumb.

"You have all your teeth," he said.

"Is that supposed to be a joke?"

"No, ma'am, it's an observation. You're also not strung out on drugs. I was a detective, and ran in my share of streetwalkers. They were all high on something."

"Well, aren't you a fund of useful information. Anything else?"

"Your necklace."

"What about it?"

"It looks real. Most streetwalkers don't wear jewelry. If they do, it's fake."

"I'll remember that. The Jayhawk is on the next block, same side of the street."

"Much obliged. Can I make one more comment?"

"Save it," she said, and walked away.

As promised, the Jayhawk was on the very next block. The marquee advertised XXX Films, Cable TV, Daily & Weekly Rates. He counted eight vehicles in the lot, but didn't spot the sedan Logan had been driving at the Citrus Park Mall. Removing the GLOCK from beneath his seat, he slid it into his pants pocket and got out of his car.

The night manager buzzed him into the office. He had a blond ponytail and bloodshot eyes. Lancaster flashed his old detective's badge, which the sheriff's department had given him in a shadowbox when he'd retired. "I'm looking for a guy named Logan Lancaster. His parole officer told me he was staying in your motel."

"I talked to Logan a half hour ago," the night manager said. "Came into the office needing a pack of matches. He's in room sixteen."

"Which car is his?"

"Doesn't have a car, at least not one that I'm aware of."

"Logan has a friend, a guy with a mustache and sideburns. Is he here as well?"

"I don't know about any friend."

"You smell like weed. Did you sell Logan some dope?"

The night manager looked like he might cry. "Yeah."

"What's your name?"

"Richard. My friends call me Skip."

"How much did you sell him, Skip?"

"A couple of joints. You're not going to bust me, are you?"

A couple of joints would get Skip the equivalent of a parking ticket. But the laws were harsh for repeat offenders, and he guessed that Skip had gotten busted before, and would go down hard for a second arrest.

"Not if you cooperate," he said.

"What do you want me to do?"

"Get Logan to open the door to his room without looking suspicious."

"How the hell am I going to do that?"

"You'll tell him he got a delivery. Do the doors to your rooms have peepholes?"

"Yeah, they have peepholes."

"Good. I need an envelope. And a pen."

Skip produced a manila envelope and a magic marker, which he put on the counter. Lancaster wrote his brother's name in big, bold letters in the center of the envelope. Below his brother's name he wrote Jayhawk Motel, and below that, the motel's address. In the upper left-hand corner he wrote the name of his brother's parole officer, Ricky Dixon, also in big, bold letters. Finished, he handed the envelope to Skip.

"Here's the plan. We're going to pay a visit to Logan's room, and you're going to knock on the door, and then you're going to identify yourself," he said. "When Logan comes to the door, hold the envelope up to the peephole, and tell him a courier delivered it to your office. Can you remember that?"

"I'll remember. What happens then?"

"When Logan opens the door, I'll take over."

"This sounds tricky."

"Don't worry, I've got your back. Let's go."

The parking lot was unlit, and their muffled footsteps were drowned out by the traffic on Nebraska. Logan's room was at the end of the row, and the curtain was drawn across the window. Skip stood in front of the door and spent a moment getting his courage up. Lancaster stood with his back to the wall by the door, out of the peephole's range. He drew his gun, then motioned with his other hand for Skip to knock.

Skip rapped on the door. "Hey, Logan, it's Skip. A guy came by with a delivery, asked me to give it to you."

The door cracked open. Lancaster pressed his back to the wall.

"What the fuck are you talking about?" his brother asked.

Skip played it cool, and held the envelope up. "It's for you."

"Fuck. It's from my parole officer. What does that stupid bitch want?"

"I don't know, man."

"Did a cop deliver it?"

"Some kid on a motorbike," he said.

"Fuck. All right, give it to me. You got any more doobie?"

"Yeah, back in the office."

"Can I buy another joint off you? It's the only way I can sleep."

"Sure. No problem."

The door opened wide, and Logan stuck his hand out. Lancaster peeled himself off the wall and stepped between the two men, aiming the gun at Logan's forehead as he did. Logan's eyes went wide, and he raised his arms without having to be told.

"Back up," Lancaster said.

He followed Logan into the room and shut the door with his heel. Logan wore nothing but a pair of Jockeys, his body hairless. From the waist up, he was built like a gladiator, with bulging biceps and monster shoulders. Below the waist, he looked like a poster boy for a rare disease, his legs thin and underdeveloped. Guys in prison who lifted weights rarely exercised their leg muscles, focusing instead on what they saw in the mirror, and he thought back to Black Bart, who had a similar physique.

"Remember me?" he asked.

"No. Should I?" Logan replied.

Something inside of him snapped. Their parents had died on the same night, in the same hospital, victims of a head-on crash. He'd been with both of them as they'd passed. Each had expressed sorrow for what had happened to their oldest son, as if blaming themselves for the litany of bad things he'd done. They'd both died worrying about Logan, and that worry had been passed on to him. Whenever he thought of his brother, be it his brother's birthday, or on Christmas, or some other important date, the thought was filled with pain, and left him feeling depressed. He often wondered if his brother had thought about him on those dates. Probably not.

"It's Jon," he said. "Your brother."

The words sparked a flicker of recognition. Logan lowered his arms and grinned. The marijuana he'd been smoking took over, and he let out a cruel laugh.

"Well, look at you. The little fat boy, all grown up."

They'd been together five minutes, and his brother was already insulting him. Some things never changed. He tossed the GLOCK into his left hand and made a fist.

"Take your best shot," his brother said with a sneer.

Moments later, he lay motionless on the floor.

CHAPTER 9

Lancaster checked the room. He would have bet good money that Logan had a gun, but he didn't find one. But he did find something strange instead. On the night table was a glossy brochure for a brand-new real estate development in Sarasota. His brother had circled one of the model houses with a pen—the house had a $300,000 price tag.

Logan lay on his back on the floor and stared at the ceiling. His eyes were swimming in his head, and he rubbed his jaw. He acted more surprised than hurt.

"Where the hell did you learn to punch like that?"

"In the navy."

"Man, you should have warned me."

"Shut up."

His brother's cell phone lay on the unmade bed. A call was in progress, and he realized that Logan had been talking to someone when Skip had knocked.

"Hello?" he said into the phone.

Silence. He looked at the number on the screen. It had an 813 area code, which was for the Tampa Bay area.

"Hello?" he said again.

The person on the other end hung up. He slipped the phone into his pocket and glanced down at his brother. There was blood in Logan's mouth, the sight of which made him wince. He grabbed the room's only chair and sat in it.

"You and I need to talk," he said.

Logan pulled himself off the floor and sat on the edge of the bed. They spent an uncomfortable moment appraising each other.

"Did you start lifting weights or something?" his brother asked.

"Why does that matter?"

"Because you were always a wimp. We fought when we were growing up, and you never won." Logan laughed at the memory. "When you came to the prison and said you were joining the navy, I figured you'd wash out for sure. Did you?"

"I became a SEAL. It toughened me up."

"You were a SEAL. Fuck. I'm impressed. How long were you in?"

"Five years. When I got out, I became a cop. That lasted fifteen years. I got sick of the bullshit, and retired. Now I'm a private investigator."

"Can't say it surprises me. Pop thought you might get into law enforcement after what happened to you at the mall. That was a close one, wasn't it?"

"It was. You saved the day."

Logan grinned. It made his face hurt, but he did it anyway. "We probably never would have seen you again. I think about that day a lot. Best thing I ever did."

"You were a hero."

"Just looking out for my baby brother." Logan paused. The stroll down memory lane had ended, and his eyes grew unfriendly. "So what the hell do you want? Or do you just like sneaking around, punching people in the face?"

"I want to talk to you about a teenage girl named Skye."

"Never heard of her."

"Her grandmother was murdered on her farm in Keystone, and Skye was abducted. I want you to tell me where the girl is."

"Like I said, I've never heard of her."

"About an hour before she was murdered, the grandmother went to the mall to do some shopping. There's a videotape of her inside a health and nutrition store, buying supplements. While she was at the register, a guy wearing a black cowboy hat showed up, and started tailing her. The cops are calling him Black Bart.

"Black Bart followed the grandmother for a while. When the grandmother went to the parking lot to get her car, Black Bart followed her. He stayed by the mall entrance. A black sedan pulled up, and the driver got out to let Black Bart take the wheel. It was just long enough for the driver's face to get caught by the mall's security camera."

Logan cursed under his breath.

"Did you finger me to the cops?" his brother asked.

"No, I didn't."

"Thanks, man."

"I have a reason. I want to know where Skye is being held. If you help me, I'll work my magic, and get the police to cut you a deal."

"If you didn't finger me to the cops, then how will they know who I am?"

"Your face is in the video."

"So what?"

Logan had been in the slammer for a long time, and didn't know the first thing about the many technological breakthroughs that had been made in solving crimes.

"The police have computers with facial recognition applications," he said. "These computers are capable of identifying a person through a digital image or video frame. The software measures different parts of a person's face, like their chin and their nose, and compares those measurements to known criminal databases."

"The cops can really do that?"

"You bet. You don't look much different than when you were sent away, so it should be an easy match. It's only a matter of time."

"What are we talking about? A few days?"

"Try a few hours. Since the crime took place in Florida, the police will start with the Florida databases, and match the surveillance video image to your mug shot. This is not going to end well. I can help you, but you're going to have to help me first."

Logan groaned and fell back on the bed. "I need a drink. You thirsty?"

"Now that you mention it, I am. What have you got?"

"Colt 45."

"Some things never change."

"What do you mean?"

"That was always your drink. You went around the house singing that stupid slogan, 'Works every time,' until Mom got pissed, and yelled at you."

Logan looked at him and laughed. Pushing himself off the bed, he went to the small fridge tucked in the room's corner, removed a bottle of Colt 45 malt liquor, took a swallow, and passed the bottle. Lancaster took a sip to be sociable and nearly spit it out.

"That's awful. How can you drink that stuff?"

"It's an acquired taste." Logan returned to the bed. "First of all, I don't know where the girl is, or if she's even still alive. She wasn't the target."

"You went there for the grandmother."

"Yeah, only she fought back, so Dexter killed her with a miniature baseball bat called a tire thumper he keeps in his car. We grabbed the girl and threw her in the trunk. Dexter dropped me off here, and left. I don't know where they went."

"What's Dexter's last name?"

"Hudson."

"Is that who you were talking to on the phone?"

"Yeah. He called to check up on me."

"How did you meet him?"

"In the joint. He recruited me to be part of his gang."

Florida's prisons were overrun with violent gangs. Many were well funded, with money coming from the outside that allowed their leaders to wield influence inside the prison. Was one of these gangs responsible for the abductions taking place around Florida? It felt like a stretch. Gangs made their money selling drugs and seldom strayed from that endeavor. Kidnapping did not pay the bills unless the victim was a celebrity or rich. As far as he knew, none of the Florida victims were famous or had wealth.

"What was your gang's name?" he asked.

"The Phantoms," his brother replied.

The name was vaguely familiar. "They're out of Central America."

"That's right. Started in Colombia and spread to Honduras and Nicaragua. They're just getting their toe in the States."

His brother stared longingly at the bottle of beer. Lancaster passed it to him, and watched its contents disappear in one long swallow.

"Is Dexter the Phantoms' leader?" he asked.

"No, but he could be. Dexter's smart, used to be with the Outlaws motorcycle gang. When he went to prison, he joined the Phantoms, and ran their smuggling operation."

"The Phantoms were smuggling stuff out of the prison?"

"No, we were smuggling shit *into* the prison. Mostly drugs and cell phones, but also laptop computers and hot boxes so we could get internet service."

"You must have had inside help."

"That we did. Dexter would bribe a guard to bring in a carton of cigarettes. Then he'd ask the guard to bring in more stuff. If the guard balked, he'd threaten to expose him, which would lead to the guard getting arrested. He turned a lot of guards that way."

"I've been inside Raiford, and security was tight. How could a guard smuggle in a laptop computer, and not get caught?"

"Dexter had an employee in the kitchen on his payroll. The laptops were hidden in a fifty-pound sack of potatoes, and the employee hid the sack in the storeroom. When you're feeding fourteen hundred guys a day, it's easy to slip stuff in."

Logan smothered a belch. The beer had loosened his tongue, and Lancaster decided it was time to find out where Skye was being held. He was going to eventually take Logan to the police, but chances were Logan would get a lawyer, and stop talking.

"Twelve women have disappeared in Florida, including the teenager you and Dexter snatched," he said. "Were you and Dexter involved in those abductions as well?"

"I sure as hell wasn't," Logan said.

"How about your friend?"

Logan's jailhouse instincts kicked in, and he fell silent. Lancaster thought he understood; this piece of information was Logan's bargaining chip, and his brother was not going to share it with him, fearing Lancaster might tip off the police and ruin whatever leverage he might have.

"If Dexter wasn't the gang's leader, who was?" he asked.

"Cano."

"Was that his first or last name?"

"I never asked. Cano's a shaman. He put spells on the guards so they wouldn't bother us. One time, I saw him wave his hands in front of a guard's face, and tell the guard to get the fuck out of our cellblock, and the guard walked out. It was crazy."

"It must have been a trick."

"No trick. Cano's the real deal. He had a crystal ball that he used to find people. Cano could track down anyone in the world using that thing."

"You believed that crap?"

"It wasn't crap. An inmate paid Cano five thousand bucks to track down some guy who'd stolen all his money. Cano found the guy, no problem."

"How did you find Elsie Tanner and Skye?"

"I just told you, Cano's a shaman."

Cano wasn't a shaman, he was a con man, and Logan had been conned. He decided to change the subject.

"You said that Cano had laptops and hot boxes smuggled into the prison. Where did he keep this stuff?"

"In our cellblock. Cano used to say that prisons work both ways. The walls keep guys inside, and they also keep people on the outside from looking in."

"Was Cano running a criminal enterprise inside Raiford?"

"That's right, little bro. Look, I've said all I'm going to say. Now I've got something to ask you. Are you going to help me, or not?"

"Yes, I'm going to help you."

- - -

Lancaster's plan was simple. He would tell the sheriff that Logan had sought him out, and offered to help run down Dexter and locate the missing women. This would put Logan in a favorable light, and let his attorney negotiate a better deal after Logan helped the police. Logan would go back to prison, but not for the rest of his life.

"You're going to lie for me," his brother said.

"That's right, I'm going to lie."

"Too bad you didn't do that twenty-five years ago."

The words stung, and he momentarily looked away.

"Put your clothes on. We need to get out of here," he said.

His brother got dressed. He wore ragged jeans and a denim shirt missing a button. His shoes were worn out, and he wore no socks. He didn't own a watch. It was a sad statement for someone who'd been on the planet for as long as he had.

They started to leave. Taking the real estate brochure off the night table, he waved it in his brother's face.

"What's this about?" he asked.

"I was going to buy a house," his brother said.

"With what money?"

"Dexter was going to give it to me."

He wanted to ask his brother how that worked, but didn't want to stay there any longer than he had to. He slipped the GLOCK back into his pocket, and they went outside to the parking lot. He unlocked his car, and Logan started to get in.

"We need to tell the manager you're checking out," he said.

"Fuck him," Logan said. "He set me up."

"We still need to tell him."

"What are you, a fucking Boy Scout?"

"Shut up, would you?"

The entrance to the motel office was on the side of the building that faced the parking lot. As they got close, a large man emerged from the shadows, and blocked their path. He was dressed in black and cradled a sawed-off shotgun. It was Dexter.

"This is what happens to rats," Dexter said.

Then he pulled the trigger.

CHAPTER 10

Logan shoved him hard.

Growing up, it had been one of his brother's favorite tricks. They'd be standing on the playground and Logan would give him a playful shove, sending him a few inches off the ground. Then his brother would laugh like hell.

This shove was harder, and he landed on the pavement, where he rolled over until he was lying on his back, looking upside down at their attacker. Without hesitating, he drew the GLOCK from his pants pocket and returned fire.

His awkward position ruined his aim, and none of his shots hit their target. Dexter wasn't interested in shooting it out, and he ran to the street, where a black sedan idled at the curb. Dexter tossed the shotgun through the open back window, then jumped in.

The sedan peeled out. By now, Lancaster was on his feet, and he ran into the middle of Nebraska Avenue and got off two more rounds. The sedan's back window imploded, and the vehicle took a corner on two wheels and vanished into the night. He could hear screaming and saw people on the corner running for dear life.

Back in the parking lot, he found Logan sitting on the pavement with his back against a car. The lower half of his body was blood soaked, his breathing tortured.

Lancaster crouched down, and Logan managed a weak smile.

"You saved my ass," Lancaster said. Then added, "Again."

"Guess I'm good at something," his brother whispered.

Skip came out of the office holding his cell phone.

"An ambulance is on its way," the manager said.

"Go out in the street, and hail it down," he said.

Skip lowered the phone but didn't move.

"You heard me," he barked.

Skip went and stood on the sidewalk to wait for the ambulance. Lancaster didn't want him to overhear their conversation, and he lowered his voice.

"How bad did he get you?"

"Bad enough," his brother said.

Logan shut his eyes and started to fade away.

"Don't you dare die on me," he said.

His brother's eyelids lifted. His eyes were swimming in his head, and he appeared stuck between the here and the hereafter. He took a deep breath and spoke, the words barely a whisper. "A priest once tried to convert me in the joint. He said that Christ saved a robber who was being crucified with him. I guess it's never too late, huh?"

"You've got to keep fighting," he said.

"It's over, Jonny. I'm done."

"Come on. You can do it."

Lancaster took his brother's bloody hand and squeezed it. Logan closed his eyes, and his head flopped to one side.

"The ambulance is here," Skip called from the street.

- - -

The EMS team took over. The lead was a feisty woman with short-cropped hair. She looked into his face and instantly knew.

"Was he your friend?" she asked.

"My brother," he said.

"I'm sorry for your loss. At least you were here to comfort him."

"I tried."

He wanted to cry, and retreated into the office. There was a folding chair beside the TV, and he dropped into it, burying his head in his hands. A strange feeling overcame him. Logan was the last relative he had, and now his brother was gone. He was alone in the world, and the feeling made him immeasurably sad.

Skip fixed him a cup of coffee from a pot that had been brewed hours ago. He sipped the hot liquid, thinking back to the cell phone he'd found on the bed in Logan's room. Logan had been talking to Dexter when he'd come into the room, and he guessed Dexter had heard enough of their conversation to decide to take Logan out of the picture.

"I saw you shoot at that car through the window," Skip said. "Did you get those sonsabitches?"

"I'm pretty sure I nailed the driver," he said.

"They'll get theirs. The bad ones always do."

He finished his drink. Logan had told him a lot of crazy stuff, and he needed to write it all down, and share it with the police. He was still no closer to finding Skye, and realized that her rescue would have to wait while he dealt with Logan's murder.

He got his courage up, and went outside. EMTs had covered his brother's body with a white sheet. It made Logan look like a ghost, and he shuddered.

A police cruiser was parked sideways in the entrance, its bubble light flashing. A pair of uniformed cops were busy roping off the area with yellow police tape. The officers wore rubber gloves, so as not to contaminate the crime scene.

Skip came outside, and identified himself to the cops. One of the officers pulled Skip aside to get a statement. There was no rushing the process, and Lancaster leaned against a parked car while he waited his turn.

His thoughts drifted back to his childhood. Logan had been screwing up for as long as he could remember, but their parents had always given him a pass. He guessed it had something to do with Logan rescuing him at the mall. Logan had saved the day, and every bad thing he'd done after that had been ignored.

The officer finished with Skip and approached him. His name tag said Montalvo, and he was a Latin guy of about thirty. Montalvo asked to see his ID. As he produced his driver's license, Montalvo spied the detective's badge attached to his wallet.

"Are you a cop?" Montalvo asked.

"Retired. I'm doing a private job," he said.

"For who?"

He handed him a Team Adam card. "I was working a case in which Logan was involved, so I came to talk to him."

"The motel manager said the deceased was your brother."

"That's right. I hadn't seen him in twenty-five years. He was recently paroled."

"What was the job you were working?"

"I was trying to find a teenage girl that was abducted in Keystone four days ago. Her grandmother, Elsie Tanner, was murdered."

"Your brother was involved in that?"

"Afraid so. I was going to turn him in, but he got shot."

Montalvo scribbled furiously into his notepad. It was every uniformed officer's dream to one day become a detective. That promotion often hinged on how the officer handled a high-profile case. If the officer did an exemplary job, the top brass would notice, and he'd get rewarded. Logan's murder was such a case for Montalvo.

"Any idea who shot him?" Montalvo asked.

"The shooter's name is Dexter Hudson," he said. "My brother and Dexter were in prison together. Dexter knew my brother was going to rat him out, so he shot him."

"Rat him out over what?"

"Dexter murdered Elsie Tanner."

"Did your brother tell you that?"

"Yes, he did."

Montalvo flipped a sheet on the notepad and kept writing. "Could you identify Dexter Hudson if you saw him again?"

"Yes."

"Describe him."

"About six feet tall, two hundred fifty pounds, a Fu Manchu mustache and sideburns. He has a muscular upper body but thin legs."

"Sounds like you got a good look at him."

"There's a surveillance video from the Citrus Park Mall that shows him following Elsie Tanner. Deputy Stahl at the District III sheriff's office has a copy."

"You know Deputy Stahl?"

"I introduced myself to him earlier tonight."

Montalvo flipped the notepad shut. "I know how difficult losing a brother is. I lost my own brother last year from an overdose. If you can find it in you, I'd like you to come down to the station house, and give us a full statement. It will really help our investigation."

Lancaster was impressed. Montalvo had revealed a piece of himself in order to gain trust. This told him that Montalvo wasn't just after a promotion, but had connected on a deeper level, and would leave no stone unturned finding his brother's killer.

"I'd be happy to help you," he said.

"Great," Montalvo said. "Would you mind waiting inside the motel office until we're done here?"

"Sure thing."

Two dark SUVs pulled up to the curb, and their doors opened. Four men and two women climbed out and stood on the sidewalk beneath the harsh streetlight. Each wore a navy windbreaker with the initials FBI stenciled above the pocket. The cavalry had arrived.

"For the love of Christ," Montalvo said under his breath.

"Something wrong?" he asked.

"You don't want to know."

"I thought the FBI were the good guys."

"Not this crew. I'll be right back."

Montalvo grabbed his partner and went over to talk to the FBI agents. It was not a pleasant conversation, and the agents rudely shone flashlights into the police officers' faces, and ordered them to stand down. The officers meekly obeyed.

He scanned the agents' faces and found Beth Daniels. Her hair was tucked under a ball cap, and her eyes bore a fury that came from a dedication to her work unlike any he'd ever seen. During their first date, she'd told him that most men didn't find this side of her attractive. He'd realized later that she liked that.

Daniels moved to Logan's body and crouched down. Holding a flashlight in one hand, she lifted the sheet and folded it back. With the same hand, she pulled back the collar on Logan's shirt, revealing a crude tattoo on his neck. It was the kind of tattoo guys in prison got because they had nothing better to do. It said 666, the same numbers spray-painted on the victim's driveway in Lakeland.

Daniels removed a digital camera from her windbreaker, and took several shots of the tattoo. She put the camera away and replaced the sheet. She rose to her full height and took a long look around the parking lot. A creepy-looking person had drifted in off the street. He looked like trouble, and refused to leave when Daniels told him to.

"You must be hard of hearing," Daniels said.

The creep outweighed Daniels by fifty pounds and was a half foot taller. But that didn't stop Daniels from twisting his arm behind his back, and marching him away from the crime scene. She gave him a shove, and sent him tumbling down the sidewalk.

"Don't come back," she warned him.

She took another look around. She still hadn't noticed him.

Lancaster felt anger boil up inside of him. She'd never returned his messages or answered his texts. He'd been jilted by women before, and had gotten over it. But this time had really stung. Perhaps it was because Daniels had told him how much she enjoyed being with him. Most law enforcement officers had a hard time letting their guard down. But it had been easy when they'd been together. It had felt real.

A hand touched his shoulder. It was one of the other FBI agents.

"Did you see what happened?" the agent asked.

He nodded.

"Go inside the office. We'll get a statement from you soon," the agent said.

He glanced at Montalvo and his partner, who now stood beside the cruiser. Montalvo could not hide his disgust and shook his head.

"Fuck you," Lancaster said.

The agent recoiled. "What did you say to me?"

"I said, fuck you, asshole. That goes for your whole team. You're a bunch of god damn dickheads. Show the cops some respect, and you might get some in return."

A flashlight's beam hit Lancaster's face. Daniels was pointing it at him.

"Jon? What the hell are you doing here?" she asked.

He glanced at Logan's body, then back at her.

"He's my brother," he explained.

CHAPTER 11

Daniels pulled him into the motel office and slammed the door. She went to the window facing the street and struggled to lower the blinds. They came down crooked, and she let out a stream of obscenities that would have made a sailor blush.

He faintly sniffed the sweet smell of pot. A half-rolled joint and a bag of weed that he hadn't noticed before lay on the counter, and he guessed Skip had been getting ready to light up a number when he'd heard the shotgun blast and stopped what he was doing to come outside. Back when he was a cop, he'd turned a blind eye to small quantities of dope when he'd run across it, believing that it was foolish to arrest people for a product that came out of the ground.

He scooped the joint and the bag off the counter and tossed them into a trash bin. Daniels was still messing with the blinds, and he went to assist her.

"Sit down. I've got it covered," she said.

"You could have fooled me," he said.

"Don't be a wiseass, Jon. I'm not in the mood."

He moved the folding chair into the middle of the room and parked himself on it. Daniels muscled the blinds down and turned to face him. Her cheeks were a pinkish salmon color, a clear sign that she was flustered.

"I didn't know Logan was your brother," she said. "I'm sorry for your loss."

"How long have you been chasing him?"

"Your brother's been on our radar for several days. I need you to explain what you're doing here. I don't want to hold you any longer than I have to."

"Is that what you're doing? Holding me?"

"Yes. The FBI believes Logan was an accomplice to a murder and a kidnapping. Since he was your brother, you might have known what he was doing. That's enough for me to hold you. If I don't like your answers, I can arrest you."

"Would you do that?"

"If I thought you were involved, yes."

"But I wasn't involved. Come on, you know me better than that."

"I'll be the judge of your involvement."

He shook his head in disbelief. He liked Beth and would have trusted her with his life. He obviously hadn't left the same impression on her.

"Now, tell me what you're doing here, and don't leave anything out," she said. Her words felt like a slap to the face. He removed a pack of nicotine gum from his pocket and popped a piece into his mouth. He'd smoked when he'd been a cop but eventually quit. When he was tired or feeling down, the cravings reared their ugly head, and he had to fight them off.

"Answer my question," she said.

"You need to talk to Deputy Stahl with the District III sheriff's office in Citrus Park," he said. "Stahl can explain everything. I also gave a statement to Officer Montalvo a short while ago. You should talk to him too."

"You're not going to tell me?"

He worked the gum hard. "Go talk to the police. They know everything."

"I want to hear your version of things."

"Afraid not."

She crossed her arms in front of her chest. "And why is that?"

"I don't have the strength to deal with you."

It was her turn to be hurt, and her lower lip trembled.

"Keep it up, and I'll run you in," she said.

"On what charge? Obstructing justice?" He shook his head. "I've been totally transparent with the police. They know everything I know. Talk to them. Good night."

He hopped off the chair and moved toward the door. It was a ploy, designed to push her buttons and get her hackles up. She took the bait and grabbed his arm.

"Where do you think you're going?" she snapped.

"I'm going to go find a bar and have a stiff drink. Logan wasn't much of a brother, but he was the last relative I had. Care to join me?"

Her face softened, and the Beth he knew rose to the surface. She released his arm and made a pleading gesture with her hands. "The sheriff isn't a fan of mine. If I ask Stahl for information, he'll stonewall me."

"You know, I think I heard that," he said.

"What did Stahl tell you?"

"Stahl said you leaked a story to the newspaper that made the sheriff's department look bad. Stahl said that you were convinced a psychopath had murdered a kid, when in fact the killer was a teenager named Lenny DeVito. Stahl said that when the DNA test implicated DeVito, you didn't own up to your mistake."

"Stahl said that about me?"

She was getting worked up into a lather, and he simply nodded.

"Let me tell you what really happened. It's the FBI's policy to review every child murder in the country. The victim in this case was named Ryan Witt, and his death was particularly brutal. An agent in our Tampa office examined the evidence and was bothered by how violently Witt died."

"Stahl said the boy was strangled."

"Witt *was* strangled. There were two broken vertebrae in his neck, and his skull was fractured. I got the file, and after reviewing the evidence, I determined Witt's killer was a psychopath. So I told the sheriff to run the DNA test on Lenny DeVito first."

"But the DNA test proved DeVito was guilty. You were wrong."

"I wasn't wrong! May I finish?"

She looked fighting mad, and again he nodded.

"Before the DNA link was made, the evidence against DeVito was weak. A judge granted DeVito bail, and he went to stay with his parents. When the FBI made the arrest, they went on DeVito's personal computer, and found evidence that he was planning to shoot up his high school and kill his classmates. In his bedroom closet was a homemade bomb and a tear gas canister. He also had a key to his father's gun cabinet, which contained an assault rifle. We got him just in time."

"Stahl never mentioned any of that."

"I'm sure he didn't. DeVito pleaded guilty, and it got buried in the court records. I wanted to share what we'd found with the newspaper, but my boss nixed the idea. He didn't want me further damaging the FBI's relationship with the sheriff's department."

"That's some story. I'm sorry I doubted you."

"Apology accepted. Now, are you going to help me or not?"

A knock on the door interrupted their conversation. Daniels jerked the door open to find one of her agents standing outside. "What do you want?"

"We just got a statement from the manager. He said Logan Lancaster has had several guests in the past few days," the agent said. "We want to search his room, but need a key to open the door. The manager said the key ring was behind the counter."

"Hold on."

Daniels went behind the counter and found a key ring hanging on a nail. She gave it to the agent and said, "I'll be right out," and closed the door in his face. To Lancaster she said, "When did your brother get out of prison?"

"He was paroled two months ago," he said.

"How long was he in for?"

"He served twenty-five years."

"So we can assume that his guests were guys he knew in prison," she said.

It was a logical assumption, and he nodded.

"Was your brother in a gang?" she asked.

"Yes. They're called the Phantoms. My brother made them sound like a cult."

"How so?"

"The leader is named Cano. My brother told me that Cano could cast spells on people and perform all sorts of other crazy stuff."

"Do you think your brother was brainwashed?"

The question gave him pause. Logan hadn't been very intelligent, and he'd been easily conned by people who were smarter than him.

"Probably," he said.

She nodded approvingly. He'd opened a door for her, and helped move the investigation forward.

"Thank you, Jon," she said.

"Anytime, Beth."

"I need to supervise the search of your brother's room. Will you stay until I'm done? I need you to tell me everything you remember from your conversation. It just might help me solve this."

Daniels could have just as easily ordered him to stay put. But she'd chosen to use a teaspoon of honey, and get back on an even footing.

"I'll stay," he said. "Go do your search."

She gave his arm a squeeze and left the office. He needed some air and followed her outside. Three members of her team stood in the parking lot wearing rubber gloves and holding plastic evidence bags. Daniels snapped on a pair of gloves and marched her team to his brother's room. There was a protocol to gathering evidence, the rules hard and fast, and she did it as well as anyone.

His brother's lifeless body still lay on the ground. A photographer from the sheriff's department had removed the sheet and was snapping photographs. The course to become a crime scene photographer took three days, the students schooled on how to control a photographic exposure in order to capture the high-quality, evidence-grade photographs required in law enforcement. What the course didn't teach was that the dead needed to be treated with dignity, no matter who they were.

Kneeling beside his brother's body, he wiped away the insects. Rising, he stepped aside, and heard the photographer mutter her thanks under her breath.

She snapped shots from multiple angles. The camera wasn't functioning properly, and she replaced the sheet, then retreated to one of the cruisers. Beneath the car's harsh interior light, she opened her camera, and tried to identify the problem.

The sheet flapped in the breeze. Logan was trying to spook him. He'd done that plenty when they were kids, jumping out from behind corners and scaring the crap out of him. It was always followed by a playful shove, and an invitation to come play with the older kids. He was still alive because Logan had come to his rescue, just like long ago. Everyone had an angel sitting on their shoulder, and Logan had been his.

His head started to spin. He alternated between wanting to scream and wanting to break down in tears. It had been a long time since he'd felt this bad.

He needed a stiff drink. Several, actually. To hell with what he'd told Beth. It would be a while before she and her team were done collecting evidence, and he couldn't hang around that long. Whatever she needed to ask him could wait.

With his phone, he found a bar called the Double Decker in Ybor City that stayed open late. His car was blocked by the police cruisers, and he decided to Uber it.

He waited by the curb for his ride. The hookers, drug pushers, and other nocturnal creatures had returned to their street corners and were back to doing business, acting like nothing had happened. Someone had died tonight, but the sad truth was, people died all the time, and it didn't change anything.

The Uber app said the driver was a minute away. He glanced over his shoulder for a final look. The photographer had gotten her camera working; she'd pulled away the sheet covering Logan's body, and was again taking pictures.

He started to choke up. The misery of being with the dead was the helpless feeling their presence invoked. You wanted to help them, only it was too late.

Logan had asked about Jesus before he'd died, wanting to know if he could still be saved. Had his brother gone to church while in prison? His final act suggested that he had. Logan was still angry at him for what had happened twenty-five years ago, yet he had not allowed his anger to cloud his judgment.

His ride pulled up to the curb, and he stole another look before getting in.

"I owe you," he said.

PART TWO

Tomorrow Never Knows

CHAPTER 12

Broward County had been a different place in the early eighties. The beach had its splashy hotels and towering condos, but the rest of the county had been farmland. Thirty miles to the south, the Miami drug wars were claiming lives every day, but that was a different world, and far removed from Broward's slow, laid-back pace.

Lancaster had grown up in an area called Southwest Ranches. The houses sat on big lots, and it wasn't uncommon to see a horse tethered to a hitching post. When people talked about predators, they meant the hawks that cut the skies, searching for prey.

One early July afternoon, his mother had gone shopping with her two sons. A flyer in the paper had announced a sale at Macy's, and she wanted to buy several items. Macy's was the anchor store in the Pembroke Pines Mall, and she parked on the building's north side. Before getting out, she made her boys promise there would be no shenanigans once inside.

Logan had broken his word as they'd neared the entrance.

"Logan hit me!" Lancaster said.

"Logan, stop tormenting your brother," their mother said.

"Jonny stuck his tongue out at me," his brother lied.

"No I didn't," he bellowed.

His mother made them stand in front of her, and pinched their chins. "That's enough out of both of you. If you don't behave, there will be no Tastee Treat during the drive home. Are we clear?"

Her sons nodded solemnly. There was no greater treat than a soft ice cream twirl from Tastee Treat, the roadside buildings designed like giant ice cream cones.

They entered the store. Just inside the doors was the toy department. The boys stopped in their tracks, transfixed by the end display on the first aisle. It was the Atari Asteroids space shooter game that was all the rage, the clamor of spaceships and cannon fire tearing up the air.

"Can we play?" they asked.

Their mother removed the flyer from her purse. One of the sale items she wished to purchase was a few aisles away in household goods.

"You may, so long as you stay together," she said.

"Yes, Mom," they said.

No sooner had she walked away than they were arguing about who should play first. Logan won out, and was soon blowing up alien spacecraft while trying to avoid being hit by counterfire. As the game progressed, the obstacles increased, and Logan became hypnotized by the machine's flashing lights.

"Let me play," Jon said.

"You're up next," Logan said.

"I want to play now."

"Stop bothering me. I'm close to making ten million points."

He'd started to sulk. Soon their mother would be finished, and they'd leave the store, and he wouldn't get a chance to play. It sucked being the younger brother.

"You stink," he said.

Logan gave him a Bronx cheer. Steaming, he walked into the appliance department, and flipped the channels on a TV with a remote while pretending it was a video game. He did not notice the strange man until he was right on top of him.

"Hey, little guy," the stranger said.

The man flashed a twisted smile, and he put the remote down and backed away from the TV. His mother had taught him not to talk to strange people.

"What's your name?" the stranger asked.

He shook his head as if to say, *Nothing doing.*

"Look at what I have. Help yourself."

The man had a brown paper bag, which he opened and shoved beneath his nose. It was filled with an assortment of mouthwatering candy. The temptation was too great, and he stuck his hand in, and pulled out a bag of M&M's. He frowned and tossed it back.

"What's wrong?" the stranger asked.

"I don't like M&M's," he said.

"That's too bad. What's your favorite candy?"

"Reese's Pieces. When we leave the store, my mother is taking us to Tastee Treat, and I'm going to get a chocolate twirl sprinkled with them."

"What's your name?"

"Jonny."

"Well, Jonny, you're in luck. I've got a big bag of Reese's Pieces in my car. Come with me, and I'll give you some. What do you say?"

"Okay."

The stranger gave another smile. His face was marred by a wandering eye that refused to stay still, and his clothes smelled dirty from days of wear. Two of the buttons on his shirt were undone, exposing a shiny purple fabric underneath.

The stranger stuck his hand out. "Let's go."

He stared at the stranger's hand and saw that it was covered in scars. A voice inside his head screamed at him. There was no bag of Reese's Pieces. The stranger was lying, and if he went outside with him, he was never going to see his family again.

"No," he said forcefully.

"Don't you want to come with me?"

"No!"

Leaning down, the stranger punched him in the stomach, which knocked the air out of him; then he grabbed his arm and dragged him out of the store. By the time they reached the parking lot, his voice had returned, and he started to scream. Several shoppers getting in their cars stopped to watch but did not intervene.

"That's enough out of you," the stranger scolded. "Now be quiet, or you won't get any dessert tonight."

He kept screaming and kicking the pavement. The man came to his vehicle, a '71 black-over-white Cadillac with a dented bumper, and dug out his keys. The man popped the trunk and lifted him off the ground by the back of his shirt.

"If you don't shut up, I'll throw you in," the man threatened.

The trunk's interior was lined with carpet. On it lay a collection of rusted tools, including a shovel and a machete. Seeing them, he stopped crying.

"That's a good boy," the man said.

He was fixated on the machete. He had seen landscape crews in his neighborhood use them to prune trees. They were dangerous, and they scared him.

"Please don't hurt me," he whispered.

The man laughed under his breath. He didn't mean for his victim to hear him, the sound born out of the sickest of impulses.

But Jon did hear him, and screamed even louder.

Fresh from conquering space, Logan burst out of the store. Seeing his brother's dilemma, he sprinted across the parking lot, and kicked the stranger squarely in the nuts. As the stranger crumpled to the ground, groaning in agony, his shirt came out of his pants, revealing a purple dress beneath.

Logan grabbed his brother's hand, and they ran back inside.

"You okay?" Logan asked.

He sucked back his tears and said yes.

"Don't tell Mom," his brother said. "If you do, we won't get ice cream."

- - -

He awoke from his fever dream drenched in sweat. Over the course of his life, he'd been in plenty of tight spots, but none of those situations had stayed with him like that day in the mall. He realized that a loud and persistent knocking on his hotel room door had woken him, so he slipped on yesterday's clothes and strode across the room to stare through the peephole. Daniels stood outside, holding a bag from Panera. He pulled back the security chain, and she entered.

"Why didn't you answer your phone? I was worried about you," she said.

"I never heard it ring."

"Check it, if you don't believe me."

His Droid sat on the night table. A notification bar on the screen said that she'd called six times. She was being truthful, and he felt like an idiot.

"I must have muted the volume. How did you find me?"

From the bag she removed a steak-and-egg bagel and a large cup of coffee. "The FBI has access to every hotel's registration in the country. It makes tracking down suspects a lot easier. You like your coffee with artificial sweetener, right?"

"Good memory. Did you get anything for yourself?"

"I did, and ate it in the car. Sorry, but I was starving. Where did you go last night? I got worried when I saw you'd left, but your car was still there."

She sat down on the bed, and he pulled up the room's only chair and dug in. The food was still warm, and he could feel it healing his insides as it reached his stomach. "I took an Uber to a bar and closed the place down. Then I Ubered it here. What time is it, anyway?"

"Eight thirty."

"Have you been up all night?"

"Afraid so." Her hand touched the sheets, and she pulled it away in alarm. "These are soaking wet."

"I was having a bad dream."

"You have nightmares?" she asked.

He said nothing and continued to eat.

"Do you suffer from PTSD?" she asked.

Daniels was not the type to let up, and he decided to answer her.

"Yes. This was something that happened to me as a kid."

"It must have been traumatic. Was your brother in the dream?"

He stared at her. "How did you know that?"

"Your brother was murdered last night. It's only natural that it would spark a memory from when you were kids. I'm sorry it was a bad one."

"So am I."

She pushed herself off the bed and came over to him. Her palm touched his forehead, and she frowned. "You're really warm. Do you feel okay?"

"I'm hungover. It was a bad night." He offered her the last bite, and when it was declined, popped it into his mouth. Done, he wiped his mouth with a paper napkin. "So what can I do for you, Special Agent Daniels?"

"You're still angry at me, aren't you?"

"A favor of a reply would be appreciated."

"What is that supposed to mean?"

"That's the line that junk mail companies print on the outside of envelopes they send out. I texted and called, and you didn't reply. Do you have any idea how crummy that made me feel?"

"I'm sorry. I should have called you back."

"But you didn't. Your niece said it was standard behavior."

"When did you talk to Nicki?"

"Why don't you call your niece and ask her yourself?" He got out of the chair, went to the bathroom, and took a cold shower to get his heart racing. She was still standing in the middle of the room when he came out. His open suitcase sat on the dresser, and he dressed in a pair of cargo fishing shorts and a T-shirt that said JIMMY BUFFETT FOR PRESIDENT while she turned her back and stared out the window.

"All done," he said.

Turning around, she eyed his wardrobe. "I thought you said you were on a job."

"I was going to Key West for some R&R when I heard about Elsie Tanner's murder and her granddaughter's abduction," he said. "It struck a nerve, and I asked the director of Team Adam if I could handle it. He agreed, and sent me the file, which I printed off my computer. Then, I drove up here."

"What do you mean, it struck a nerve?"

"I was nearly abducted as a kid, and I screamed my head off. The file said the granddaughter's scream was heard all over the neighborhood. That nerve."

"I'm sorry. I didn't know."

Their relationship hadn't progressed enough for him to feel comfortable talking about his first brush with evil, or its aftermath, and he slipped on his Top-Siders.

"How about a lift to my car?" he asked.

"Sure, Jon," she said. "Whatever you'd like."

CHAPTER 13

Florida was bursting at the seams. Every day, the state added a thousand new residents, not including newborns. The population growth wasn't expected to stop until it reached thirty million residents. By then, all the desirable places to live would be taken, and hopefully the out-of-staters would stop coming.

Living in the Sunshine State wasn't paradise, not with monster hurricanes and man-eating alligators that appeared on golf courses and front lawns. But it was nicer than anywhere else on the East Coast, so the people kept on moving down.

Because of the growth, traffic was a nightmare, and the major roadways often resembled parking lots. Tampa was no exception, and they crawled down the four-lane Veterans Expressway with Daniels manning the wheel.

"We need to talk about what happened at the Jayhawk," she said. "I know it's painful, but I've got to do it."

"No such thing as a free meal, huh?" he said.

"Jon, please let me do my job."

"Did you get in hot water for letting me walk away last night?"

She nodded stiffly. "My boss chewed me out pretty good."

"I'm sorry, but I couldn't stay there."

"There's no need to apologize."

"Instead of grilling me, may I suggest another approach?"

"What would that be?"

"Let me tell you what I think is going on. When I'm finished, you can ask me all the questions you want. Okay?"

"Sure."

He spent a moment collecting his thoughts. He had worked cases with the FBI before, and knew how their agents operated. There was a voice-activated tape recorder in Daniels's purse, and everything he was about to say would be recorded, and later analyzed. He couldn't blame Beth for this; Logan was an accomplice to a murder and a kidnapping, and he'd been the last person to talk to Logan before he'd died.

"Let's start with the facts. A dozen women have been abducted, and there are no clues to their whereabouts. That's hard to fathom, considering the resources the state uses to find missing people. There are high-resolution surveillance cameras embedded in light poles on every highway, and in traffic lights at major intersections. The images are fed into computers with facial recognition software programs, which lets law enforcement capture bad guys on the run. It's also a handy tool when looking for missing people, because the only way to get around in the state is by car. Yet, so far, there have been no hits." He paused. "Sound about right?"

"You're on fire. Keep talking," she said.

"You were brought in to run the investigation because you're an expert in human trafficking. Correct?"

"Correct."

"Now, I'm going to go out on a limb, but I'm pretty sure that you started working the case from the start. Am I right?"

"How did you know that?"

"Personal history."

"What is that supposed to mean?"

"The first victim was abducted four weeks ago, which is when you stopped talking with me," he said. "Then another woman vanished, then another. You got so wrapped up in your investigation, that you shut out the real world. You didn't talk to me, or your sister, or your niece. Total tunnel vision. Am I right?"

"Yes, you are. I get wrapped up in my cases, and stop talking to people. I was going to call you once I was done. I enjoyed our dates."

"So did I. The people behind these abductions have done this before, haven't they?"

Her jaw tightened. "Who told you that?"

"You just did."

"Why, what did I say?"

"You confirmed that you started working the case at the beginning. The first victim was a Hispanic woman from Miami in her late forties. Your specialty is finding missing kids, not middle-aged women. The Miami abduction must have matched an abduction that took place somewhere else, where a juvenile was taken."

"You don't miss much. The Miami abduction matched a case in Jacksonville where a teenage girl disappeared three months ago. I worked the Jacksonville case, so my boss gave me the assignment."

"What made the cases similar?"

A driver in the left lane needed to move over. She let the vehicle cut in front of her, then said, "I can't tell you that. It's against bureau rules."

"Can I guess?"

"Fire away."

"Were there demonic symbols left at the crime scenes?"

"Who the hell told you that?"

"My brother had a 666 tattoo on his neck, and there was a 666 spray-painted on the victim's driveway in Lakeland. Sorry, cat's out of the bag."

"Please don't go around repeating that. We don't need wild stories about devil worshippers splashed across every newspaper in the country."

"The sheriff in Polk County already leaked it to the media."

"He's a fucking idiot. No one's going to believe him."

"My lips are sealed."

"Thank you."

"If you want my opinion, the guys who are behind these crimes aren't really devil worshippers. It's a smoke screen. You should ignore the demonic symbols."

"If they're not devil worshippers, then what are they?"

"They're criminals. While in prison, my brother was recruited into a gang whose leader is named Cano. Logan said that Cano would cast spells over the guards, and get them to secretly bring laptops and cell phones into the prison. Logan made it sound like Cano was a witch doctor who could track people with his spells."

"You think it's a bunch of bull?"

"Of course it's bull. Cano is from Colombia. When I was a SEAL, I did several rescue missions in Colombia, and got to know the country pretty well. There's an indigenous tree called the borrachero that produces beautiful white-and-yellow trumpet flowers. When those flowers are ground up, they become a drug called scopolamine, which the locals call Devil's Breath. Blow some in a person's face, or slip it into their drink, and they turn into a zombie. My guess is, Cano got some Devil's Breath smuggled into the prison, and is drugging the guards."

"So Cano's a fake."

"Absolutely. If Cano can perform black magic and cast spells, what does he need laptops and cell phones for?"

"Good point."

Tampa International Airport abutted the highway they were driving on. A jumbo jet flew directly over their vehicle with its landing wheels down, the sound making conversation impossible. Daniels exited onto Interstate 275 north, and soon they were driving past Tampa's jagged skyline of office buildings and new construction.

"Is that it?" she asked.

"I have one more thing to share. Call it a suspicion," he said. "I think the gang behind these abductions is in the Tampa Bay area." He paused. "Am I warm?"

"That's the assumption we're working off. How did you know?"

"Two things tipped me off. Dexter Hudson murdered Elsie Tanner and took her granddaughter. Last night, he murdered my brother. Dexter could have taken off between murders, but that's unlikely. I'm guessing he's hiding out in this area."

"One guy doesn't mean the whole gang is here."

"I said there were two things."

"Yes, you did. What's the second?"

"Tampa is ground zero for the FBI's investigation. You're camped out at the Marriott on State Road 54, and are taking people there to be questioned. You're also butting heads with the sheriff's department, which tells me you have a lot of agents sniffing around. There could be only one reason for that."

She let out a frustrated sigh. "Are we making our presence that obvious?"

"Yes, but I don't think you have a choice. This gang is here, and you need to find them. Hiding your presence won't accomplish anything. May I ask you a question?"

"What's that?"

"What led you here?"

"We had a report in Miami of a guy with a Fu Manchu and sideburns in the neighborhood where the first abduction took place. He showed up again in Orlando, then was spotted in Keystone. He got spotted several more times in Tampa after that, leading us to believe he's camped out here with his gang. Everything you've told me confirms that."

"So the key to solving this is Dexter."

"It certainly seems that way."

- - -

A few minutes later she pulled into the Jayhawk's parking lot. It looked worse in the daylight, the sidewalks cracked and buckled from the relentless heat. All that remained of last night's shooting was a chalk outline on the pavement where Logan had fallen and died. It still wasn't sinking in that Logan was gone, and he wondered if it ever would. When this was over, he planned to bury his brother next to his parents at the cemetery in Fort Lauderdale. Maybe then he could achieve some kind of closure.

"Are you okay?" she asked.

"Not really," he admitted.

The office door opened, and Skip came outside. Seeing Lancaster, he tipped his head and gave him a two-finger salute. It was not a mocking gesture, but a way of saying thanks for hiding the bag of dope that Lancaster had found on the desk.

Skip went back inside. Lancaster undid his seat belt and turned to face her.

"I can solve this thing," he said.

Her eyes went wide. "Your brother told you how to find Dexter, didn't he?"

"In a manner of speaking, yes, and it shouldn't take me very long. Once I find Dexter, you can put his feet to the fire, and get him to tell us where the victims are. Case solved."

"You've got this whole thing figured out, don't you?"

"Yes, but I can't do it alone. We need to team up. You need to let me join the FBI's investigation."

"I'd get fired if I did that."

"Ask your boss for permission. If he says yes, you're in the clear."

"What if my boss says no?"

"Then I'll round up my old SEAL buddies, and find Dexter myself."

"My boss is going to want to know what your brother told you. Are you going to tell me what he said?"

Lancaster shook his head. Daniels exploded and grabbed his arm.

"God damn it, Jon! You agreed to answer my questions," she said angrily.

"I changed my mind. Either we solve this as a team, or I'll do it on my own. Take it or leave it."

A long moment passed. She was still holding his arm. They'd hugged and kissed on their dates, and he'd enjoyed the intimacy, but this was different; if she didn't let go, whatever thing they'd shared would be destroyed.

"Call me when you've made up your mind," he said.

She let go of him, her lips moving in silent rage. He climbed out of the car and slammed the door. His own vehicle was where he'd parked it last night, the roof covered in bird droppings. He backed out and tried to leave. He couldn't get past Daniels's vehicle and had to drive over the chalk outline. An unearthly chill passed through his body, and he turned onto Nebraska and hit the gas.

CHAPTER 14

Daniels found a service station and filled up her tank. She was ready to erupt and took several deep breaths to calm herself down. Jon's refusal to answer her question had made her so angry that she considered dragging him to the nearest police station, and throwing him into a cell. She'd done that with uncooperative witnesses before, and it always paid dividends.

Only she'd let him go. That wasn't like her, and she supposed it was the nagging desire to rekindle their relationship, and start dating again. It was weird. She liked athletic-looking men, and Jon wasn't that. Nor was he handsome or debonair. His wardrobe left a lot to be desired, and the blond stubble that covered his chin would never pass as a beard. So what was the attraction? She wasn't entirely sure, just that it was real, and that she wanted to see him again.

She entered the station's convenience store to buy a water and spied three teenage boys hovering around the register. They wore heavy gold chains and looked like trouble. She placed her purchase on the counter, tossed her money down, then pulled back her blazer to show them the sidearm strapped to her side.

"Get out of here," she said.

"You can't order us around. We didn't do nothing," the tallest one said.

She showed him her badge. "I'm with the FBI, and I can do whatever the hell I want, which includes searching you. If I find any drugs or weapons, I'll arrest you. Now get your sorry asses out of this store, and don't come back."

The teens took off. Through the store window she watched them race down the sidewalk as if their pants were on fire. It lifted her spirits, and the manager gave her an appreciative smile along with her change.

She drove north on the interstate. A few miles before her exit, she got a call from her boss. His name was Joseph Hacker, J. T. to his subordinates, and he was the acting director of the FBI's Criminal Investigative Division. They had worked together for over a decade, and J. T. was responsible for her rapid rise within the department.

"Good morning, J. T.," she said.

"Hello, Beth. Are you on a speakerphone?"

"Yes. I'm in my car, driving back to the hotel."

"Are you alone?"

The question caught her by surprise. "I am," she replied.

"Good. This conversation goes no further."

"Understood."

"Have you had a chance to question Jon Lancaster?"

"We just finished up. Jon did most of the talking. He knows a lot."

"Do you think he's involved with the gang behind these abductions?"

"Absolutely not. Jon is here on behalf of Team Adam, and discovered that his brother Logan was involved in Elsie Tanner's murder and her granddaughter's abduction. That's the story Jon gave to the police, and I have to believe that it's true."

"Will Jon help us?"

"That's up in the air. Jon wants to join my team. In return, he'll help us track down the gang's ringleader, Dexter Hudson."

"What did you tell him?"

"I didn't give him an answer."

"But you're considering it."

"I don't have much choice. Our investigation has hit a brick wall. If Jon can find Dexter, then I need to bring him on board."

"I'm not comfortable with this, Beth. Call me on Skype when you reach your hotel. We need to talk this over further."

J. T.'s voice had turned cold. That wasn't like him, and she sensed that she'd said the wrong thing. She agreed and ended the connection. Her exit was up ahead, and she flipped her indicator on. The bureau had forty-five directors who dealt with everything from domestic terrorism to cyber security, and they'd all been walking on eggshells since Deputy Director McCabe had been fired and stripped of his pension. It was a hard time to be in the FBI, and she assumed that J. T. didn't want his career to go down in flames because one of his agents had done something stupid.

- - -

The Residence Inn by Marriott on State Road 54 was tucked behind a complex of commercial development and invisible from the street. She used a plastic key to take the elevator to the basement where the conference rooms were located, and walked down a hallway to an unmarked door, which she rapped softly upon.

The door swung in, and she entered. Her team had seven members including herself, and the others sat around a conference table, poring over reports. Photos of the victims were thumbtacked to a cork bulletin board, while a whiteboard contained the details of each abduction. To help them keep their geography straight, a map of Florida was taped to a wall, with gold stars applied to each city where a woman had vanished.

The room also had a flat-screen TV, and it contained a live feed of surveillance cameras from Tampa's highways and roads. The images were sharp, the faces of drivers and their passengers being compared to the victims on a software program. So far, there had been no hits, but there was always the chance.

She murmured hello, and got several muted greetings in return. She didn't need to ask them how things were going; the worry on their faces said it all.

She entered a breakout room, and shut the door. Taking her laptop from her purse, she put it on the table, and sat down in front of it. The FBI had switched to using Microsoft Surface Pros, which were the size of a tablet but more powerful than most PCs.

She got on to Skype and found J. T. in her contacts. Moments later, his face filled the screen. He was pushing fifty but looked older, his face lined with worry. His unhappiness was more evident than it had been during their phone conversation.

"I'm not comfortable with this situation," he said, forgoing the usual hello. "Jon Lancaster is the brother to a suspect in this investigation. He's also your boyfriend. How the hell do we put these things into a report?"

"He can find Dexter Hudson. I have to use him," she said defensively.

"Please answer my question."

"My relationship with Jon has no bearing on the case. I wasn't planning to include it in my report."

"But what if your investigation breaks bad?"

She shook her head, not understanding. J. T. gave her a slow burn. He didn't like to explain himself, and she found the ensuing silence unbearable.

"We're going to find these guys," she said. "They're hiding out in the Tampa Bay area, and we're going to sniff them out. It's just a matter of time."

"But what if one of their victims is dead?" he said. "You know how the families react when a loved one dies. They blame us, and we end up in court."

One of the sad truths about performing rescues was that the victim's family was often not prepared to deal with tragedy. If a victim died in captivity, there was nothing the FBI could do about it. But that didn't stop the grieving family from filing a wrongful death lawsuit, which would lead to the bureau having to turn over the investigation's reports, and the agents who'd handled the case being deposed. Daniels had been on the receiving end of these lawsuits before, and they were never fun.

"That wouldn't be good," she admitted.

"Actually, it would be a shit storm," he corrected her. "If it came out that you and Lancaster were romantically involved, and that his brother was a suspect, we'd all go down hard. I could lose my job, and so could you."

"What do you think the odds are of that happening?"

"You mean of a lawsuit?"

"Yes."

"If there were only one victim, I'd say the odds were slim. But because there are so many victims, the odds are much higher. We already have our lawyers gearing up for it, just to be safe."

Her mouth had gone dry. Their work was hard enough without throwing a bunch of lawyers into the mix. She took the water bottle from her purse and had a drink.

"There's another problem with Lancaster," he said.

The words caught her by surprise. She didn't date men with problems, and she wondered what J. T. had unearthed in Jon's past.

"What's that?" she asked.

"I called the Broward County Sheriff's Office this morning, and had an off-the-record conversation with Jon's former boss, Sheriff Dempsey. I asked Dempsey if he believed Jon might be involved with these abductions."

"What did he say?"

"Dempsey didn't think Jon was capable of doing such a thing."

"Then what's the problem?"

"Jon worked for the sheriff's department for fifteen years. I asked Dempsey if there were any blemishes on Jon's résumé."

"Were there?"

"That's the interesting part. After Jon became a detective, he was accused of breaking the rules during several investigations. These accusations came from attorneys whose clients Jon had busted. The accusations were formally reviewed by the sheriff's department, and Jon was cleared of any impropriety."

Lawyers were paid to get their clients off, and she wanted to ask J. T. why he was bringing this up. She bit her tongue and waited for him to continue.

"Sheriff Dempsey confided that he believed that Jon *had* broken the rules during these investigations, but had cleaned up his transgressions," he said. "The sheriff said, and I quote, 'Jon is a master at covering his tracks.'"

Jon often talked about his cases as a police officer, and he was rightfully proud of his record while on the force. Not once had he mentioned tampering with or destroying evidence, which was what J. T. was inferring that Jon had done as a detective.

"Did Sheriff Dempsey offer any proof?" she asked.

"No, he didn't. But he seemed convinced of it."

"I don't think we should judge Jon based upon what his ex-boss thinks he may have done. Jon has been fighting the good fight a long time, and the world is a better place because of it."

"Are you in love with him?"

It was a fair question, one that she'd asked herself when they'd dated. Jon wasn't her type, yet she'd found herself drawn to him.

"I don't think *love* is the right word," she said.

"Then what?"

"I admire him."

The answer caught J. T. off guard, and he gingerly touched his stomach. From his desk drawer he removed a box of antacids, popped two tablets into his mouth, vigorously chewed, and then washed them down with a glass of water.

"So what do you want me to do?" she said.

"The way I see it, you're stuck between a rock and a hard place," he said. "Your investigation is stalled, and more women are disappearing. The only person who can help you is also capable of ruining your career. That's a no-win situation."

"I know it is," she said.

"I'd *like* to offer my opinion, but I don't know enough about Lancaster to do that," he said. "The decision rests squarely on your shoulders. It's your call."

The FBI usually stood behind its agents, but there were always exceptions, and she supposed this was what happened when people were made to work in a climate of fear. "I need to think about this. I'll call you later," she said.

"I'll be here," he said.

She hit a command on her keyboard, and the screen went dark.

CHAPTER 15

Leaving the Jayhawk, Lancaster drove to the county medical examiner's office on North Forty-Sixth Street. It was a depressing place, the soulless brick building sitting on earth so brown that it looked scorched.

He spent a half hour waiting in line to claim his brother's body, and another half hour arranging for Logan to be transported home to Fort Lauderdale after the medical examiner performed an autopsy. The process was draining, and he went outside to the parking lot and sat in his car for a while.

He'd discovered the music of Jimmy Buffett after getting out of the navy, and had been a fan ever since. He listened to the steel drum happiness of Buffett's classic song "Volcano" on his car's CD player, and gradually started to feel better.

He was having a hard time accepting that Logan was dead. It wasn't easy having your brother in prison for twenty-five years, and he'd convinced himself that someday, when he and Logan were old men, they'd reunite, and become friends again. Maybe it was a fantasy, but it had made the situation a lot easier to accept.

His cell phone vibrated on the passenger seat. He flipped it over and saw a strange number with an 813 area code. He was in no mood to talk and let it go into voice mail.

A minute later the same person called again.

Then they called again.

Pissed off, he answered it.

"Jon, is that you?" a female voice asked.

"Who is this?"

"Lauren Gamble with the *Tampa Bay Times*."

"Yeah, it's me."

"Are you okay? You don't sound like yourself."

He asked himself why Gamble was calling. Had she heard about Logan's murder, and figured out they were brothers? He hadn't seen any reporters milling around the Jayhawk last night, and told himself to stop being paranoid and talk to her.

"My sinuses are bothering me," he said. "What's up?"

"I'm in Gainesville working on a story about yesterday's kidnapping," Gamble said. "There are some eerie similarities with the victim's background and Elsie Tanner's."

"Like what?"

"The victim's name is Audrey Sipos, and she's a thirty-year-old nurse practitioner who lives in a remote area several miles outside of town. My GPS couldn't locate the address, so I had to ask directions."

"Just like Elsie's place."

"Correct. Sipos left work yesterday and went to the mall to do some shopping. Her kidnapper abducted her about a half hour after she returned home. The timeline is similar to Elsie visiting the Citrus Park Mall."

"This is very helpful. Good job."

"There's more. Sipos works at Shands Hospital, which is part of the University of Florida. Every person I spoke with at the hospital told me how compassionate Sipos is, and how she always went out of her way to help patients and their families."

"Another Good Samaritan."

"That's right. Sipos studied nursing at UF, and was a member of the Alpha Chi Omega sorority. I visited the sorority this morning, and discovered that there's an award named after her."

"What did she do?"

"She saved a sorority sister who was being raped by a guy who picked her up in a bar. This happened when Sipos was a sophomore."

The last three kidnapping victims had made it their mission to help people, and he wondered if that were the case with the previous victims as well.

"Did you share this information with the Gainesville police?" he asked.

"Not yet. I wanted to call you first."

"I appreciate that. But you should tell the police what you've learned. It might help their investigation."

"I'll call them after we hang up. Do you have a minute? I'd like to talk to you about your work with Team Adam. It will help me with my story."

The conversation had taken a bad turn. He didn't want Gamble's story to be about him, and why he'd chosen to join Team Adam after retiring from the police force. That wasn't anybody's business, and he planned to keep it that way.

A black woman clutching a baby to her chest came out of the medical examiner's building and walked past his car. She'd been behind him in line, and had scowled when he'd offered his spot to her. She was racked with sobs, her face awash in tears.

"Let me call you right back," he said.

He ended the call and got out. The woman was trying to get her keys out of her purse while not losing her baby. He offered to help, and this time she accepted. He fished out her keys and manually opened the car, then opened the back door so she could secure her child into a baby seat in the back. The child was fussy, and it took a while.

"Would you like a water? I've got one in my car," he said.

"No, but thank you," she said.

"My name's Jon."

"Shawnda."

He dug a wad of Kleenex out of his pocket and gave it to her. She dabbed at her eyes and tried to pull herself together. "Came here to claim my sister's things, only her stuff's down at the police station," she said. "Got to go down there and go through this nonsense all over again. Why didn't they put a sign up saying that?"

For Shawnda's sister's body to be here meant she hadn't died of natural causes. The poor woman was barely holding on, and he wished there was more he could do.

"I'm sorry for your loss," he said.

"Why are you here?" she asked.

"To claim my brother."

"World isn't a safe place anymore."

"No, it's not."

She thanked him for his help, and drove away. He returned to his car and got directions to his hotel. Back on Interstate 275, he got a call from Gamble and let it go to voice mail. A minute later, she called again. Then, she called again. She was like a dog that refused to let go of a bone.

"Sorry about that," he answered, "but I needed to help a lady in distress."

"You enjoy doing that, don't you?" Gamble said.

"I guess. Look, I would really prefer if you didn't focus on me when you write your story. There are a lot more important people in this investigation."

"The managing editor at my paper feels otherwise. I told him how you volunteered to work this case, and he thought that was fascinating."

"I'm actually a pretty dull guy," he said.

"You could have fooled me," she said. "So here's what I want to ask you. I did a search on the internet, and found a photo on the front page of the *Times-Picayune* that was taken after Hurricane Katrina hit New Orleans. It shows you standing on an airport tarmac with a bunch of kids who got separated from their parents. There's another man in the photo named Andy Vita, who's identified as being a member of Team Adam. Were you doing a job for them?"

"No. I didn't even know what Team Adam was back then."

"Was Andy Vita the reason you joined?"

"Andy was part of the reason. He had amazing resources. With one phone call, he could move mountains. That stuck with me."

"So he was your inspiration. What exactly did he do?"

"How much do you know about Katrina?"

"Not much. I was in middle school."

"It was chaos. New Orleans was under martial law, and law enforcement agencies from all over the country sent teams to help out. I led the team that was sent by the Broward Sheriff's Office. There were ten of us. We were taking boats into flooded areas and pulling kids out of trees and off rooftops who'd gotten separated from their families. We'd take them back to the camps so the doctors could check them out, and then do it all over again. It went on for days."

"How many hours a day?"

"All day, all night."

"You didn't sleep?"

"We couldn't. The kids had no food or water. If we didn't find them quickly, they'd starve to death."

"How many did you save?"

"We had four small boats. Probably fifty kids a day."

"You must have been exhausted by the time it was over."

While training to become a SEAL, he'd often stayed up for seventy-two hours straight while preparing for missions. It had taught him how far his body could go.

"I don't remember. It was a long time ago," he said.

"How did you connect with Andy Vita?"

"That happened at the end. Most of the kids were reunited with their parents. But there were about twenty that weren't."

"Their parents abandoned them?"

"It was nothing like that. Millions of people had to evacuate, and families got separated. Then the floodwaters rushed in, and people ran for their lives. It was like a war zone."

"Didn't the kids have cell phones?"

"These kids were poor. Besides, the flooding took down the cell towers. There was no communication, except by walkie-talkie."

"That sounds like a nightmare."

"It was. We eventually tracked the parents down. They'd gone to live with other family members, and were scattered all over the country. Houston, Atlanta, even Chicago. That presented a problem. How were we supposed to reunite them? We couldn't just put the kids on a Greyhound bus and say good luck. That's where Andy Vita and Team Adam came in."

"They saved the day."

"I'd never seen anything like it. Andy arranged for private jets to fly into New Orleans, and take the kids to the cities their parents were living in. I personally put every kid on one of those jets to make sure they got out okay. Andy was with me the whole time."

"Who paid for the jets?"

"Team Adam has arrangements with the major airlines. If a child needs to be flown across the country, an agent can arrange for a private flight at no charge. For the NOLA operation, the jets were supplied by Delta and Southwest."

"That's way cool."

He'd been enjoying their conversation up until that point. Rescue operations were often mired in red tape and politics, and as a result, innocent people suffered. Vita had demonstrated that there was a better way to get things done.

"Have you ever covered a disaster?" he asked.

His question caught her off guard.

"No, I haven't," she said.

"Saving lives hinges upon everyone working together. While Vita was reuniting those kids with their families, people were dying inside the Superdome because there weren't any doctors. Ten miles outside the city there were truckloads of medicine waiting to be sent in, only they weren't."

"Why not?"

"Because the mayor of New Orleans and the governor hated each other, and never got on the phone. They had a pissing contest, and innocent people died because of it."

"Thank you for telling me that. It explains a lot."

He didn't know what it explained, nor did he care. He had a job to do, and talking to Gamble wasn't getting it done.

"I've got to run," he said.

Then, he hung up.

- - -

Twenty minutes later, he parked beneath a shady tree in his hotel's parking lot. It was noon, and he was surprised that he hadn't heard back from Beth. At the end of the day, it really didn't matter what she said. Dexter Hudson was the key to solving this puzzle, and he was going to track the bastard down, with or without the FBI's help.

Daniels awaited him in the lobby. She had her cell phone out, and slipped the device into her purse as he came inside. Her badge was clipped to her lapel, indicating that this wasn't a social call.

"I was just about to call you," she said.

"My ears were burning. What's up?"

"We need to go for a ride. I want you to take a look at something."

"Are you taking me up on my offer?"

"We can discuss that in the car."

They headed for the door, and she pulled her car keys out.

"I'll drive," she said.

"What exactly are you taking me to see?"

"A body."

CHAPTER 16

With Beth, it was all about being in control. She insisted on driving, even though she was unfamiliar with the area. Arguing with her was usually a losing proposition, and he strapped himself into the passenger seat of her vehicle.

"Where are we going?" he asked.

"A little town called Tarpon Springs. Are you familiar with it?"

"Yeah. Although I haven't been there since I was a kid."

She drove west until she reached US 19 and headed north. US 19 was an ugly eight-lane highway with long uninterrupted stretches. Driving on it felt like NASCAR.

"Whose body do you want me to look at?"

"We're not sure. It got hauled up in a fishing boat's nets early this morning. It's a white male approximately six feet tall and a hundred sixty pounds with a bullet hole in his back. He wasn't carrying any ID. I need you to take a look, and see if you think it's the driver from last night that you shot at."

"It doesn't sound like a match."

"How can you say that without looking at him?"

"I shot at that bastard twice."

"Maybe one of your bullets missed."

In the navy, he'd shot over ten thousand rounds of ammo from a variety of different weapons and had won medals for his marksmanship.

"I don't miss at close range," he said.

"Take a look anyway," she said.

"You're the boss. Have you made a decision on my offer?"

"Let's talk about it over lunch. I have a proposition for you."

They came to a busy intersection, and Daniels turned onto Tarpon Avenue. The scenery dramatically changed, and she drove down a narrow cobblestone street lined with stately Victorian houses with gabled roofs. It led to the historic downtown, which had gone through a transformation, the dusty antique and consignment shops he remembered as a kid replaced by trendy eateries with outdoor seating and a microbrewery.

Soon they were at the sponge docks, and she looked for parking. Sponges had once been Florida's biggest industry, and Tarpon Springs had been its capital. The divers who risked their lives every day needed to eat, and the main drag was filled with restaurants that had sprung up to serve them and continued to thrive.

She parked in a gravel lot. Across the street was a waterfront restaurant called Rusty Bellies that also had a seafood store. Three police cruisers were parked in front of the restaurant with their lights flashing. Next to the cruisers was an unmarked van that he guessed was a CSI team.

They had to walk up a flight of stairs to enter the restaurant. A group of waiters sat at a long table, talking among themselves. Otherwise, the place was empty due to the crime scene out back.

They passed through a pair of doors to a balcony that overlooked the Anclote River. Down below was a dock where two commercial fishing boats were moored. A body covered in a bright-orange tarp lay on the dock. There was a breeze, and the tarp was waving like a flag. The cops stood around the body, talking in low voices.

They went down a short flight of stairs, and Daniels identified herself.

"Who's in charge?" Daniels asked.

"That would be me," the female officer said.

"Where's the crew that found the body?"

"I had them go inside the fish store," the female officer said.

"Do you know these men?"

"I do. My kids go to school with their kids. They're good people."

"I need to ask you a question, and I want a straight answer. Do you think one of them might have removed a wallet from the dead man's pocket? Be straight with me."

The female officer hemmed and hawed.

"I don't see any of them doing a thing like that," she finally said.

Daniels wasn't convinced. To Lancaster she said, "I'll be right back," and she left with the female officer in tow. Beth was an aggressive interrogator, and he pitied the fishermen if they decided not to cooperate with her.

Kneeling, he lifted the tarp. The dead man lay on his stomach. He had stringy hair and a nasty tattoo of a snake on his neck. A body thrown into the ocean sank to the bottom as its lungs filled with water, and stayed submerged until bacteria in the gut produced enough gas to bring it to the surface, which usually took a day or so. The corpse on the dock hadn't been dead very long.

But was it the same guy he'd shot in the fleeing car outside the Jayhawk? The stiff's T-shirt had a bullet hole right between the shoulder blades. With his fingertips, he gently opened the tear for a closer look. The wound was larger than normal. That decided it. Daniels returned a few minutes later.

"Any luck?" he asked.

"The fishermen are telling the truth. They didn't steal the dead guy's wallet," she said. "How about you?"

"It's him," he said.

"You sure?"

"Positive."

"I thought you said you shot him twice."

"I did shoot him twice. Both bullets entered through the same hole in his back. That's why the wound is larger than normal."

"Come on, that's not possible."

"See for yourself."

They both knelt down, and he lifted the tarp and showed her the enlarged wound.

"If you don't believe me, ask the pathologist after the autopsy is performed. They're going to find two slugs in the same hole." He stood up and dusted off his knees. This bastard had been an accessory to his brother's murder, and he stared at the body long and hard. Rot in hell, he thought.

He offered Daniels his hand, and she rose as well.

"Where are you taking me to lunch?" he asked.

- - -

They took a walk down the street to Hellas. It was one of the first restaurants to serve the sponge divers, and was decorated with furniture and artwork that had been shipped over from Greece many years ago. The outdoor seating area was full, and Daniels asked the hostess for a secluded table inside.

The interior was deceptively large. Waiters wearing white shirts set fire to skillets of saganaki and shouted "Opa!" while diners gorged on octopus and souvlaki. In the back of the room was a garish blue neon bar that could have been a set in *Pulp Fiction*. The hostess seated them at a raised table, and handed them oversize menus.

"Your waiter will be right over."

She departed. Daniels put her elbows on the table and looked him in the eye. Her face softened, and she gave him a rare smile. Beth could be charming when she wanted to be, and he told himself to be careful.

"I talked to my boss about your offer to join my team," she said.

"What did he say?"

"He was against it, but said it was ultimately my call. I want you on board, provided you do as you're told. Think you're up to that?"

"What do I have to gain from disobeying you?"

"You want to pay Dexter Hudson back for murdering your brother. I saw it in your face last night. And don't you dare tell me that isn't true."

FBI agents were trained in the art of reading facial expressions. He broke eye contact and stared at the table, which was covered in aqua-blue tiles.

"Look at me," she said.

He lifted his gaze and saw the fire in her eyes.

"Dexter is our key to finding the victims," she said. "If you kill him, which you're perfectly capable of doing, we may never find them. I can't let that happen."

"Can I kill him after we rescue the victims?"

"That's not funny."

Their waiter came. Daniels ordered a Greek salad for two and the broiled seafood combo to share. Glasses of water appeared along with a basket of bread and a plate of olive oil. He dipped a piece of bread and popped it into his mouth.

"You didn't answer me," she said.

"It's your show, Beth," he said. "I'll do whatever you want. But . . ." He let the sentence hang and popped another piece of bread into his mouth and chewed. "I won't be your lapdog. I'll share with you what my brother told me, provided you share with me. Otherwise, no deal."

"Fair enough. Should I go first?"

"That would be a good start."

She reached into her purse and produced a sleek black Droid, which she placed on the table between them. "This cell phone was found in the driveway of one of the Miami victims. We're certain that it fell out of the kidnapper's pocket before he fled the scene. The phone is encrypted, and had its microphone, camera, and other connectivity functions disabled."

He picked up the phone and examined it. Logan's phone had also been a black Droid, and he wondered if the two things were connected.

"The phone also contains a privacy app called KYTS, which stands for Keep Your Texts Safe," she said. "The app looks like a calculator, and can be used to do simple equations. But it's really a communication device. By entering a four-digit PIN and password, the user enters an encrypted vault, and can store text messages and videos."

"Is that legal?"

"There's nothing illegal if a person wants to keep their communications hidden. But if the phone is being altered and sold for criminal activity, then it's illegal, and the manufacturer will be prosecuted."

"My brother had a black Droid. Was it altered in this manner?"

"Yes. And it also had a KYTS app."

"Did you find anything valuable on it?"

"Unfortunately, it had been scrubbed clean by the time we examined it."

His cheeks burned. He'd been the last person to handle Logan's cell phone. Did Beth think he'd gone and erased the information on it? She seemed to know what he was thinking, and she reached across the table and touched his wrist.

"Don't worry, you're not a suspect," she said. "The KYTS app lets anyone who knows the phone's number remotely wipe away the data, provided they have the PIN and password. We think your brother's phone was scrubbed after he was shot last night."

"By a member of his gang?"

"That's our guess."

"If the data's been erased, what good is it to your investigation?"

"The company that made your brother's phone, as well as the phone we found in Miami, is called Phantom Communications. This same company also developed the KYTS app. Guess where they have an office."

"Tampa?"

"You got it. All roads lead to Tampa."

The waiter brought their Greek salad. Beth didn't think the scoop of potato salad was large enough considering she'd ordered a salad for two, and she made the waiter take it back. She'd done that in restaurants before, and it always amused him.

"Should I assume you're going to raid Phantom Communications' Tampa office, and seize their files and computers?" he asked.

"Our lawyers are drawing up a search warrant, and plan to take it to a judge tomorrow," she said. "Our evidence is circumstantial, so we need to word the warrant correctly, otherwise the case might later get tossed."

"Everything by the book."

"That's right, Jon. It's how the FBI works."

She tore off a piece of bread and chewed. She'd shared a valuable piece of information with him, and he needed to do the same. He'd lied earlier when he'd said he could find Dexter. The truth was, he could find people that knew where Dexter was hiding out, and with Beth's help, would get them to cough up the information.

The waiter returned with a new Greek salad, which Beth inspected.

"Don't send it back. I'm hungry," he said.

She decided the salad was fine, and they both started eating.

CHAPTER 17

Along with being a picky eater, Daniels was hell on wheels, and the forty-five-minute trip from Tarpon Springs to the Florida Department of Law Enforcement's Regional Operations Center in Tampa took less than half an hour. She parked in a visitor spot and killed the engine before addressing her passenger.

"Are you sure this is going to work?" she asked.

"Positive," he said.

"Let's go over it again, just so I'm clear."

He'd already explained how he planned to track down Dexter, and didn't see the need to repeat himself. "What aren't you clear about?"

"I want to make sure we're not breaking any laws," she said.

"Dexter is a member of the Outlaws motorcycle gang," he said. "When Dexter was in Raiford, he joined the Phantoms out of necessity. But he never stopped being an Outlaw. The gang's motto is 'Once an Outlaw, always an Outlaw.'"

"And you think the local gang in Tampa knows where he is?"

"I'm sure of it. When Dexter got released from prison and relocated to Tampa, he would have checked in with the leader of the local club."

"What would he gain from doing that?"

"Motorcycle gangs are tribal, and hold loyalty to a high standard. Dexter would tell the head of the local club that he's available if they needed him. That's important to these guys. I dealt with them as a cop, and know how they behave."

"And you think that you can persuade the leader of the local club to tell us where Dexter is hiding out. Isn't that a bit of a stretch?"

"Not if you help me."

She arched an eyebrow. "How does that work?"

"You grab your team, and we all go pay the local club a visit."

"What do you plan to do, threaten them?"

"In a manner of speaking, yes. But I won't break any laws."

"I'm going to hold you to that."

- - -

The FDLE's primary job was to assist local police when dealing with homicides, drug trafficking, and missing person cases. The Tampa office was one of seven statewide, and employed over two hundred officers, who actually seemed to enjoy their jobs. The receptionist wore a creaseless beige uniform and a shiny gold badge. She handed back their credentials with a smile.

"How may I help you?" she asked.

"We're here to see Missy Hopkins. She's expecting us," Lancaster said.

"I'll tell Special Agent Hopkins you're here. Please make yourselves comfortable."

They moved away from the reception area. Daniels never stopped asking questions when working a case, her brain on overdrive.

"What's your relation to Hopkins?" she asked.

"Our paths crossed after I joined Team Adam," he said. "Missy posted an alert on the Missing Endangered Persons Information Clearinghouse about a missing girl named Tammi. Missy had gotten a tip that Tammi was living in Fort Lauderdale with a couple who were living under assumed names."

"What was their motive?"

"They couldn't have a child of their own, so they stole someone else's. The couple had been seen driving around the neighborhood in a pickup, and they abducted Tammi out of her backyard while she was in a kiddie pool. I was given the case, and I decided to play a hunch. My hunch was that Tammi was enrolled in a public school in Fort Lauderdale, and wasn't at a private school or being homeschooled."

"What did you base this upon?"

"Two things. The pickup was in bad shape, which meant the couple didn't have money. That ruled out private school. They could have homeschooled Tammi, but a neighbor who spotted them said they looked like hillbillies. Parents that homeschool need to get certified by the state. This couple didn't sound like they'd pass."

"It's flimsy, but go on."

"The school district police liaison is named Valerie Richter. I emailed Valerie, and requested that she ask the county's elementary principals if there were any seven-year-old girls suffering emotional problems or depression."

"What led you to that?"

"Kids who get kidnapped have a hard time adjusting if they're older than five. Tammi was seven, and I was thinking she might be struggling with her new life."

"I can see that. What happened?"

"Valerie came back with several leads. I worked through them, and one stood out. A seven-year-old girl named Tina was having outbursts. Tina's parents had enrolled her into Embassy Creek Elementary a few months before. The timing was right, so I got permission to visit the school.

"I watched Tina in the playground. Her hair was a different color, and I wasn't sure it was her. When school let out, I changed my mind. Tina was on a bench with a group of kids, waiting to be picked up.

When the parents came, the kids ran to the cars. Not Tina. She let her mother come to her."

"Tina didn't want to go with her."

"Not in the least. That night I contacted Missy, and told her what I'd found. She drove down the next day, and took over."

"You let Missy rescue the kid? That was nice of you."

"She deserved it."

Many cops enjoyed the limelight, and actually seemed to thrive under it. He'd tasted fame as a cop, and hadn't enjoyed it. To do his work, it was better to be a face in the crowd, and blend into the woodwork. He heard his name being called, and saw Hopkins standing by reception. She was a twenty-year veteran, and her eyes had an ever-present, slightly disapproving look.

"There she is," he said. "Let me introduce you."

- - -

Hopkins's office was adjacent to the crime lab. Each FDLE operations center had a crime lab, which police departments relied upon when dealing with difficult cases. As a result, the labs were always busy, and Hopkins shut the door to keep out the noise. She offered them chairs in front of her desk, then sat behind it.

"It's good to see you, Jon. It's been too long," Hopkins said. "I heard through the grapevine that there's a movie in the works."

"Shooting begins this summer," he said. "Would you like a part?"

She laughed. "No, but thanks for offering."

"I have a favor to ask," he said. "Special Agent Daniels and I are planning to visit the local Outlaws Motorcycle Club. If I remember correctly, the FDLE was working a case against the Outlaws last year, and you were in charge. I'd like to ask you some questions about that case."

He'd hit a nerve, and Hopkins shifted uncomfortably.

"I really don't want to talk about that," she said.

"One of their gang is a suspect in two murders and a kidnapping, and we need to find him," Daniels said. "We'd really appreciate it if you helped us."

Beth was being polite. The FDLE was the most powerful law enforcement body in the state and reported directly to the governor. But the FBI was more powerful, and Hopkins could get herself in hot water if she didn't cooperate with them.

"All right," Hopkins said. "What exactly do you want to know?"

"If I remember correctly, your case was tied into amphetamines," he said. "The Outlaws were cooking speed and supplying it to long-distance truckers, and the Saint Petersburg and Fort Lauderdale clubs were involved. What I'd want to know is, are they still dealing?"

"I could lose my job over this."

"It goes no further than this room," Daniels said. "You have our word."

"Yes, the Outlaws are still dealing speed," Hopkins said. "The operation was in full swing the last time I checked."

"Which was when?" he asked.

"A few weeks ago. It pissed me off that we never busted them. Hopefully, one day we will, and they'll go to prison."

"Why didn't you?" Daniels asked.

Hopkins made a face, the memory eating at her. "I'll give you the official version, and then I'll tell you the real version. We were ready to shut the Outlaws down when we got word from Tallahassee telling us to suspend the operation, and to put our resources against fighting the opioid epidemic, which is one of the governor's top priorities. We had five thousand people die from overdoses last year, so it made sense, at least on paper."

"Are you saying the governor protected the Outlaws?" he said.

"That's right. He protected them."

"Why on earth would he do that?"

"One of the governor's top advisers is Claude Littlejohn, the owner of the King Grocery chain, which is the largest in the state," Hopkins said. "Littlejohn is a wealthy man who wields a big stick. It's rumored that you can't get elected if he isn't backing you. It was Littlejohn who convinced the governor to drop the investigation."

"Why?" Daniels asked.

"Because his business depends on trucking," Hopkins said. "Truckers are supposed to follow something called hours-of-service limits, which is federal law. A trucker is not allowed to drive more than eleven hours straight, but many of them break that rule, and drive sixteen hours or more."

"Are they on speed?" Daniels asked.

"Most of them are. Get on the interstate at night, and watch the semis fly down the road at ninety miles per hour. It's scary as hell. I was told that Littlejohn saves millions of dollars by having his drivers break the rules. Not that he needs it. He's a billionaire."

It was not the first time a politician had put a donor's wishes over the welfare of his constituents, and it probably wouldn't be the last. Hopkins excused herself and left the room. When she returned, she was holding a file, which she gave to them.

"The Outlaws are still under surveillance," she said. "The FDLE considers them a threat, so we monitor their activity. This file contains a log showing every vehicle that comes to their local club. Every vehicle that isn't a motorcycle is carrying speed."

"Can we have this?" Daniels asked.

"Not unless you want to get me fired. Photograph the pages you want on your cell phones. I'm going to the cafeteria for a cold drink. Want something?"

They both declined. Lancaster followed Hopkins into the hall to thank her. She was taking a huge risk, and he wanted her to know how much he appreciated it.

"My name can't be associated with whatever you're doing," Hopkins said.

"You have my word," he said.

She glanced at the door. "What about your friend?"

"Beth's good people. She knows how to keep a secret."

"I don't like the FBI, Jon. They're a bunch of arrogant assholes."

FBI agents weren't known for their bedside manners. But there was a difference between bruising feelings and betrayal, and he had never known Beth to break her word.

"Please don't worry," he said.

"I'll try not to," she said, and walked away.

CHAPTER 18

The Outlaws' headquarters in Saint Petersburg was listed as a nightclub on Google Maps. It was actually a fenced compound in a residential neighborhood that contained a pair of white two-story buildings, neither of which had windows.

They sat in Daniels's vehicle at the end of the block. Lancaster was watching the house through a pair of binoculars while Daniels was on her cell phone arranging for a helicopter to fly over the compound for the purpose of scaring the daylights out of the bikers inside. It was dinnertime, and the neighborhood was quiet.

"Done," Daniels said, ending the call. "The chopper's pilot will text me when they're in range. How are things looking at the club?"

"I think we just got lucky." He passed the binoculars so she could have a look.

"I'm seeing a purple minivan drive into the compound and a wooden gate being pulled back by two guys wearing leather," she said. "Now the van's inside and the gate's being closed. Think it's a shipment of speed?"

"I do. The timing's right."

"How so?"

"Truckers use speed to stay awake at night, and buy it at truck stops on the interstate. The one percenters wait until dark to make their deliveries."

"What's a one percenter?"

"It's what the Outlaws call themselves. Ninety-nine percent of bikers are law-abiding citizens. The other one percent are criminals."

"So they're proud of breaking the law. What degenerates."

She pulled out her cell phone to read a text. "We caught a break. The FBI's crime lab identified the body the fishermen pulled up in Tarpon Springs. His fingerprints were altered by the salt water, but his neck tattoo did the trick. His name is Skyler Seeley, and he served ten years in Raiford for raping a woman in Miami."

She passed him the phone, and he studied Seeley's mug shot. Rapists were on the low rung of the genetic totem pole, and Seeley looked like a Neanderthal. When he'd left the force two years ago, identifying criminals through tattoos had been an inexact science. He didn't like challenging Beth, but wanted to be certain they had the right guy.

"How many bullets did he have in him?" he asked.

"Two. Both in the same spot. Nice shooting."

"Thanks. How do you positively identify someone by a tattoo? Back when I was a cop, that wasn't very reliable."

"It is now. When a person gets arrested, their physical description is put in a police report, including weight, height, hair color, and any tattoos. Since most criminals are inked, the bureau thought it would be a good idea to compile a Tattoo Recognition Database. By getting a tattoo, these idiots make it easier for us to track them down."

She got another text. "The team's ready and so's the chopper. Let's roll."

Her team was parked at the other end of the block in two black SUVs. Each vehicle carried three FBI agents dressed in body armor and carrying assault rifles. They would come running the moment she hit a button on her cell phone.

They crossed and walked up the front path. He pulled a pack of chewing gum from his pocket and offered her a stick. She declined with a shake of her head.

“Take one anyway. It will make you fit in,” he said.

“Is that the deal? I should have worn my leather jacket.”

She popped the gum into her mouth and blew a bubble. They reached the front stoop, and he noticed there was no bell to ring, or welcome mat. He rapped on the front door, and a moment later it opened a foot; a wild-looking guy wearing a leather vest with nothing underneath stuck his head out. He was missing both front teeth, and every word that came out of his mouth was accompanied by a whistle.

“What the fuck do you want?” the wild man said.

Daniels blew a bubble and popped it. Lancaster laughed and said, “I just got out of Coleman, and was friends with Snivelhead. He wanted me to pass a message to the head of your club. Is he around?”

The wild man’s eyes narrowed. “I didn’t catch your name.”

“Jon, my friends call me Jonny.”

“If you knew Snivelhead, tell me his real name, and how long he’s in for.”

“Snivelhead’s real name is Willy White. He’s a lifer.”

“Who’s the bitch?”

“She’s my parole officer.”

“Is that a joke? I’m not laughing.”

“She’s my girlfriend. Not that it’s any of your god damn business.”

Daniels popped another bubble, and the door was closed in their faces. In a whisper Daniels said, “How do you know Snivelhead?”

“He ran the Fort Lauderdale operation for the Outlaws,” he whispered back. “I helped put him away.”

“What for?”

“He decapitated a guy that he didn’t like.”

“How charming.”

The ruse worked, and the wild man returned. “Hawk said you can come in.”

He ushered them inside. The club took up the downstairs and was a paean to the biker lifestyle, with a pool table, a long bar that took up a wall, and assorted black leather furniture. A Lynyrd Skynyrd song about white supremacy played on a flashing jukebox, while a trashy woman in a tank top was passed out on the couch. A leather-clad man at the bar spun around on his stool. He sported a purple Mohawk and had muscles on his muscles. This had to be Hawk. He growled like a junkyard dog, and the pool players stopped their game and fell silent.

"Dirty Pete said you had a message from Snivelhead," Hawk said. "What is it?"

"I lied. There is no message," Lancaster said.

"Is this a joke?"

"No. But we do want to talk to you about Dexter Hudson."

"Who?"

"Dexter Hudson. He's a member of the Outlaws."

"Never heard of him. I think you have the wrong address." The pool players all laughed. To the wild man he said, "Dirty Pete, show these nice people out."

"Let's go," Dirty Pete said.

"We're not done," Daniels said.

"Oh yes, you are. Start moving."

Dirty Pete placed his hand on Daniels's shoulder, which was a mistake. When they were dating, Lancaster had learned not to initiate physical contact with Beth, but to let her take the lead. She had been abducted by a pair of serial killers while in college, and thrown in the trunk of a car. By a stroke of luck and the grace of God she'd managed to escape, and as a result of that experience, she'd developed an aversion to men who thought they had the right to place their hands upon her.

She kicked Dirty Pete in the groin with enough force to make every male in the room wince. He groaned in agony, and sank to his knees. Pulling her wallet from her purse, she tossed it onto the pool table so her badge was showing.

"FBI," she said.

Out came her cell phone. She pressed a button on the screen, summoning the troops. Hawk watched her with a bemused look on his face.

"Where's your search warrant?" he asked.

"I don't have one," she said. "I came here to ask you a few questions, which I'm legally entitled to do, and one of your men assaulted me. You're all under arrest."

"You're arresting us?" Hawk said in disbelief.

"That's right."

"God damn bitch," Dirty Pete said, choking in pain.

Daniels grabbed Dirty Pete's ponytail and jerked his head back. "Open your mouth again, and I'll stick my shoe in it."

The clubhouse began to vibrate, and the walls shook. It felt like an earthquake, and Hawk took a cell phone off the bar and pushed a button. Lancaster assumed he had an app that allowed him to view the surveillance cameras on the property, and was now looking at the police chopper dancing over the house and the small army of armed FBI agents poised to break down the front door and rush inside. Hawk let out a curse and tossed the cell phone back onto the bar, knowing he was beaten.

"Dexter isn't here," Hawk said. "He came by a couple of months ago, said he'd just gotten released from Raiford, and wanted to check in. He played some pool and drank some beer and then split. Haven't seen him since."

"Where's he staying?" Daniels asked.

"The hell I know," Hawk said. "I'm not his mother."

One of the pool players snickered. Daniels clenched her jaw.

"We're going to check the place anyway, just to be sure," she said.

"I know my rights," Hawk said. "You can't do that without a search warrant."

"Have it your way," she said. "I'll place you and your asshole buddies under arrest, and then I'll get a search warrant. I happened to see a van pull into your compound earlier. We'll start looking there first."

It was a masterful stroke. Daniels had nailed Hawk without revealing that she knew the van was loaded with speed and compromising the source of her tip.

"All right, you win," Hawk said. "Dexter is staying up in New Port Richey. He's got a room in the back of a strip club he's living in. The owner's an old friend of his."

"What's the club's name?"

Hawk looked to the pool players for help. Dirty Pete cleared his throat. Daniels put her hands on her hips and gave him a hard stare.

"Spit it out," she said.

"It's called Barely Legal," Dirty Pete said.

"I take it you and Dexter are friends."

"Yup. We've been running together a long time."

"When was the last time you saw him?"

"'Bout a week ago. We went drinking, shot the shit."

"What did you talk about?"

"Pussy."

She cuffed Dirty Pete in the side of the head and made him see stars. Facing the others, she said, "Your friend is wanted for two murders and a kidnapping. So let this be a warning. If you contact Dexter, and we find out, you'll be charged as an accessory to these crimes. Am I making myself clear?"

"Loud and clear," Hawk said, as if putting an exclamation point on things.

Lancaster was impressed. Beth had used the right amount of aggression to convince the bikers that it was in their best interest to play ball. Their business was done, and he grabbed her wallet off the pool table and tossed it to her.

Only they weren't done. The girl passed out on the couch hadn't stirred, not even when the chopper had shaken the walls. Daniels sat down on the cushion beside her, and gently slapped the girl's cheek to wake her up. The girl's eyelids fluttered but remained shut. Daniels slapped her a little harder, and got the same response. A dark cloud passed over her face, and her mouth silently moved up and down. She stood up and parted her jacket, exposing the sidearm strapped to her side. It was a menacing gesture, meant to invoke fear. It worked.

"What the hell you doing?" Hawk said.

"Tell me about the girl," she said.

"What do you want to know?"

"Her name would be a good start."

"Tina."

"She your girlfriend?"

"She's everyone's girlfriend."

It was the wrong thing to say. Daniels stiffened, and Hawk got visibly smaller on his stool. The others turned to stone, including Dirty Pete.

"What's she on?" Daniels asked.

"Ludes," Hawk said. "She took some speed and started bouncing off the walls, so I gave her a lude to calm her down, and she fell asleep."

"Wake her up."

"How the hell am I going to do that? She's passed out."

Daniels cursed him. She got behind the bar and grabbed a bottle of Jack Daniel's and a glass, then sat down next to Tina and poured a few fingers of whiskey into the glass, which she put under the girl's nose. When that didn't produce the desired effect, she poured some whiskey into Tina's open mouth, sending half down her chin. Tina came to and coughed violently.

"Who the hell are you?" the girl said.

"Special Agent Daniels, and I'm with the FBI." Daniels paused to let the words sink in. "I want you to answer some questions for me. What's your name?"

"Tina Hixby."

"How old are you, Tina?"

"Nineteen."

"Do you have a job? Or go to school?"

The girl shook her head.

"Then what do you do?" Daniels asked.

"I hang out," she said.

"Where did you meet these guys?"

"We hooked up at a bar called Harlie's."

"Are you here because you want to be, or because they brought you here?"

Tina hesitated, and Daniels took the girl's wrist and gave it a squeeze.

"I'm here because I want to be," Tina said.

"Have you ever tried to leave, and one of these men stopped you?" Daniels asked.

"It's not like that."

"Have any of these men ever forced you to have sex?"

Tina's eyes touched on each biker's face. Every night, Lancaster guessed.

"Never. I fuck 'em because I want to," Tina said.

Daniels had heard enough, and she returned the bottle of whiskey to the bar. To the bikers she said, "Remember, boys. If you contact Dexter, I'll hunt you down and throw your sorry asses in jail. That's a promise you can take to the bank."

She moved to leave. Lancaster was a step ahead of her, and he opened the front door. Looking over her shoulder, she gave Tina a parting glance.

"You have poor taste in men," Daniels told her.

CHAPTER 19

Daniels was on a mission. Her body language gave it away. There was a bounce to her step that hadn't been there before, and a heightened alertness. Dexter was hiding in New Port Richey, and she would not rest until he was apprehended and the twelve women whom his gang had abducted were rescued.

The chopper had left, and except for a barking dog, the neighborhood was quiet. She addressed the FBI agents assembled on the sidewalk, and told them what she wanted done. Finished, she marched down the street to her vehicle and climbed behind the wheel. Lancaster barely had his door closed as they took off.

"Your plan is flawed," he said.

They were in a residential neighborhood. The posted speed limit was thirty miles per hour, and she was doing fifty. She eyed him without slowing down.

"Why didn't you say anything back there?" she asked.

"Professional courtesy," he said.

"What's wrong with it?"

"You want the guys on your team to enter Barely Legal tonight, mingle with the customers, and root out Dexter. That's not going to work."

"Why not?"

Using Google Images, he pulled up a photograph and showed her. "It's a hellhole, and the clientele are lowlifes. Your guys look like Boy Scouts. It won't work."

"You've been in this place?"

"No, but I know what to expect. There are two types of strip clubs in Florida. The clubs that cater to businessmen have nice addresses and are upscale. The clubs that don't have nice addresses are dives. I visited New Port Richey once to pick up a guy who skipped bail. The town is the pits, and I have to assume Barely Legal is a toilet."

"So what do I do? Put my team in disguise?"

The guys on her team had short haircuts and were physically fit. Those two things alone would set off alarms.

"Let me go inside instead," he said. "I'll unbutton my shirt and let my belly hang out. I'll look just like every other slob in the place."

"And let you handle Dexter alone? Not a chance."

"I promise, I won't kill him. I'll corner him inside the club, and text you. Then your team can come in, and make the bust."

A sign directed them to the interstate, and she didn't reply until they were heading back to Tampa. "But Dexter knows what you look like. If he spots you inside the club, he might try to shoot it out."

"He's not going to spot me," he said. "Back when I was a SEAL, I was the front man. Blending in is my specialty."

Beth said nothing, which he didn't take as a good sign. She had looked into his eyes the night before at the Jayhawk, and seen the hatred burning in his soul. It was the type of wound that would not begin to heal until justice was served, no matter what promises he made.

- - -

Thirty minutes later, she pulled up to his hotel in Oldsmar. Through the front windows he could see guests enjoying the complimentary happy hour. She still hadn't responded to his offer.

"So what do you want to do?" he asked.

"I need to think about it," she said.

He took that as a no, and climbed out. It was Beth's show, and he had to play by her rules. He had the hotel door open when she called out to him.

"I'll call you in an hour." Then she added, "Promise."

He grabbed a cold beer on the way up to his room. As he keyed his door, his cell phone vibrated. He'd gotten a text from Nicki. Her CSI class had researched the other kidnapping victims, and she wanted to share their findings. The beer could wait, and he put it in the fridge before calling her.

"Are you still in Tampa working the case?" the teenager asked.

"Yes, indeed. Guess who I joined forces with? Your aunt Beth."

"That's so cool. I bet you guys make a great team."

"We're trying. So what did your class find?"

"You're going to like this. We checked to see how many of the victims were involved in community service, just like you asked us. It turns out all of them were. They did volunteer work for the handicapped and all sorts of other neat stuff. I put a list together, and emailed it to you."

"Hold on a second. Let me see if I got it."

He retrieved his laptop from the wall safe. Booting it up, he went into his inbox and found Nicki's email, which had been sent hours ago. It had an attachment, which he opened, and the victims list filled the screen. It was in chronological order, starting with the first victim and ending with the last. His eyes briefly touched upon each name.

1. Gloria Joiner*—Habitat for Humanity
2. Diane Clancy—Meals on Wheels
3. Angie Bracco—Guardian ad Litem
4. Torrie Walters—Bible School volunteer
5. Tarah Gray—Works with special needs kids
6. Phoebe Ellington—Trains service dogs

7. Kendra Mundy—Runs local civic association
8. Lisa Vondle—Neighborhood watch group
9. Lindsay Vanhoesen—Hospital volunteer
10. Amy Potter—Wildlife animal rescue
11. Lisa Catherine Tanner—Community activist
12. Skye Tanner—Volunteer with handicap riding program
13. Audrey Sipos—????

Picking up his cell phone, he resumed talking to Nicki. "I'm staring at your list right now. Your class did an awesome job."

"Thank you. We couldn't find out much about the victim in Gainesville, Audrey Sipos, except that she's a nurse who lives by herself," Nicki said.

"That's already been done. Sipos is big on helping people. She even has an award named after her."

"Wow. So all the victims were Good Samaritans."

"That's right. They share a behavioral trait. I'm sure there are others."

"What do you mean?"

"I'd bet you a dollar that none of them has ever been arrested, or broken the law," he said. "Good people tend to be good all the time."

"That makes sense."

"The first name on your list, Gloria Joiner, has an asterisk. Why's that?"

"She was mentioned in a newspaper article that I found online," Nicki said. "Her neighbors' house was broken into, and she called the police, and helped get the burglar arrested. The newspaper called her a hero."

The story had a familiar ring. Audrey Sipos had come to the aid of a girl being raped, and helped send her rapist to prison by testifying at his trial. Had Gloria Joiner testified at the burglar's trial? It was another link that needed to be pursued.

"How long ago was this?" he asked.

"It happened ten years ago."

"Did the article publish the burglar's name?"

"Yep. Get this. His name was Charlie Bandit."

They shared a laugh. He now had enough information to move the investigation forward. He thanked Nicki, and started to say goodbye.

"So what's the deal with you and Aunt Beth?" the teenager said. "Are you going to start seeing each other again?"

"We haven't discussed it," he said.

"Do you want to?"

"I wasn't the one who broke things off."

He regretted the words the moment they came out of his mouth. They sounded bitter, and that wasn't how he felt about his relationship with Beth. "I like your aunt a great deal," he added. "Hopefully, she feels the same way about me. I've got to get back to work. Thanks again for the help."

"Tell Aunt Beth I said hi," Nicki said.

"I'll do that," he said, ending the call.

He drank his beer while studying the list. He hadn't known that Elsie Tanner's name was actually Lisa Catherine, and the name struck a nerve. He shut his eyes, and after a long reflective moment he realized where he knew her from. Twenty-five years ago, inside a cramped courtroom in Broward County, Lisa Catherine Tanner had been the star witness at his brother's trial, and had helped send Logan away to prison.

\- - -

Lancaster got on the Broward County Clerk of Courts website, and did a search on the name Charlie Bandit. Had Charlie had a lick of common sense, he would have changed his last name, or gotten into a different line of work. When no records came up, he did a second search, and typed in the name Charles Bandit. That proved to be a gold mine, with over a dozen case files appearing.

He read each one. Bandit had been born to steal; he started shoplifting as a teenager, and then he graduated to burglary. Each file contained a criminal affidavit, which had been written by the arresting officer. In several of the later files, the arresting officer had stated that Bandit was high on drugs, and had resisted arrest.

He found the case when Gloria Joiner had sicced the cops on Bandit. The arresting officer's name was familiar, Frank Maraca. Years ago, Maraca's wife had gotten sick, and several officers had subbed for him so Maraca could be with her at the hospital. He had been one of those officers, and hoped Maraca would remember him.

He called around to his cop friends and finally got Maraca's number. He placed a call, and Maraca's voice mail picked up.

"This is Frank. I'm busy right now. Leave a message and I'll call you back."

"Hey, Frank. This is a voice from the past, Jon Lancaster. I'm working a case in Tampa, and need to pick your brain. Call me when you get this. Later, man."

- - -

The hotel's business center was behind the front desk. It was empty, and he keyed the door and entered with his laptop tucked under his arm. The room contained a PC, and a printer. He powered up the printer, and connected his laptop through the hotel Wi-Fi. Then, he made copies of Nicki's list. Her class had hit a home run, and he needed to share the information with Beth.

As he left the business center, he got a series of texts from his buddies in Key West. They had sent him photographs they'd taken while out snorkeling earlier in the day. There was also a message. **Weather is here, wish you were beautiful.**

"You bastards," he said.

Behind the hotel was a smoking area. He went there and sat on an empty bench. He'd smoked as a cop before deciding it was slowing him down and he had to quit. But he still had the occasional craving, and he filled his lungs with secondhand smoke.

It felt good, and he slowly exhaled.

He looked through his buddies' photographs. They had gone snorkeling at Fort Zachary Taylor beach on the southernmost tip of Key West, and the photos showed a school of dolphins playing offshore. It was here that the Atlantic Ocean met the Gulf of Mexico, and he'd always believed that the waters had a special power, and could soothe the most troubled soul. Closing his eyes, he imagined he was floating, with the sun burning his face. He could hear the gulls and the sounds of breaking waves but not cell phones or the annoying beeps of electronic devices summoning their owners to do their bidding. He was free of the constraints of modern life, and had never felt happier.

He opened his eyes. His cell phone was calling him.

"Hello?"

"Jon! This is Frank Maraca. How are you doing, my friend?"

"I'm good. How have you been? How's your wife?"

"She's doing great, thanks for asking. We're celebrating our anniversary next week and going to Bimini. Your message said you needed my help. I'm here for you."

"I'm in Tampa working a case, and the name Charlie Bandit came up. Does that ring any bells?"

"I've got a knot on the bridge of my nose because of that piece of shit. Bandit played possum after I arrested him. Then, he coldcocked me, and split my nose open."

"How well do you remember his arrest?"

"Like it was yesterday."

"The witness who called in the robbery was named Gloria Joiner. Do you know if she testified against Bandit at his trial?"

"She did. Bandit pleaded innocent, claimed the police framed him. Luckily, Joiner saw the whole thing. She was the prosecution's star witness."

He found himself nodding. One by one, the pieces of the puzzle were falling in place, the picture getting a little clearer. Like Audrey Sipos in Gainesville, Gloria Joiner had helped stop a crime, then helped put the perpetrator behind bars. He felt himself growing excited, and stood up from the bench.

"Were you there at Bandit's sentencing?" he asked.

"After he broke my nose? You bet I was."

"Where did they send him?"

"Raiford," Maraca said.

All roads continued to lead to Raiford.

"I don't mean to pry, but what's this about?" Maraca asked.

"I'm sure you've heard about the women disappearing around Florida during the last month," he said. "Gloria Joiner was the first victim, and I think a gang of ex-cons that did time out of Raiford is responsible."

"She was? Jesus, how did I not see her name in the paper?"

"You were probably busy. Do you know if Bandit is still in the joint?"

"I haven't kept tabs on him. I'm sitting in front of my computer. Want me to go on the DOC offender site, and run him down?"

"That would be great."

Maraca hummed as he did the search. "Nothing comes up."

"Try Charles instead of Charlie."

"Gotcha. You were right—Bandit's file is staring me in the face. He got his sentence reduced and was paroled a few months ago. Could he have been responsible for Joiner's abduction?"

He nearly said yes, but stopped himself. If Bandit had wanted revenge, he would have murdered Joiner. That was how criminals enacted payback against people who crossed them. But Joiner had been kidnapped, which took planning. It was not the kind of crime that scum like Bandit were known for.

It didn't add up. And until it did, he had to keep digging.

"Maybe," he said. "Thanks for the assist."

"Happy to help," Maraca said.

He ended the connection and called Daniels. He had promised to share whatever leads he came across, and be a team player.

Her voice mail picked up.

"Call me when you get this," he said.

CHAPTER 20

The ringtone on Daniels's cell phone was a police siren. Police sirens were meant to instill fear in criminals, while telling victims that help was on the way. Her niece had given it to her as a present, and she'd fallen in love with it.

She put down her infrared binoculars to stare at the cell phone's screen. It was Jon. She didn't want to talk to him right now, and let voice mail pick up.

She raised the binoculars to her face and continued her surveillance. She was parked in front of Dino's Pizza and Subs, where a sign proclaimed EVERY DAY IS TWO FOR ONE! Barely Legal, the adult club where Dexter Hudson was hiding out, was next door.

The club was a dive. But that didn't stop the locals from dropping by to stare at the naked ladies, and the parking lot was filled with dirty pickups and beaters. She had conducted busts inside of strip clubs before. Based upon what she'd learned from those investigations, strip clubs were money-losing propositions, the markup on watered-down drinks not large enough to cover the overhead. The real money came from peddling drugs and prostitution, which made the clubs nothing more than fronts.

But she wasn't there to make a drug bust, or stop the club's owner from pimping. She was there to arrest Dexter Hudson, and she'd brought her team to do the job.

She'd split the agents into two teams. The first team's job was to drive around the club, and count the exits. When the bust went down, she would have an agent guarding each exit in case Dexter tried to run.

The other team was inside the club, looking for Dexter. She'd decided to ignore Jon's warning, and had sent them in. She'd been inside strip clubs, and they were as dark as caves. Her team wasn't going to be made.

Her cell phone beeped. She dialed into voice mail and punched in her password. Jon's voice greeted her. "Call me when you get this."

She erased the message and lowered her phone.

Did Jon really have something? Or was he itching to join the bust, and creating an excuse to get a call back? Having Jon join her team was a risk. He'd promised not to hurt Dexter, only she knew that was a lie. If Jon got his hands on Dexter, there was no telling what he'd do.

She resumed her surveillance. A group of back-slapping guys went into the club. They were feeling no pain and laughing hoarsely. She gazed at each of their faces through her binoculars. None of them resembled Dexter.

The first team pulled into the lot and parked. Special Agent Gary Safko got out, and rapped his knuckles on the passenger window of her vehicle. Safko was a rookie, and a little too cocky for her taste. She unlocked the doors, and he got in.

"How many exits did you find?" Daniels asked.

"We found two exits in the rear of the club," Safko said. "Both feed into the parking lot. If our suspect has a car parked in back, he might escape."

"He's one man. You should be able to stop him."

"Not if we wait on the street."

"Why would you wait on the street?"

"There are surveillance cameras on the roof and motion detector lights. If we get too close to the building, someone inside the club might spot us, and alert him."

Safko was starting to annoy her. Where there was a will, there was a way.

"You outnumber him three to one," Daniels said. "When the bust goes down, your team will cover the exits. If Dexter makes a run for it, take him down."

"You want us to shoot to kill?"

"No. Shoot to wound. I need to question him."

Safko didn't seem happy with her decision. She looked sideways at him.

"Is this not to your liking?" she asked.

He wilted beneath her stare. "It sounds risky."

"How so?"

"You said that this guy is wanted for two homicides, and was recently released from prison. He might come out with guns blazing."

"That's highly unlikely. If Dexter runs, it will be because he's scared, and people like that rarely shoot it out," she said. "If he tries to escape, wait until he's close to his car, and is getting his keys out. It will be enough distraction for you to subdue him."

Safko swallowed hard. "That will work."

The remark angered her, and she wondered if Safko would have made these comments if he'd been talking to a male superior instead of her.

"Didn't they teach you anything at Quantico?" she snapped.

- - -

The second team came out of the strip club ten minutes later, and strolled down the sidewalk to the sandwich shop. Two members of the team went inside to get something to eat, while the third member got into Daniels's car to give her an update. His name was Otto West, and like her, he was a runner, with a lean body that looked good in clothes. There was lipstick smeared on the collar of his shirt, and he reeked of cheap perfume.

"Sampling the merchandise?" Daniels asked.

"I got made inside the club," he said, embarrassed.

"For the love of Christ. How did that happen?"

"I let one of the girls drag me to a VIP room for a lap dance. I wanted to check out the back to see where Dexter might be hiding. I sat down on a couch, and she shut the door and then parked herself in my lap, and started kissing my neck. Before I knew it, she was running her hands over my body like she was frisking me. She found my gun, and said, 'You're a cop.' I said, 'Aren't cops allowed to have fun?' and she told me that I had to leave."

"Do you think she was prepped?"

"It sure felt that way. I was in a strip club a few weeks ago, and there was no touching. I'm guessing Barely Legal got raided, and the management told the dancers to check out the customers, and ask them if they're cops."

"You go to strip clubs often?"

"Actually, I avoid them. It was a bachelor party."

"Do you think Dexter's hiding inside the club?"

"I do. When the girl was taking me to the VIP room, we passed a door with a sign that said, STAY OUT. It made me think Dexter was in there, so I played drunk, and banged the door with my shoulder. The girl got mad, and told me to cut it out."

"What was security like inside the club?"

"A bouncer at the door, two more inside."

The other members of West's team came out of the sandwich shop holding bags of food. West lowered his window, and was handed a large cup of coffee and several packets of sugar.

"I'm sorry, I should have asked if you wanted anything," he said.

"But you didn't," Daniels said.

"I said, I'm sorry."

"Apology accepted."

West fixed his coffee. He was starting to fade, and he smothered a yawn. She wanted to chew him out, but bit her lip. That was the problem with the agents on her team. Being in the FBI was just a job to them. Their passions lay elsewhere, either with their families or the hobbies they pursued on the weekends. They didn't love their work, or derive the same satisfaction from making a bust that she did.

She realized that she missed Jon. Jon loved his work, and his level of energy was amazing. While in the military he'd been trained to stay up for days at a time, while still having enough energy to run over mountainous terrain with a rifle strapped to his back. There was no yawning in Jon's world, his passion undiminished.

If anyone could go inside that club and root Dexter out, it was him. But could she keep him under control? Could she rein in Jon's primal impulses, and prevent him from harming Dexter once he found him?

"I need some privacy," she said.

"Want a coffee?" West asked. "On me."

"No, I'm fine. Thanks for offering."

Daniels waited until West was gone before calling Jon back. He picked up on the first ring, his breath tinged with excitement.

"Lay it on me," she said.

"Nicki and her class helped me make another connection with our case," he said.

"I need you to hold that thought, and hear me out," she said.

The connection went silent, and she wondered if he was still there.

"Jon?"

"I'm listening," he said.

"I'm at Barely Legal with my team, and we think that Dexter is hiding inside the club near the VIP rooms. I want you to go in there, and smoke him out."

"I'm on my way."

"Hold on. There's a caveat. To make sure that you don't hurt Dexter, I'm going to accompany you inside the club. With me so far?"

"I'm with you."

"If you harm one hair on Dexter's head, I'll arrest you on the spot. I mean that, Jon. I need Dexter Hudson intact. That's the deal. If you agree, say yes."

"Yes, ma'am," he said.

"Good. Get your ass up here."

CHAPTER 21

Florida was strange. The wealth was centered around the cities and their airports. The farther away you drove from these locations, the poorer and more downtrodden the landscape became. It was the land of haves, and have-nots.

He sped up US 19, his heart pounding in his chest. Beth, being an FBI agent, had thought she could smoke out Dexter on her own, and had discovered that she was out of her element. It happened to the best law enforcement agents when they conducted investigations in the Sunshine State. The rules were different here.

Barely Legal's neon street sign wasn't working, and he passed the club. The automated voice on his cell phone told him to make a U-turn and head back. He didn't like it when robots gave him instructions, but he begrudgingly turned his car around.

He pulled into the parking lot of Dino's and did a double take. Beth stood in front of the establishment, wearing ripped jeans and a tank top, her hair brushed back, her face painted with lipstick and mascara. She looked like the kind of babe you saw riding on the back of a motorcycle with her boyfriend, tough and alluring. He got out and approached her. Several clever lines came to mind, all of which he shelved.

"Got here as fast as I could. Nice outfit," he said.

She eyed him warily. "Are you being sarcastic?"

"Not at all. You'll fit right in. Where's your team?"

"They've split up. One team is covering the back of the club, the other is parked by the main entrance, covering the front. Are you carrying?"

"Of course I'm carrying."

"You need to lose your weapon. One of my agents got made by a dancer. She ran her hands over him, and found his gun."

"We're going into the club unarmed? That's not wise."

"I've got a gun in my purse. We're good."

"So I'll be unarmed, and you won't be."

"I've got your back, Jon. You'll be safe."

He wanted to disagree, but arguing with Beth was a waste of time. He went to his vehicle, popped the trunk, and put his weapons into the large plastic bin where he kept his firearms and ammo. He was carrying a gun around his ankle, another in his pocket, and a third tucked away in his pants pocket. She stood behind him, shielding his actions from any patrons inside the sandwich shop. When he was finished disarming himself, they walked together down the sidewalk toward the club.

"Let me ask you something," she said. "What kind of women patronize strip clubs? That's a new one to me."

"Women who like to watch other women get naked," he said. "I once dated a woman that liked going to strip clubs. She claimed that watching the dancers take off their clothes made her horny."

"Lovely."

They entered the club's property and crossed the parking lot. Every space was taken, the vehicles filled with rowdy guys drinking beer and getting stoned. One of the vehicles contained Beth's team, although it was difficult to determine which one.

He stopped by the front door. The walls of the club were vibrating, the pounding music coming from within shaking the building.

"We should be arm in arm. Otherwise, some drunk will get the wrong idea, and start hitting on you," he suggested.

"I can take care of myself," she said.

He gave her a look that said please, do it my way, just this once. Her eyes narrowed, and he braced himself for a tongue-lashing. The moment passed, and she slipped her arm through his, pressing her body against him.

"Lead the way," she said.

"I'll need to buy you a drink once we're inside. What's your pleasure?"

"Glass of chardonnay. Something from California, if they have it."

He realized she was making a joke. She didn't do that enough, and it caught him by surprise. Her eyes twinkled with amusement.

"Jack and coke," she said. "Now, let's bust this asshole."

- - -

The club was jumping, the dancers performing naked gymnastics on an elevated stage to the accompaniment of rap music. The patrons were throwing money on the stage, wanting to see the girls bend over. It was a mean crowd.

He went to the bar and yelled out his order. As a cop, he'd dealt with strippers, and had discovered that most of them were financially burdened single moms trying to make ends meet. They didn't like the work, but it paid the bills.

Two drinks set him back twenty bucks. Beth had found a booth, and he slipped in. They drank and watched a few dances. Knowing that one of her team had been made had turned them both cautious, and they didn't want to arouse suspicion.

He scanned the room. The patrons around the bar were three deep, all male. Based upon his experience, patrons of adult nightclubs fell into three categories. Young single guys were usually pretty vocal, while lonely old men were silent, their eyes fixed upon a particular dancer whom they believed they would "save" by night's end. Then there were the married men clutching wads of bills, often with a twenty or fifty showing.

"Any sign of Dexter?" she whispered.

He shook his head. "Nope."

"One of my agents said there's a door on the way to the VIP rooms with a sign telling people to stay out. We need to check that room out."

Dexter knew what Lancaster looked like, which was a problem. That wasn't true for Beth, who would be a stranger.

"Do you mind drawing him out?" he asked.

"What do you have in mind?" she said.

He explained his plan. Beth would be the beard, and he'd be her backup. It had a degree of risk, yet she immediately agreed.

They slid out of the booth. Beth unclasped her purse in case she needed to draw her weapon. The club's DJ was having issues with his equipment, and the music suddenly died. Up on stage, the dancers jerked like puppets having their strings pulled in the wrong direction. The boorish patrons grew uneasy without the wall of noise.

A narrow hallway led to the VIP rooms. He lifted his drink so it was partially hiding his face, just in case there was a surveillance camera in the ceiling. They stopped at the door with the warning sign. Daniels stood in front of him and knocked.

"Anybody home?" she said loudly, slurring her words.

He'd suggested that she pretend to be drunk to help sell the play. The door swung in, and a bald guy with circular piercings in both ears glared at her.

"Can't you read?" he said. "This room is off-limits."

"I left my cell phone in the ladies' room. Was it turned in?" she asked.

"No."

She pointed past him into the room. "That cell phone on the table looks like mine."

Confused, the bald guy spun around. She seized the opportunity and stuck her head into the room to have a look around. She pulled back as the bald guy turned.

"What the hell are you talking about?" he said. "That's a pack of butts."

"Sorry. Guess I've had too much to drink."

The bald guy pointed at Lancaster. "Make him take you home, he got you drunk," he said, and slammed the door in their faces.

They went outside to talk. A pair of souped-up cars on US 19 blew past the club at warp speed. Daniels waited until they were gone before speaking.

"I think Dexter's blown out of here," she said. "There was a folded-up cot leaning against a wall, and a hot plate sitting in a cardboard box. One of his biker buddies must have tipped him off, so he split."

"If he ran, one of the girls probably knows where he went," he said.

"You mean one of the dancers."

"That's right. They usually know the score. I'll get one of them to take me to a VIP room, slip her some money, and see what I can find out."

"You think you can get a girl to open up?"

"It shouldn't be too hard. Did you see the girls up on the stage? None of them looked very happy. A couple of hundred bucks should do the trick."

"I can put it into my expenses, and get you paid back."

"Don't worry about it. I'm flush these days."

"I'll be next door at the sandwich shop."

He went back inside the club. The DJ had gotten his equipment working, and a hip-hop number called "I Luv Dem Strippers" by 2 Chainz and Nicki Minaj rocked the house. A seat at the bar opened up, and he grabbed it and ordered a beer. From his wallet he removed five hundred-dollar bills, and tossed them on the bar.

Then, he waited.

The money was the bait. The bartenders would see it, and one of them would communicate to the dancers that they had a "live" one. The dancers worked in rotation, and the next girl up would come down off the stage, and get up close to him. She'd start flirting, and convince him to follow her to a VIP room, where she'd offer to exchange sexual favors for some, if not all, of his money. If he wasn't careful, she'd slip a pill into his beer, and he'd be running to the toilet before she fulfilled her end of the bargain.

It took only a minute until he was proven right. A dancer wearing a pink G-string walked down a short flight of steps next to the bar, and soon was standing next to him.

"My name's Chanty," she said. "Buy me a drink?"

He sized Chanty up. Everything about her was fake: fake tits, fake hair, fake smile. Her pupils were dilated, and she was flying high—probably on Ecstasy, or maybe cocaine. In his experience, people who were high did nothing but lie.

"I don't think so," he said.

"Let me guess. You're the bashful type. I can fix that."

He ignored her and drank his beer. Another dancer on stage caught his eye. She was young, and had a hint of innocence. Inked across her tummy was an Outlaws skull and crossbones tattoo. The tattoo was fresh, the dead skin still flaking.

"You know her?" he asked, pointing.

"Maybe," Chanty said.

He took a hundred off the bar, tore it in half, and gave her one of the pieces.

"I want to meet her. Make it happen, and I'll give you the other half."

Chanty made a face. "Why'd you do that? Bill's no good torn in half."

"Sure it is. Just scotch-tape it back together, and take it to the bank."

"Bullshit. They won't take it."

He asked one of the bartenders to settle the argument.

"I get bills taped together every day," the bartender said. "They're good."

Clutching the torn half in her hand, Chanty returned to the stage, and whispered in the young dancer's ear. The dancer smiled mischievously, and together they came down off the stage and made a beeline to where he sat. He handed Chanty the other half.

"Thanks," he said.

The young dancer smiled at him. Up close, the years fell off her face, and he didn't think she was more than seventeen. That meant she was dancing illegally, and could get in a world of trouble if caught.

"I'm Echo," she said. "I hear you want to meet me."

"I do," he said.

"It's so noisy in here. Let's go someplace quiet."

As he followed Echo to the VIP rooms, Daniels texted him, asking if he'd made any progress. He texted her back a thumbs-up emoji.

"Your wife checking up on you?" Echo asked.

"Just someone from work," he said.

- - -

He sat down on a red leather couch, and she crawled into his lap. Her hands were lightning fast as she frisked him.

"Whatever happened to foreplay?" he asked with a grin.

"Got to check for guns. House rules. You're not a cop, are you?"

"Do I look like a cop to you?"

"No, you look like Santa Claus."

Echo unbuttoned his shirt and started to rub his big, round belly. She was surprised at how hard his stomach was, and gently poked at it like a kid testing the air inside a balloon. Knowing she was underage made him uncomfortable, and he pulled out his wallet and flipped it open, revealing his detective's badge pinned to the inside. Her smile vanished.

"Shit. I guess you're not Santa Claus," she said. "You going to bust me?"

"Let me ask the questions. How old are you? And don't lie to me."

"Seventeen."

"Where are you from?"

"Atlanta."

He pointed at the scabbing tattoo on her stomach. "What's the story here?"

"My boyfriend made me get it."

"You didn't want a tattoo?"

"I thought it was ugly. Made me look like a whore."

Tears welled in the corners of her eyes. It was not uncommon for bikers to make their girls get a tattoo so that they could take possession of them. Echo had gotten the tattoo, but she hadn't liked it, and that said a lot.

"Is your boyfriend a biker?" he asked.

She nodded, and a tear rolled down her cheek.

"What's his name?"

"Dexter. He threatened to hurt me and my baby if I disobeyed him."

"Does Dexter have a droopy mustache and sideburns?"

"Yeah. You know him?"

"I do. Would you like to get away from Dexter? I can help you do that."

Her face turned to stone. Seventeen, raising a child, forced to strip to make ends meet, her life filled with broken promises. She had no good reason to believe anything he said.

"Can I show you something?" he asked.

She shrugged. "I guess."

He opened the gallery app on his cell phone, and clicked on an album of photographs taken at Amber Glen Ranch, a rehabilitative facility outside of Nashville. It was here that Team Adam sent victims of kidnapping and sexual assault so they could heal their damaged psyches and reconnect with the world. The therapy included working in gardens, doing chores on the farm, and caring for horses.

He scrolled through the collection. "See the girl riding the horse? Her name is Stacy Lynn. She was kidnapped when she was fourteen, and kept in a cellar. Her captor raped her every day. I rescued her a year ago, and arranged for her to go live on a ranch. A team of therapists are helping her get better."

One photo showed Stacy Lynn picking tomatoes. She wore jeans and a T-shirt and looked like a normal teenager. When he came to the last photo, he stopped. It was of the two of them, holding a basket of tomatoes that Stacy Lynn had picked. He'd gone to see her while chasing down a lead in Nashville, and been thrilled at how well she was doing.

Echo stared longingly at the photo, then gazed at him. The suspicion in her face had evaporated. "Can my baby and I live in this place?"

"I can arrange that. But you've got to help me find Dexter."

"Is that a promise?"

"Yes, it's a promise. All I have to do is make a phone call."

It was a big decision, and Echo thought about it long and hard.

"Dexter's down in Saint Petersburg, getting ready to kidnap a woman," she said. "He told me the other night before he left, said he'd kill me if I talked."

"Does Dexter live with you?"

"Yeah. I share an apartment with another dancer. Dexter decided to move in, and threw my roommate out. Couple of nights ago he got drunk, and told me how he was part of a gang that was kidnapping women. He even showed me a video of the women. I think they were being kept somewhere."

He sat up straight on the couch. "How did they look?"

"I don't know what you mean."

"The women—were they healthy?"

"They looked okay. None of them looked beat up, or anything."

"Did you meet any other members of his gang?"

"His buddies came over a few times. Their names were Skyler and Logan."

It was a small world. Echo had known his brother, and she'd also known Skyler Seeley, the man he'd shot twice in the back outside the Jayhawk Motel who'd later died.

"What did Dexter tell you about the job in Saint Petersburg?" he asked.

"Dexter said he was meeting up with a guy named Jake Williams, who he'd known in prison. They were going to track this woman down, and kidnap her. Dexter said this woman had an unlisted address and unlisted phone numbers, but that didn't matter, because he could still find her."

"Did he say how?"

"Dexter said he could find people just by having their email address."

Lancaster knew a great deal about cyberstalking through his work with Team Adam, and was not aware of any method of finding a person solely through their email address. It simply wasn't possible, and he guessed Echo had misunderstood what Dexter had said to her. The door opened, and a mean-looking bouncer stuck his head in.

"Time's up," the bouncer said. "Get back to work."

The bouncer glared at them and slammed the door. Echo started to tremble, and she looked like she might start crying again. "That's Marcus. He's one of Dexter's biker friends. Always checking up on me. I've got to go."

She climbed off his lap, and went to the door. The Outlaws did not tolerate disloyalty and liked to say that while God forgives, Outlaws don't. He knew that he'd placed Echo in danger.

"When do you get off work?" he asked.

"Couple of hours," she said.

"Give me your address, and I'll pick you up. You're not safe around here."

Echo gave him her address. The look on her face said she didn't think she would ever see him again. They both returned to the club. She climbed onstage and started dancing with the other girls. He tried to make eye contact, but she wouldn't look at him.

- - -

He made sure he wasn't being followed before going outside. The temperature had dropped and made his skin tingle.

He felt elated. Echo had shared two important pieces of information. The victims were still alive, and Dexter was preparing to abduct another woman with a new partner. He knew enough about the gang's motives to believe that he could figure out the new victim's identity, and stop Dexter and his partner in the act.

He walked down the sidewalk toward the sandwich shop. Beth was going to be happy with his progress. She'd been working the investigation for a month, and the emotional wear and tear was showing. She needed to take a vacation after it was wrapped up, and he knew a perfect spot in the Keys that he planned to recommend.

Dino's lot had a single car parked in it. His. Beth and her team were gone.

He checked his phone to see if she'd left him a message. There were none.

The owner of the sandwich shop was cleaning up. He banged on the window, and the owner unlocked the front door. "We're closed."

"There were three cars parked in your lot. Did you see them leave?"

"Yeah, about ten minutes ago," the owner said.

Furious, he got in his car and called her. Beth and her team were backing him up, and could have at least given him the courtesy of a text message saying they were pulling out. Her voice mail picked up.

"Where the hell are you?" he asked.

CHAPTER 22

The message had said to come alone.

Daniels saw the exit signs for Tampa International Airport and flipped on her blinker. The expressway was quiet, and she'd spent the drive wondering what she was about to walk into. To be forewarned was to be forearmed. To be in the dark was to be helpless.

There were two dedicated lanes leading into the airport. She stayed in the right-hand lane and reduced her speed. At the exit for cargo, she got off and drove up to the gate. The female security guard was all business, and didn't seem impressed by her credentials. Handing them back, the guard said, "You been here before?"

"First time," Daniels replied.

She emerged from her booth and knelt down next to the driver's window. "This is a big place, and it's easy to get lost. Here's what you need to do."

Daniels memorized the guard's instructions and thanked her. The gate was raised, and she entered the cargo area, drove around several buildings, and crossed an empty tarmac to an unmarked hangar. A Gulfstream G550 private jet was parked in front and was being serviced by a maintenance crew. A handsome pilot stood a few yards away, talking on his cell phone. The FBI owned a fleet of G550s, which were housed at Dulles International Airport and were at the disposal of the bureau's directors.

She parked and got out. She expected someone to greet her, and explain what was going on, but there was no one. She didn't think the pilot or maintenance people knew the score, so she climbed up the portable stairs and stepped into the small aircraft.

The interior was plush, with facing leather chairs and HDTVs on the walls, as well as computers built into several small desks. The G550s were often used as command centers in remote areas, and had every modern convenience.

"Anybody home?" she said.

"Back here," a familiar voice replied.

She followed the voice to the rear of the plane. Joe Hacker sat by himself in the last row. His eyes were ringed from lack of sleep, and gray stubble dotted his chin. The remains of a meal sat on a plastic tray in the seat beside him. He acknowledged her with a weary nod and pointed at the empty seat across from his.

Daniels sat down. "Hello, J. T."

"Hello, Beth." He sounded exhausted. "How's the investigation going?"

"I think we're close to apprehending one of the members of the gang. I was at a stakeout when I got your message. Is something wrong?"

"You and I have a problem."

"We do?"

"Yes, and his name is Jon Lancaster."

Daniels stiffened. She wanted to think she'd been keeping Lancaster on a short leash, and was conducting her investigation by the book.

"I learned about an incident involving Lancaster that took place outside the Jayhawk Motel in Tampa," Hacker said. "Do you know what I'm referring to?"

Learned from who? she nearly asked.

"You mean the shooting," she said instead.

"Correct. According to the report I was given, a man named Dexter Hudson shot and killed Lancaster's brother outside the Jayhawk last night. Lancaster chased Hudson, and fired his handgun into a moving vehicle. The driver of the vehicle later turned up dead. Does this sound right?"

She nodded stiffly. She had typed up a report of the shooting with the intention of including it in her final report when the investigation was complete. For J. T. to have this information meant that a member of her team had secretly made a copy off her computer and emailed it to him. She had been betrayed.

But by whom? Was it Gary or Otto? Or had another member stuck the knife in her back? It really didn't matter. J. T. had the report, and she needed to deal with it.

"I also got my hands on the police report," Hacker said. "The Tampa police don't have a problem with Lancaster, and aren't going to charge him with shooting the driver. Well, I do have a problem, and so should you."

"He was chasing down a suspect," she said defensively.

Hacker grew in his seat. "He fired his gun in the middle of a busy street, and put innocent lives at risk. He could have missed and hit a bystander."

"But he didn't," she said.

"You think this is correct behavior?"

"The Tampa police didn't have a problem with Jon's actions, and neither do I."

"You're missing the point," he said.

"Which is what?"

"He's a liability. Or are you too blinded by your feelings to see that?"

The words stung like a slap in the face. She counted to three, and collected her thoughts before replying. "Jon is helping move the investigation forward. We were spinning our wheels until he showed up," she said.

"But what if this happens again?" Hacker said. "What if Lancaster shoots his gun, and an innocent person gets wounded or killed? If the media finds out that he's assisting the FBI, we could both lose our jobs, not to mention the shit storm it would create."

"That's a lot of ifs," she said.

Hacker was not used to being challenged. His face turned red, and he started coughing. She hurried into the rear of the plane and found a bottled water.

He downed the water in one long gulp. "Thank you."

"You're welcome," she said.

There were times when she wished she'd never been promoted to run a division within the FBI. If she'd learned anything, it was that the higher she rose in the bureau, the more the job centered around good PR, while battling crime took a back seat. "How long have we known each other?" he asked.

"Since I graduated from the academy," she said.

"Do you feel you know me pretty well?"

"Yes, J. T., I do."

"Then read my mind. What am I thinking?"

"You want me to cut Jon loose."

"That's right. Think you're up to it?"

"I'll do whatever you feel is best."

"Good answer. Wrap things up with him tonight. After that, there will be no more communications. If you wish to see him when the case is over, that's your call. But if I find out that you're talking to him while the investigation is proceeding, I'll ask for your resignation. Am I making myself clear?"

"Loud and clear."

"Please don't disappoint me, Beth."

He sounded just like her father, who had been a domineering asshole. It made her want to strangle him, and she rose from her seat.

"I'll try not to," she said.

"One last thing. You are not to enact any payback within your team."

She raised an eyebrow. "Sir?"

"You know what I'm talking about. The agent who shared your report with me wasn't being vindictive. He was simply doing what was best for your team."

Hacker had just narrowed the list of suspects to the other male agents on her team. She would find out which one was responsible, and have a word with him.

"No payback. Got it, sir," she said.

"Glad we're on the same page. Good night, Beth."

- - -

Back in her car, Daniels pulled out her phone. Jon had called, and left a voice message. She had bruised his feelings when they were dating, and she could only imagine what this new development would do to their relationship.

As she called him back, she realized her hand was trembling.

CHAPTER 23

"I'm sorry," he heard Beth say.

His face was burning up. Beth had just explained why he was being yanked off the investigation. Like so many government law enforcement agencies he'd dealt with, the FBI was placing its own well-being above the people it was sworn to protect.

He decided not to go down without a fight.

"But I'm about to crack this thing wide open," he protested.

Beth's sharp intake of breath sounded like a gun going off. He knew her hot buttons. Nothing would have made her happier than breaking this case wide open.

"The victims are still alive," he added.

"Who told you that?" she asked.

"A dancer named Echo. I spoke with her in a VIP room at the club. She's Dexter's girlfriend. Dexter showed her a video of the victims. They're still alive."

"Does she know where they're being kept?"

"No. Echo told me that Dexter has a new partner, and is about to abduct a woman in Saint Petersburg. I thought we might bust them together."

The connection went silent. He was sitting in his car in the parking lot of Ashton Oaks Apartments in New Port Richey, waiting for Echo to come home. Echo and her baby were not safe here, and he needed to move them tonight.

"I can't talk to you anymore," she said. "For all I know, my cell phone may be bugged. The bureau's done that before."

"To you?"

"Not to me, but it's happened to other agents they put under the microscope. If an agent gets in hot water, the bureau will monitor their cell phone calls, and also read their emails and text messages. My boss gave me permission to talk to you a final time. If I do it again, and he finds out, I'm history."

He punched the wheel in anger. This was not right, and they both knew it. A Prius with a damaged bumper drove into the complex and parked by the entrance to one of the apartments, a building three stories tall with window AC units. Echo jumped out and glanced furtively over her shoulder before hurrying inside. She was dressed in torn jeans and a Mickey Mouse T-shirt and looked scared.

"My services are needed. I have to run," he said.

"Where are you?" Daniels asked.

"At an apartment complex in New Port Richey. The dancer I was telling you about just came home. I promised to move her and her baby to a safe location."

"Is she in danger?"

"I think so. A bouncer at the club caught us talking. He's a friend of Dexter's, and a member of the Outlaws."

"I wish I was there to help you."

But she wasn't here, and that bothered him. The rules and regulations that FBI agents were sworn to uphold often proved to be the chains that held them down, and sometimes prevented them from bringing bad people to justice.

"Do you remember what I said about the Outlaws calling themselves one percenters?" he asked.

"I remember."

"Well, you and I are part of a different one percent. We belong to the one percent that has sworn to fight evil. We're the last line of defense against the monsters that make our lives miserable. It's why you joined the FBI, and why I'm sitting in this parking lot instead of in a bar, drinking a beer and taking in a basketball game."

She exhaled into the phone. "I know that, Jon. It's why I'm attracted to you."

"And it's why I'm attracted to you. So get over here."

"I can't. Let me rephrase that. I can, but my boss will find out, and I'll get fired. What good am I if I lose my job?"

She had a point. His window was open, and in the distance he heard cars drag racing on US 19, which seemed a common occurrence in these parts. He opened his door and put one foot out.

"I've got an idea," he said. "I'll figure out a way to feed you information without jeopardizing your job."

"How do you plan to do that?"

"I don't know, but I'll figure out something."

He grabbed a ball cap off the passenger seat and slipped it on. Then he got out, popped the trunk, removed a SIG SAUER P365 from the plastic bin where he kept his guns, and tucked it behind his belt buckle. Closing the trunk, he began to walk toward the apartment's front entrance.

"Are you still there?" Beth asked, sounding worried.

"I'm here," he replied.

"Be safe."

"I'll try."

- - -

The elevator was on the blink. As he trotted up the stairs, he called Echo on his cell phone. She answered without saying a word. A baby cried in the background.

"This is Jon," he said. "I'm coming up the stairs. What's your apartment number?"

"You're here?" she said, sounding surprised.

"Damn straight, I'm here. You need to leave soon. What's the number?"

"Apartment 303. When you come out of the stairs, go left. I'll be waiting for you."

He took the stairs two at a time. At the third-floor landing he went left, and saw a shaft of light streaming out of a partially open door at the end of the hallway, which he ran toward. The floor was concrete, and his footsteps sounded like cannons going off. As he neared the door, it opened fully, and Echo greeted him with her baby in her arms. He was tiny, maybe six months old, with a head of black curls and dark, unblinking eyes. Seeing a stranger approach, he buried his head into his mother's bosom.

Lancaster followed Echo into the apartment. Another woman sat on the floor in front of the TV, looking strung out, and he guessed she took care of the baby while Echo stripped at the club. The woman was a train wreck, with rotted teeth and sallow eyes, but he supposed it was better than leaving the kid alone.

Echo grabbed his wrist with her free hand, and pulled him toward the bedroom.

"We need to get out of here," he said.

"Don't you want to see the video of the girls?" she asked.

"You have it?"

"It's on a private channel on YouTube. I'll show you."

The bedroom had a futon and a desk with a computer. A pile of dirty men's clothes—Dexter's, he assumed—lay heaped in a corner. Echo handed him her baby and got on the computer's keyboard, which she handled like a pro. The computer had a separate hard drive that made a whirring sound as the screen came to life. YouTube allowed users to create private channels where unlisted videos could be shared with people who knew the link. The private channel that Echo pulled up had a large library. Based upon the titles, it appeared to be the property of the Outlaws motorcycle gang.

The kid gave him a mean stare, which he ignored. Bike Week had just finished in Daytona Beach, and the recent videos were of gang members attending the event. Echo scrolled down to an untitled video posted eight days earlier and clicked on it. The video started to play. Clutching the baby to his chest, he leaned in and peered at the screen.

It was in black and white, and was taken from a camera perched high above its subjects, possibly a ceiling mount. It showed the interior of a spacious kitchen with an island in its center. The kitchen had two sinks, two ovens, and an assortment of pots and pans dangling from metal hooks.

A small army of women were busy fixing a meal. Several diced vegetables on cutting boards, while others cut meat into bite-size chunks. Still others added the meat and vegetables into pots simmering on the stove. There was also a cleanup crew, which washed and dried dishes and mopped the floor.

There were eleven women in all. They wore identical aprons and facial expressions that reminded him of prison inmates, all hope extinguished from their faces.

He searched the group, looking for Skye Tanner, whose face he had memorized from the photograph that Team Adam had sent him. She didn't appear to be in the group. Then it clicked. The video had been taken before Skye's abduction. But that didn't make sense—Skye was the eleventh victim, and there were eleven women in the video. So who was the extra woman? The baby started to cry, and he passed him back to his mother.

"How did you find out about this video?" he asked.

"Dexter got drunk, and he showed it to me one night," she said. "He told me that if I didn't behave, I'd end up with the women in the video."

"You mean you'd end up a slave."

"That's right. One of the girls was my friend."

"You know one of the women in the video?"

"Yeah. Her name is Lexi. She used to dance in the club, and we got to be friends. One night, she didn't show up for work. The other girls figured she'd gone to another club, but when Dexter showed me the video, I knew otherwise."

That explained the eleventh woman in the video.

"Did you tell anyone about what happened to Lexi?" he asked.

Echo shook her head. It angered him, and he gave her a reproachful look.

"I didn't want Dexter to hurt me. Or my baby," she explained.

He had heard enough. They went into the next room, and Echo grabbed a paper bag off the dining room table that he guessed contained the things she wanted to take. As they moved to leave, the strung-out woman by the TV began to shriek.

"What's her problem?" he asked.

"I'm all she's got," Echo said.

No further explanation was forthcoming. But he could assume. The woman was an addict, and without Echo paying her to babysit the kid, her income would dry up, along with her ability to score the drugs that kept her going. He crossed the room and shoved money into her face.

"Take it," he said.

The woman fell silent. She held the bills up to the light, checking to see if they were real. Her face filled with bliss.

"Thank you so much," she whispered.

He returned to where Echo stood holding her baby and her paper bag. The apartment window was open, and outside he heard the roar of a convoy of motorcycles entering the apartment parking lot.

"Stay behind me, and do exactly as I tell you," he said.

"I'm scared," she said.

"Don't be."

- - -

He opened the door and stuck his head into the hallway. It was empty, which he found surprising. The smart move for the bikers would have been to send members of their gang into the apartment building before making the ruckus outside. He would have been hard pressed to defeat a gang of men in close quarters, especially with Echo and her baby nearby. But the bikers hadn't done that, which told him that they were amateurs.

He had dealt with their ilk before, and knew what to do. As he walked down the hallway toward the stairwell, he drew the SIG. Outside, the motorcycles were revving their engines, the bikers waiting for him. It reminded him of lions roaring at the zoo.

Reaching the stairwell, he glanced at Echo, who was trembling in fear.

"Say the word *Hooyah*!" he said.

She stared at him, not understanding.

"It's a battle cry, and will give you courage," he explained.

"Hooyah," she whispered.

"Say it like you mean it."

"Hooyah!" she said, much louder this time.

"There you go. Hooyah!"

Fear was contagious, and had cost more than one brave soldier his life. He gave her his best smile, and she found the courage to smile back. Pointing the SIG at the ceiling, he headed down the stairs.

CHAPTER 24

It was like a scene out of the old biker movie *Easy Rider*.

The bikers were in the parking lot, racing their hogs in a circle, making it all but impossible for Lancaster to get to his car and escape with Echo and her baby. In a way, it was a smart move, since they weren't breaking any laws, except disturbing the peace.

Lancaster stood at the apartment building's entrance, watching through a crack in the door. He put the gang's number at fourteen, although that was just a guess, since they were moving too fast to accurately count. It was a big number, and it gave him pause.

"What are we going to do?" Echo asked, her voice trembling.

"Maybe we should call an Uber," he suggested.

She looked ready to cry. They had run out of options. Even if he had decided to shoot them, his SIG had only ten bullets, which would have left four bikers for him to deal with. He could hold his own in a fight, but Echo and her baby were a handicap.

Without a word, Echo started to walk past him.

"What are you doing?" he asked.

"I'm going to go talk to them," she said.

"That won't work. They're animals."

"Do you have a better idea in mind?"

Out in the parking lot, one of the bikers had popped a wheelie, and was driving on his back wheel, grandstanding for his friends. He drove a hundred feet, brought the front wheel down, then spun around, and raced the bike back the same way he'd just come while doing another wheelie. It was illegal to drive a bicycle without a helmet in Florida, but not a motorcycle, and the biker's long hair flapped in the wind.

The rest of the gang stopped to watch. It looked like fun, and a second member popped a wheelie and rode alongside his friend on one wheel. It wasn't long before the rest of the gang joined in, and rode back and forth on one wheel.

It was grandstanding, and it changed his opinion of them. Either they were drunk, high, or just plain stupid, and because of this, they didn't feel threatened. That was a huge mistake. During his training to become a SEAL, his rigorous schedule had included classes called evolutions. Only when he passed the necessary tests could he evolve to the next level. One of his first classes had taught readiness, and how a SEAL could never let his guard down, no matter what the situation. The bikers had let their guard down, and the first rule of warfare was never to do that.

"Hide behind me," he said.

"What are you going to do?" Echo asked.

"Just do as I tell you. Okay?"

"Are we going out?"

"Yes, we're going out. On the count of three. One, two, three."

Holding the SIG at his side, he marched out of the apartment building with Echo right behind him. His steps were fast and deliberate as he went down the brick path. The outside lighting was poor, and he didn't think the bikers would see his sidearm right away.

Reaching the end of the path, he halted. One of the bikers roared past on one wheel, and flipped him the bird. It was the wild man who'd greeted him and Daniels at the clubhouse in Saint Petersburg. He tried to remember the guy's name.

Dirty Pete.

He lifted the SIG and aimed at Dirty Pete's rear tire. He squeezed the trigger, and the tire exploded, sending shards of rubber into the air. The motorcycle flipped backward, and landed atop Dirty Pete, pinning him to the pavement.

Lancaster stepped into the parking lot. The rest of the gang was still showboating. As they swerved to avoid hitting him, he shot out their rear tires. It was like shooting ducks in a barrel, and their bikes either flipped in the air, or spun wildly out of control.

The carnage was intense. One bike crashed into a parked car, and sent the driver airborne, his arms flapping like a bird. Another bike skidded across the pavement, and took out several other bikes before crashing, its driver howling that his leg was broken. Not one bike stayed upright. The four bikers who did not get their tires shot out had their own problems. Two crashed into other riders who were lying on the pavement, while the other two smacked into each other and caused a pileup. No one escaped unscathed.

Echo hovered beside him. He put his arm protectively around her shoulder, and led her to his vehicle. Her baby hadn't made a sound. Great kid.

"Oh no," she said.

Out of the corner of his eye, he saw three bikers walking toward them. One had blood on his face, while the other two were limping. Some guys just never learned.

"Stay behind me," he said.

When they were within striking range, he lunged at them. It was a tactical move, and got the desired reaction. The bloodied biker jumped backward, while one of the limpers halted. Only one of the bikers kept coming forward.

Lancaster feigned throwing a punch, but kicked the biker in the groin instead. The man doubled over in pain, leaving his chin open for a knee, which snapped his head back. He crumpled to the pavement in an inglorious heap and did not move.

The second limper knew karate, and took a little longer to subdue. He managed to get a roundhouse kick in, and Lancaster briefly saw stars, before sweeping the biker's legs out from under him, taking him down. As his vision cleared, he heard a stream of curses, and spun around to find Echo spraying a can of Mace into the face of the bloodied biker, who appeared to be blinded. She emptied the can, and he stumbled away, screaming in agony.

She tossed the empty can away, then picked up her paper bag.

"Let's go," she said.

Her baby still hadn't made a sound.

With Echo acting as copilot, he drove east on State Road 54 and eventually got onto the Suncoast Parkway. A few miles later the parkway ended, and he merged onto the Veterans Expressway, and headed south toward Tampa.

Echo rode shotgun and sang to her baby. Instead of caving under pressure, she had shown character. Although her future was uncertain, he knew she'd come out okay.

"What's your son's name?" he asked.

"Hector. We named him after his daddy," she said.

He wanted to ask the father's status, but knew that was none of his business.

"ICE took my boyfriend away six months ago," she said, as if reading his mind. "He's living in Mexico, trying to figure out a way to come back to Florida, and be with us."

"I'm sorry," he said.

"My boyfriend is smart. He'll figure out a way. Where are you taking us?"

"To a hotel near the Sarasota airport. Once I have you and your baby in a room, I'll connect with my people at Team Adam, and have them send a private plane to fly you to the horse farm in Tennessee that I told you about earlier tonight. You'll be safe there."

- - -

The Veterans Expressway had an express lane that ran for most of its length. He wasn't keen on using it and paying the additional toll, but did so anyway, wanting to concentrate more on talking to Echo than maneuvering his car in the heavy traffic.

"I want to ask you some questions about Lexi," he said. "Are you okay with that?"

Echo rocked her baby in her arms. "Sure."

"You said that Dexter kidnapped Lexi. Why do you think he picked her?"

"I asked myself that same question," she said. "Why take Lexi, and not one of the other dancers, or me? I think it was because Lexi was alone. She didn't have any family or a boyfriend. When she didn't show up for work, no one missed her."

"Except you."

"Yeah. Lexi babysat for me a few times. She was nice."

"Was Lexi the first girl to be kidnapped? Or were there others?"

"I think there were others."

"Why do you think that?"

"I heard stories about other dancers disappearing. The girls were like Lexi, and didn't have anyone in their life, so no one reported it."

It was a common refrain when people went missing. A victim without family or friends would disappear, and soon be forgotten. And the sad part was, it happened every day.

They did not speak for the rest of the way. He went on to Spotify and played a list of favorite Jimmy Buffett songs that he'd compiled and shared with other subscribers. Echo seemed to enjoy the music, and he caught her softly singing along.

Before reaching their destination, they drove across a four-mile-long bridge called the Sunshine Skyway. It was so long that it stretched over three counties, and Echo pressed her face to her window, oohing and aahing at the spectacular view.

- - -

The Sarasota-Bradenton International Airport serviced national and international flights. Expedia showed eight nearby hotels, and he chose the Knights Inn because the rooms were accessible from the street. After pulling into the hotel, he parked by the front entrance and killed the engine. He handed her the keys.

"I'm going inside and booking you a room," he explained. "I want you to lock the doors when I get out. If someone suspicious gets near the car, beep the horn."

"Okay." She hesitated. "I don't have money for a room."

"I've got it covered. Did you eat earlier?"

"No. I brought formula for my son."

"But nothing for yourself. I'll get you something. Back in a few."

He started to get out, and she grabbed his wrist.

"I'm frightened," she said.

"Don't be. I'm going to get you and your boy out of here. You'll get to start your life over, and not worry about the past."

She flashed a hopeful smile. It quickly faded, the reality of her situation creeping in, and erasing hope. He tousled her son's hair, then hopped out of the car and closed the door behind him. No sooner was it shut than he heard the doors click.

Inside the hotel's brightly lit registration office, he found a clean-cut night manager who looked like he'd played football in college and, when the pros hadn't come calling, decided to go into hospitality management. His eyes were cold and unfriendly.

"Can I help you?" he asked stiffly.

His radar went on full alert. He took a Team Adam card from his wallet and placed it on the counter. With his fingertips, he slid the card across the marble counter, and waited a beat so the night manager could read what it said.

"My name is Jon Lancaster, and I work with Team Adam, which is affiliated with the National Center for Missing and Exploited Children," he said. "There is a young lady sitting in my car who was nearly a victim of an abduction earlier tonight. There will be a private plane coming to the Sarasota airport to get her out of here. In the meantime, I need to book a room for her. Do you think you can help me out?"

The night manager stared at the card. "Is this legit?"

"Feel free to call the 1-800 number," he said. "The operator will put you through to a hotline. Whoever answers will verify who I am."

"Hold on."

The night manager punched the number into his cell phone. Lancaster stepped back from the counter and waited. Forty million people around the world were victims of human trafficking. Many of the victims were young women, who were sold into slavery. No country was immune to the problem, not even the United States of America.

There were seven global organizations dedicated to stopping this problem. These organizations spent a large portion of their budgets educating the airline and hospitality industry on how to spot traffickers, since hotel and airline people came in contact with traffickers and their victims on a regular basis.

When a person in the airline or hospitality industry spotted a customer they believed was engaged in human trafficking, it was hoped they would call a toll-free number, and report their suspicions. To help facilitate this, the airline industry distributed pamphlets to its employees, as did the hotel industry.

This pamphlet spelled out telltale signs of trafficking. A teenage girl traveling with an older male was one sign. A lack of luggage was another, and the girl's inability to communicate with the people around her. The male paying in cash for airline tickets or a hotel room was another giveaway.

Not every hotel got these pamphlets. But those hotels situated near airports that serviced international flights *always* got the pamphlets, because more often than not, traffickers on international flights made layovers with their victims.

No doubt, the night manager at the Knights Inn had read the pamphlet. Seeing Lancaster pull in, he had become suspicious when he'd spotted Echo in the passenger seat. She was seventeen, and Lancaster was forty, and that was a red flag.

"Good evening, this is Eric Richmond, the night manager at the Knights Inn at the Sarasota International Airport," he said into his cell phone. "I have a man named Jon Lancaster wishing to book a room for an underage girl into my hotel. Can you please verify that Lancaster is a member of your organization? Yes, I'll hold."

Richmond rested the phone in the crook of his neck. "You better be who you say you are," he said to his guest.

"I wouldn't lie to you," Lancaster replied.

"Do you know how many times customers have said that?"

"Too many, I guess. But I'm not one of them."

"What is Team Adam? I've never heard of it."

"It's a group of retired law enforcement agents that work missing persons cases. Mostly CIA, Secret Service, FBI, and ex-cops."

"Which are you?"

"Ex-cop."

Richmond looked at his guest's protruding belly and scowled. His call was put through, and he started asking questions. The NCMEC ran a twenty-four-hour hotline, and there was always a knowledgeable person working the phones. Richmond's attitude changed. Hanging up, he said, "You check out with flying colors. My apologies."

"Better safe than sorry."

"There you go. How do you want to pay?"

"All my money's tied up in cash," he said.

Richmond laughed and got on his computer. "Do you have a preference on the room?"

"First floor. I'm going to sit outside in my car to make sure she's safe."

"Got it. I'll put your friend in room 16L. It's at the end of the building. You can park your vehicle right in front of the door."

"That works. I'm also going to sit in my car with a shotgun in my lap. Just in case these guys who are after her tailed us."

Richmond blew out his cheeks. "These sound like bad people."

"That would be an understatement."

"My brother-in-law is a cop. If I call him, he'll be here in two minutes."

"I may take you up on that."

"How will I recognize these guys if they show up?"

"They'll be riding motorcycles."

- - -

Lancaster got Echo and her son situated in their room before again asking Echo if she was hungry. She said she was, and he bought bags of chips and nuts from a vending machine, plus a bottled water, and brought them to the room before explaining what came next.

"I'm going to put a call into Team Adam, and request a private jet come to the Sarasota Airport to fly you and your son to Nashville. Depending upon which airline has an available plane, this can take anywhere between three and six hours. In the meantime, I want you to stay in your room, and chill out."

"I'm not sleepy," Echo said.

"Then watch a movie on cable. You need to relax, and take your mind off things. I'm going to park my car in front of your room, and stand guard. If you need anything, or just want to talk, open the blinds to your window, and I'll come running."

It took a moment for the words to sink in. When they did, she visibly relaxed. He thought he understood. She had expected that he wanted to have sex, because that was what Dexter had done, and probably other men who had offered to help her. Sleep with me, and I'll help you. That was how the deal went.

But that wasn't his deal. Never had been, never would be. Echo was pretty and had a great figure, and saying he didn't find her attractive would have been a lie. But that didn't mean he was going to take advantage of her during a time of weakness.

She knew this, and it made her feel safe. Standing on her tiptoes, she kissed him on the cheek. "Thank you for saving me and my baby," she said.

"You're welcome. Get some rest. You're going to need it."

He went outside and moved his vehicle into the parking space in front of her door. Then he got out and opened the trunk and removed the Mossberg 590 Shockwave pump-action shotgun that he kept with his other firearms. With a pistol grip and antijam elevator, the 590 Shockwave was a nasty weapon at close range, and many states prohibited its sale. Luckily, Florida wasn't one of them.

He got behind the wheel and laid the shotgun across his lap. He left the engine running so he could listen to his Jimmy Buffett playlist on Spotify without draining the car's battery. Then he called the restricted Team Adam number on his cell phone and heard an operator pick up.

"This is Claudia. Who am I speaking with?" the operator asked.

"This is Jon Lancaster, code name Margaritaville."

"Good evening, Margaritaville. What can I do for you?"

"I have an emergency transport request for a seventeen-year-old female and her six-month-old baby son, to be transported to the farm in Nashville. They are currently staying at a motel near the Sarasota-Bradenton International Airport. The girl and her son are in imminent danger, and need to be moved tonight."

"Understood. Hold the line."

The operator put him on hold, and silence filled his ear. A motorcycle blew past the motel, followed by another, and he got out of his car holding the shotgun to his waist and the cell phone stuck between his shoulder and his neck. The two bikes faded into the night, and only when he felt sure they were gone did he get back in.

The operator returned. "Still there?"

"You bet. What have you got for me?"

"The kind folks at Delta Private Jets have stepped up to the plate. They have a Hawker 800 at the Fort Lauderdale Airport and have called one of their pilots to fly to Sarasota, and transport the girl and her son to Nashville, where a private car will take them to the farm. I'll text when the plane departs Fort Lauderdale, and give you its estimated landing time in Sarasota."

"That works. Thanks for the assist."

He ended the call. Delta Private Jets was a subsidiary of Delta Air Lines, and had a fleet of seventy small jets that were used throughout the Southeast. The company had transported more of his rescues than any other airline, always for free. It was why he tried to fly their parent company whenever possible.

He killed time listening to music. He knew every line to every Jimmy Buffett song, and he sang along while tapping his fingers against the wheel. The light in Echo's room went off, and he guessed she was trying to get some sleep. Echo was a decent girl, and from what he could tell, not horribly damaged by what life had dealt her. With some help, she and her son just might get their lives back to normal.

Echo was lucky, and had caught a break. But what about the enslaved women he'd seen on the YouTube video in Echo's apartment? Were they going to be able to one day resume their lives? Or would they forever be locked away, forced to cook and clean, and do their owners' bidding?

Next to murder, there was no greater crime than human trafficking, and thinking about their situation made him angry. They'd done nothing to deserve such a horrible fate, and had become prey to their captors, who were monsters.

He wanted to help them. If he put his mind to it, he just might be able to figure out where they were being held. He shut off the music, deep in thought.

The video had shown the women in a well-equipped kitchen, with multiple sinks, two refrigerators, and enough pots and pans for a small army. He put the room's size at two hundred square feet, which made it larger than a kitchen in an ordinary house. It made him think that the women were being held in a building where a large kitchen was necessary.

Kitchens were expensive, and he estimated that the one in the video had cost $100,000 or more to build. Were the women in an abandoned hotel, or an empty school? He didn't know the answer, but he did know this: the size of the kitchen indicated that it was a large facility, which he guessed had extensive sleeping quarters for the women, and probably their captors.

To keep such a facility going cost money. Money to pay the rent, the taxes, the power, and the grocery bill. It was an expensive proposition, and he wondered where the funds were coming from.

Not Dexter Hudson. Dexter was fresh out of prison, and was alternating between living in the back room of a strip club and shacking up with Echo. The rest of Dexter's gang was also recently released from prison, and didn't have the means to support such an enterprise. Which meant someone else was funding it.

He thought he knew who that was, but needed to be certain. He climbed out of his car and laid the shotgun on his seat. Going to the door to Echo's room, he rapped gently. He saw the lights come on through the window, and the door cracked an inch.

"Sorry to bother you," he said, "but I need to ask you a question."

Her eyes were half-closed, and her hair was a sleepy mess.

"Sure," she said.

"You said that other dancers at the club have disappeared. When did they disappear? Was this in the past few weeks, months, or years?"

"Last couple of years," she said.

"You're sure about this."

"Yeah."

"Thank you. The private jet will be here in a few hours. Go back to sleep."

She closed the door, and he got back into his vehicle. Echo had answered his question and solved the riddle. Dancers at Echo's club had been disappearing long before Dexter and his fellow ex-cons had gotten released from prison, and he had to believe that the Outlaws motorcycle gang was behind it. The Outlaws had the financial means to fund such an operation, and were also the types of soulless individuals who would kidnap women and later sell them into slavery. The kitchen he'd seen in the YouTube video was part of their operation, and Dexter was using it to house his victims.

It was a joint operation between the bikers and Dexter's gang of ex-cons.

The door to the front office opened, and Richmond came outside. In his hand was a steaming Styrofoam cup. Lancaster lowered his window.

"I thought you might need this," the night manager said.

It was coffee, strong and black. He took a sip and smiled.

"You have no idea how good that tastes," he said.

PART THREE

Whoever Fights Monsters

CHAPTER 25

The noise was short and persistent. Three long buzzes, then silence, followed by three more long buzzes. It came over and over again, refusing to die.

Daniels pulled a pillow over her head, and tried to block the noise out. She was exhausted, and had crashed on the bed in her room at the Marriott still fully dressed. Sleep had come instantly, and her thoughts had drifted far, far away.

Then the noise had started. It was still pitch dark, and she'd refused to fully awaken, but had forced herself back to sleep. She wasn't like Jon, who could run on five cylinders without sleep for days at a time. Her body needed rest; without it, she was nothing more than a zombie.

The noise didn't care. It invaded her dreams, first posing as a yellow jacket banging against a screen door, and then as a dentist's drill bit. She was allergic to bee stings and hated going to the dentist, and the dreams had felt like punishment.

At six a.m. she caved, and opened her eyes. Her hotel room was dark, the blinds tightly shut, the digital clock's face the room's only light. The sound was gone, and she tried to gather her thoughts, and figure out where it had come from. It wasn't a fire alarm, nor was it emanating from her laptop. What the hell.

She heard it again. This time, it was accompanied by vibration. Her eyes had adjusted to the darkness, and she shifted her head on her pillow. Her cell phone was doing a little dance on the night table. She'd muted the volume, but not the vibrator. Someone had been texting her, and when she hadn't responded, had kept at it. This was the sound that had plagued her all night.

She fumbled to turn on the bedside light. The only messages that were delivered at night were bad ones. Something horrible had happened while she'd been sleeping, and she could only guess what it was.

She wasn't ready to deal with bad news just yet, and fixed a pot of coffee in the machine supplied by the hotel. While it brewed, she stood in front of the bathroom sink, brushed her teeth, and then ran a wet washcloth over her face, the water good and cold. Only when she felt connected to the real world did she sit down on the bed, and sip the scalding brew.

The coffee brought her around. When the cup was empty, she picked up her cell phone and had a look. She'd gotten sixteen text messages during the night. No wonder she'd had such a hard time sleeping.

She punched the "Message" icon with her finger, and entered the area where the messages were displayed. They'd all come from her boss, J. T.

"Jesus Christ," she said aloud.

She started with the first message, which had come in right after she'd gone to bed. J. T. was asking if she'd seen the news, and for her to call him right away. J. T. had always been good about respecting her privacy, and she guessed that something truly horrific had taken place last night.

She scrolled through the rest of the texts. The messages were similar to the first, with J. T. asking her to call immediately.

This had disaster written all over it. It would have helped if J. T. had sent her a link to the news story that had prompted his first message, instead of leaving her in the dark. She had no idea what she was stepping into, and that was never good.

She pulled up the blinds, and let the early-morning sunlight wash over her. It gave her strength, and she pulled up her boss's private number and placed the call while staring at the parking lot. It rang four times before being patched into voice mail.

"This is Special Agent Joseph Hacker with the Federal Bureau of Investigation," the prerecorded message said. "I'm away from the phone at the moment. Leave a brief message along with your phone number, and I'll return your call upon my return."

A long beep filled her ear.

"J. T., this is Beth. I was asleep when your text messages came in. I didn't see the news, and don't know what's going on. Call me when you can."

She ended the call. The room had a workstation on which her laptop sat. She got on the internet and searched the different news sites, hoping to find the story that J. T. was referring to. Plenty of things had happened since she'd gone to bed, with most of the stories posted in the last hour. She read through them, but found nothing relative.

She shut down her laptop in disgust. That was the maddening thing about the internet. A hot story might be replaced by another story so quickly that the original one became lost and forgotten. The old expression, here today, gone tomorrow, was no longer relevant. Now it was here today, gone in a second.

She placed another call to her boss's private number. It was not like J. T. not to immediately call back. The prerecorded message played. The beep that followed was longer than the previous one, which meant that J. T. hadn't picked up her message.

She hung up.

She poured herself more coffee. When you were in law enforcement, there was nothing worse than being in the dark, especially when working a case. She needed to find out what was going on, quickly.

There were two types of agents within the FBI. Early risers, and night owls. She was a night owl, while many of her peers worked better in the morning. On the hunch that one of them was now at work, she called the main switchboard, and tried different extensions.

On her first five attempts, she struck out. Number six was the charm.

"This is Special Agent McDonald," a female voice said. "May I help you?"

"Karen, this is Beth Daniels," she said. "I'm down in Florida working a case, and need to get ahold of J. T. He isn't answering his phone, and I'm worried about him. Do you know how I can reach him?"

"Hey, Beth, I hate to be the bearer of bad news, but J. T. collapsed this morning and was rushed to the hospital. They think he had a stroke."

"Oh my God. Do you know his condition?"

"He's critical. J. T.'s been under a lot of stress lately."

McDonald's voice trembled. Daniels wanted to console her, but stifled the urge. They were soldiers in a war, and were expected to deal with adversity without flinching. It was hard when one of their own went down during the fight, but those were the breaks. "Would you shoot me a text when you get an update?" Daniels asked.

"I'd be happy to. Should I use this number?" McDonald said.

"Please. Keep the faith."

"I will. I said a prayer for J. T. earlier. It felt like the least I could do."

Daniels didn't believe in God, but she feared him greatly. She ended the connection and said a prayer for her boss as well.

- - -

A hot shower helped clear her head. As she was toweling off, she had an unsettling thought. If J. T. didn't pull through, she might never learn the meaning behind his text messages.

She took her time dressing. Whoever fought monsters often paid the price for their service. Insomnia, weight loss, and depression were not uncommon among people in law enforcement whose daily jobs brought them face-to-face with evil. Alcohol abuse was rampant, and so were broken marriages. Evil was corrosive, not only for the criminals, whose souls it burned away, but also for agents of the law whose psyches became singed each time they were forced to stare into the abyss of human depravity.

J. T. had paid the price. Over the course of his career, he'd apprehended his share of serial killers and mass murderers, and seen more bad things than most soldiers on the battlefield. It had worn him down. He drank more than was healthy and still smoked. His home life was no picnic either. After his kids had gone to college, he and his wife had divorced, then reconciled, and tried to piece things together. He'd joked to Daniels that a six-month sabbatical would have saved his marriage the first time, only the bureau wasn't in the habit of giving those.

And now he'd had a stroke. Everyone had seen it coming, but they were powerless to do anything about it. They were trapped in a war without end, and the only way out was to retire, or to be felled by one's own health.

- - -

Next to the front desk was an alcove that sold cold drinks and snacks. If a customer didn't see what they needed, they could leave a list with the manager on duty, and it would be there in the morning.

"Daniels, room 237. I put an order in last night," she said.

The manager handed her a paper bag. She crossed the lobby to be out of range of the TV, and ate her breakfast of grapefruit juice, a banana, and plain yogurt sprinkled with granola. As she finished, her cell phone rang. She took it from her purse, hoping it was McDonald with news about J. T. To her surprise, it was her niece, Nicki. They hadn't spoken in a while, and she wasn't in the right frame of mind to talk about teenage girl stuff. Better to wait until the weekend to engage in that kind of conversation.

Then she had a thought. Nicki and her classmates were doing sleuthing for Jon, trying to help him break the case. Maybe Nicki was calling to share their findings. Daniels needed all the help she could get, and decided to take her niece's call.

"Good morning. How's my favorite niece?" she said.

"I'm okay. I know you're working a case, but I had to call," Nicki said.

Her niece was breathing hard, betraying her anxiety.

"Is something wrong?" Daniels asked.

"I guess that depends on what your definition of wrong is."

"Come again?"

"Something tells me you haven't seen the video that was posted on YouTube last night. It's already gotten three hundred thousand views."

Daniels sat up straight in her chair. Was this what J. T. had been referring to when he'd texted Daniels, and asked her if she'd seen the news? The timing was right, and the video had obviously caused a sensation to generate that many views.

"No, I haven't seen the video," Daniels said. "But something tells me you have. What's on it?"

"Jon takes on a gang of bikers," Nicki said. "It's epic."

CHAPTER 26

Lancaster's cell phone had also woken him up early in the morning. Not many people had his number, and as a result, he didn't get many calls, so he rarely muted the volume before hitting the sack.

His cell phone was plugged in on the other side of his hotel room. By the time he'd switched on the night light and climbed out of bed, the ringing had stopped.

He checked the call directory. The last call had a 305 area code, which was Dade and Monroe County, but otherwise was unfamiliar, and he chalked it up to a wrong number.

Although he'd slept only a few hours, he felt rested. The Hawker had touched down at the Sarasota Airport at two a.m., and he'd checked out the pilot's credentials before allowing Echo and her baby to board. He'd heard stories of victims disappearing while in transit because they'd mistakenly gotten on the wrong plane, and he'd vowed that would never happen on his watch.

It was the right pilot, so everything was good. But then a bad thing had happened. Echo had experienced a meltdown, and began hysterically crying while standing on the tarmac, which had caused her son to also cry. She was going to a strange place with strange people, and the thought terrified her.

He couldn't let Echo leave in such a bad state. So he'd led her into a building that had restrooms and vending machines, and asked her to sit in a stiff plastic chair. He sat down beside her, and showed her a short video stored on his cell phone of the farm that he'd taken during his last visit. It was a slice of heaven, and he'd turned up the volume so she could hear the birds singing in the background, and the content voices of the people living on the farm as they groomed horses as they stood in cross ties. When the video was over, she'd asked to see it again. After the second viewing, she took a deep breath and visibly relaxed.

"My new home," she whispered.

"Yes, your new home," he'd said.

They went back outside, and this time, she boarded without crying. But before she did, she hugged him so fiercely that he thought his rib cage might break. As the Hawker took off, he stood on the tarmac and watched it ascend into the heavens, not willing to leave until the private jet had disappeared from view.

While he was brushing his teeth, his phone pinged, indicating his caller had left a message. Intrigued, he went into voice mail and keyed in his password. The raucous laughter of his friend Beecher Martin, who he was supposed to be partying with in the Keys, came out of the phone.

"Hey, Jon, it's your old buddy Beech. Like a dumb shit, I dropped a bag with all our cell phones in the water, so I have to call you from a pay phone at the motel we're staying at. Clive and Ray also say hello."

Clive's and Ray's drunken voices chorused in the background.

"We just closed down an after-hours bar," Beech said proudly. "Right when we were paying the tab, there was a video on a TV of a guy I swear was you. The guy's wearing a Yankees baseball cap and shooting up a bunch of bikers in a parking lot. Clive and Ray think the guy in the video is somebody else, so we made a little wager. A hundred bucks says I'm right, the guy is you. I'll call you back later to confirm. Be safe, my friend."

He erased the message. This complicated things, and he brewed himself a pot of coffee, then drank a cup while thinking back to the shootout at Echo's apartment. He was good at taking in his surroundings. He hadn't noticed any surveillance cameras at the building earlier in the evening, and he'd assumed the owners were too cheap to install them. Had he spotted cameras, he would have shot out their lenses, which had been standard operating procedure when he was a SEAL. The Taliban, Al-Qaeda, and other terrorist organizations were fond of sacrificing innocent women and children while secretly filming American soldiers as they mistakenly shot these people to death. The videos were posted on social media and used as recruiting tools. To stop the practice, the SEALs were trained to disable any surveillance cameras they discovered during a mission.

Had someone filmed him from inside the apartment building? That was a distinct possibility, especially considering the quality of videos that could be shot on smartphones.

There was only one way to find out. The best place to start was the news organizations. Opening his laptop, he got on the internet, and first checked CNN, then Fox News, and finally MSNBC. The video wasn't on the home pages of any of those sites, which made him feel better, if only for a short while.

Next stop was YouTube. He typed the words *motorcycle gang shootout* into the search engine. This produced a hundred videos of crazed bikers firing at each other in such towns as Waco, Albuquerque, Las Vegas, and the South Side of Chicago. He decided to add the word *Florida* to his search to see what happened.

He hit the jackpot. A video of the shootout from Echo's apartment had been posted at around midnight the night before. The video was in color, and had been taken from inside the building on an upper floor. Although up for only a few hours, it had already gone viral, and garnered three hundred thousand views.

On the video, the Outlaws could be seen riding in circles around the apartment parking lot. He hadn't been able to accurately count how many there were earlier in the evening, but did so now. There was an even dozen in all. There was enough light in the lot to reflect their faces, and they all looked good and drunk.

After completing several loops, one of the bikers got bored, and popped a wheelie. The biker did the wheelie in a straight line, then brought the front wheel down, braked, turned around, and popped another wheelie and drove back in the same direction. He had a glazed expression on his face, and was howling at the moon.

The other bikers started doing wheelies with their buddy. The video had audio, and he could faintly hear the bikers' hoots and hollers beneath the engines' mighty roars.

In the lower left-hand corner of the screen, he saw himself exit the building with Echo and Hector. They walked down the path to the edge of the parking lot and halted. His Yankees ball cap was pulled down low, the brim hiding his face from the camera.

So far, so good.

On the video, he watched himself raise his gun, and shoot out the bikers' back tires as they flew past. The resulting mayhem was nothing short of spectacular. Three bikes on the edge of the pack flew over the trunks of parked cars, while those in the middle hurtled into each other, and sent their riders crashing to the pavement. It was a shame they weren't wearing helmets.

Twelve bikes, and they all went down hard. He couldn't have planned it better if he'd scripted it. He paused the video and stared at the screen. He was a shadowy figure, and nothing more. No wonder Clive and Ray didn't think it was him.

But why did Beech?

He resumed the video. Three of the bikers had untangled themselves from their damaged machines and were marching toward him, ready to do battle. On the screen, he turned to confront them. The air caught in his throat. If the camera caught his face—even for an instant—he was screwed. There were dozens of photographs of him on the internet from his police days, including a YouTube video that showed him shooting two guys to death who'd been trying to kidnap a little girl, and it would be easy for someone to make a match.

The fight was short and sweet. He knocked two bikers out cold, while Echo immobilized the third with Mace. Adversaries often let their guard down because of his pot belly. The truth be known, a guy could be of average height and have a gut, and still be absolutely lethal. Only, the average schmuck didn't know that.

His face wasn't caught by the camera due to the parking lot's dim lighting, and partly due to luck. On the screen, he escorted Echo and her baby to his car, and made a hasty getaway.

He paused the video again, and tried to see if the license plate on his car was visible. The numbers and letters were hidden, again by the poor lighting. He was home free, and broke into a smile.

Or was he? Beech had been willing to bet a hundred bucks that it was him on the video, even though his face wasn't clearly identifiable. What exactly had Beech seen that made him feel it was his old buddy Jon? And would other people see it as well?

He didn't know. All he could do was deny that it was him, and hope for the best.

He decided to go for a run. The rear of the hotel was connected to a running path, and he needed to clear his head. As he laced up his sneakers, Beth called. The timing wasn't good, and he guessed she'd seen the video as well.

"Good morning," he answered cheerfully.

"You are one crazy son of a bitch," she said.

CHAPTER 27

Daniels was in her hotel room staring at her laptop, the shootout video having just finished playing. She'd watched it three times, just to be certain the cowboy on the screen was Jon. When she'd decided it was him, she'd made the call.

"What did I do?" he asked innocently.

"You know exactly what you did," she said, unable to hide the anger in her voice.

"No, I don't. Please illuminate me."

"Stop playing games. You opened fire on a motorcycle gang in the parking lot of an apartment complex in New Port Richey last night. A renter in the building filmed the encounter, and posted it on YouTube. The god damn thing has gone viral."

"It wasn't me."

"Oh, come on! I knew the moment I saw the video that it was you. Same build, same cocky attitude, and deadly with a handgun. The fact that the shooter's face is hidden by a Yankees baseball cap doesn't hide who it was. You did it."

"It wasn't me. I hate the Yankees."

"Are you trying to be cute? Because it's not working."

"Your case is flimsy, to use your favorite expression. Lots of guys look like me, and I'm sure plenty know how to handle a firearm. I didn't shoot up a gang of bikers."

"No? Well, then let me add this to my argument. The gang that got shot up was the same guys we confronted in the clubhouse in Saint Pete."

"What a coincidence."

"The local newspaper posted a story a little while ago. Every single biker suffered a major injury because of what you did. The paper said the gang sustained three broken arms, four broken legs, two concussions, two broken backs, a broken jaw, a crushed pelvis, and a broken neck, not to mention a whole bunch of broken ribs. It's a miracle that you didn't kill any of them."

"That's sad. I hope they had insurance."

"You're saying it wasn't you, is that what you want me to believe?"

"Correct. Until someone proves otherwise, please stop saying I'm to blame."

"What about the girl with the baby in the video? That's the stripper from the club that you talked to, isn't it? What if she steps forward, and says it was you? How do you plan to wiggle your way out of that?"

"That's not going to happen."

"You're saying that she's gone in the wind?"

Jon said nothing, confirming her suspicion. Every person that broke the law screwed up, even the smart ones. She wasn't ready to let go just yet.

"The video has over three hundred thousand views," she said. "A viewer is going to notice the way you beat those guys up. You knocked out one with a knee to the jaw, and the second by sweeping out his legs from under him. You told me that's part of your SEAL training. Don't use your fists because it's too easy to break your hand. Better to use your head, or an elbow, or a knee. This is going to come back and bite you, Jon."

"Not using your fists is part of most martial arts training." He paused. "The guy in the video could have been anyone. Stop saying it was me, or I'll hang up."

"You are something else."

"My turn. Last night, you told me that your boss told you to take me off the case, and that we couldn't talk anymore. What changed?"

"Nothing changed. I just had to call you."

"I hope it doesn't lead to trouble."

There was real compassion in his voice, and she realized that he meant it. That was the thing about Jon; she could dress him down, call him terrible names, and it didn't seem to diminish his feelings toward her.

"Nor do I," she said.

She heard a click, indicating another call had come in. She pulled her cell phone away from her face and stared at the screen. It was Karen McDonald calling, perhaps with an update on J. T.'s condition. Bringing the phone back to her face, she said, "I've got another call from a colleague. I'll call you later. Please try and stay out of trouble."

"Yes, ma'am," he said.

She disconnected and picked up Karen's call.

"Hey, Karen. Any news?"

"The hospital just released a statement," her colleague said. "There's good news and bad news. The good news is that J. T.'s a strong son of a bitch, and is going to live. The bad news is, the stroke occurred on the left side of his brain, so the right side of his body was affected. He has partial paralysis and can't speak. With therapy, the doctors think he's going to be okay, but it's going to take time."

Daniels realized she was crying. Wiping away the tears, she said, "J. T. not able to speak? I can't imagine that."

"You and me both."

"Is there anything I can do?"

"Keep praying. I'll call you with any updates."

"I will. Thanks, Karen."

Ending the call, she went into the bathroom and washed her face. J. T. wasn't the easiest boss, and had always pressed her to do better. But he'd always had her back, and like a safety net, he had been there to catch her when she'd screwed up.

She thought back to their last conversation. J. T. had flown to Tampa for the express purpose of telling her to pull Jon off the case. In hindsight, she realized how unusual that was. When an FBI director issued an order, it was done in memo form, which was emailed to the agent, with a copy put in the agent's file. That way, if the agent did not comply, there was documented evidence that could lead to the agent being punished or dismissed.

But J. T. hadn't sent a memo. Or had he? She got dozens of emails a day, and there was the chance that J. T.'s memo had escaped her notice. She needed to check, so she got on her laptop and loaded her email, where she found sixty-five messages waiting in her inbox.

She read every single one. None were from J. T. There was no evidence of him telling her to pull Jon off the case. It was like it had never happened. And with J. T. now in the hospital, unable to speak, she could safely say that it hadn't happened. Everything was status quo.

She wanted to call Jon back, and relay the good news. But before she did that, there was the matter of the agent on her team who'd betrayed her. She'd never had a knife stuck in her back before, and it hurt like hell.

- - -

Her team was buried in work when she entered the basement conference room. A box of freshly baked Dunkin' Donuts sat on the table, and she peeked inside. They had saved her one. She didn't believe in beating around the bush, and she crossed her arms and told everyone to stop what they were doing. Closing their laptops, they turned in their swivel chairs to face her.

"As you've probably heard, J. T. suffered a stroke and is in the hospital," she said. "The word from the doctors is he's going to survive, but his recovery will be slow. Please say a prayer for his speedy recovery.

"Last night, I learned that one of you went behind my back, and contacted J. T. in order to voice your displeasure over the fact that Jon Lancaster was brought into the investigation. I have a problem with that, and I'm going to explain to you why.

"I don't expect for you to agree with every decision I make, but I do expect you to respect my decisions, nonetheless. If you think I've done something wrong, I expect you to come directly to me. Not doing that is a betrayal.

"I handpicked each one of you to be on my team, and would like to believe that I've been a pretty good boss. One of you obviously feels otherwise.

"I want to know who did this. I can find out one of two ways. I can confiscate your cell phones and laptops, do a search, and see which one of you contacted J. T. I personally find this approach distasteful, because it means that I have to look at everyone's communications, and I'm sure you all have things you'd wish I didn't see."

Her team shifted uncomfortably in their chairs. Hurting all of them because one had erred wasn't fair, but she didn't care. She was going to get to the bottom of this, one way or another.

"The second option is that the guilty agent come forward. By doing that, the rest of the team won't suffer. There's a smoking area behind the hotel. I'm going there to wait. If the guilty agent doesn't come out in five minutes, I'll confiscate your devices."

She uncrossed her arms and searched their faces. To say that she'd put the fear of God into them was an understatement, and she hoped it produced the desired result. She took the last doughnut before leaving.

- - -

The smoking area was shaded and had a bench. She sat on one end and muted her cell phone. She was betting that the guilty agent was apologizing to the rest of the team for bringing this on them, and would be joining her shortly.

A minute later, Otto West came outside. He was her favorite on the team, and she was saddened by his poor choice. She patted the bench, and he sat on the opposite end.

"It was me," he said.

She waited for more, and realized that nothing was forthcoming.

"Are you going to apologize, ask me not to fire you?" she asked.

"If I did, I would be lying," he said.

"So you think I made a bad choice. Why not come to me, and say so? We could have gone for a run, and you could have brought it up, and said what was on your mind. I wouldn't have had an issue with that."

West rested his elbows on his knees and looked straight ahead. She always considered it a bad sign when a person wouldn't look her in the eye during a conversation; it was an indication that a trust had been broken.

"This is different," he said.

"How is it different?"

"Jon Lancaster is a loose cannon. He does things that would get any of us fired. We all watched a YouTube video of him shooting two guys who kidnapped a little girl. He shot them on the side of the highway, with cars flying by. That's crazy." He paused, then added, "I don't want my career cut short because of him."

"You should have told me that."

"Really? You and Lancaster have dated. I think it's safe to say that you have feelings for him," he said, still looking straight ahead. "We've all noticed it."

The words were slow to sink in. Was this a group decision, with Otto picking the short straw and being the one to contact J. T.? If that was the case, then she had a much bigger problem on her hands.

"I dated Jon for a month. We had a great time, and I enjoyed his company," she said. "When J. T. put our team on this case, I stopped communicating with him because I was afraid the distraction would impair my ability to do my job. Just so you know, I rarely talk to my family or friends when I'm working an investigation. It makes for a lousy social life, but that's my decision."

"I didn't know that." Then he added, "I'm sorry, Beth."

"If you'd known this, would you still have contacted J. T.?"

"Probably not."

"There's more. Would you like to hear it?"

"Please."

"Months ago, Jon helped me catch a pair of serial killers that had been eluding us for years. I'll never forget it. I was with Jon in his apartment, and we'd been working the case nonstop for two days. We were poring over a file when I suddenly ran out of gas, and passed out on his couch. Has that ever happened to you before?"

"Sure. The mind says yes, but the body says no."

"That's right. The desire is there, but not the physical strength."

"Happens to the best of us."

"Not to Jon."

Otto stared at her. "He doesn't get tired?"

"Not as quickly as you and I do. It gives him an edge when working a case."

"I'll say."

"Several hours after I fell asleep, Jon woke me up. He'd cracked the case. I remember looking at him, and thinking, 'How are you still functioning? How does that work?' I asked him on our first date. He explained that to become a SEAL, each recruit is trained to stay awake for several days at a time. While awake, the recruits have to run mountain courses, detonate explosives, and train underwater in scuba equipment. It's grueling, and those that can't do it, flunk out. The navy toughened Jon's body and also his mind."

"That's impressive. You wouldn't know that to look at him."

"Looks can be deceiving."

Otto shifted on the bench to face her. He didn't seem fully satisfied by what she'd told him, and after a moment he explained why. "Several of the team checked out Lancaster online. Based upon the articles we read, it seems like he never stopped being a SEAL. That's the part none of us understand."

"How so?"

"Were you in the military?"

Daniels shook her head.

"My older brother was in Army Special Forces and did two tours of Afghanistan," Otto said. "When he got out, he came home, got a job, got married, and raised a family. He put on weight, and drank beer with his buddies on the weekend. He started acting like a civilian, and stopped being a soldier. That isn't the case with Lancaster. He went from being a SEAL to being a cop, and now he's with Team Adam. He's always armed and doesn't run from trouble. If you ask me, he's fighting his own private war."

Otto had nailed it. Jon was pushing back against the darkness, just as she was. Her battle had started when she'd been tossed in the trunk of a car by a pair of serial killers while in college, and by a stroke of luck managed to escape. She'd been fighting evil ever since, and felt like she was winning. That was good enough reason to keep going, even if she didn't have much of a personal life. But she didn't know much about Jon's motivation, or what drove him to sacrifice his time to help people he didn't know.

She rose from the bench. Otto slowly stood up as well.

"Am I fired?" he asked.

"No," she said.

"Do you want me to resign?"

"I'd like you to stay. Just don't betray me again."

They went to the exit that led back inside the hotel. Otto reached to open the door for her, then said, "Are you going to bring Lancaster back on board?"

"I want to, but not at the risk of alienating you and the rest of the team. Something tells me that you're not the only one who feels this way."

"Everyone on the team is worried."

So it was a group sentiment. She needed to handle this right, or risk alienating them. "Here's what I'll do. I'll sit down with Jon, and voice your concerns. If I can rein him in, I'll bring him back. If not, he's history. Sound fair?"

"I guess. Do you really think you can control him?" Otto asked.

She stared at her reflection in the door's glass partition. She didn't consider herself attractive, yet knew that most men *did* find her attractive, and would lavish attention on her, if given the opportunity. Jon had made her feel like a princess the times they'd gone out, and she felt certain that she could use that to her advantage.

"Jon will do what I want him to do." She didn't believe in loose ends, and wanted to be sure they were on the same page. She put her hand on his sleeve.

"Are we good?" she asked.

"Good as gold," he said.

CHAPTER 28

There was no such thing as luck. That had been drilled into Lancaster's head over and over during his military training. Luck was a by-product of hard work, intense preparation, and showing up. As the Norwegian explorer Roald Amundsen once said, "Victory awaits him who has everything in order."

The unexpected phone call came right after he hung up with Daniels. The area code wasn't familiar, and at first he thought it was a robocall offering him a free line of credit or help dealing with the IRS. He almost didn't take the call, but an itch in his gut said that it was important, so he answered it.

"Hi, this is Echo."

"Hey there," he said, smiling into the phone. "How was your trip? Are you at the farm? Is everything okay?"

"The trip was fine. We arrived about fifteen minutes ago. The farm is more beautiful than I could have imagined. Thank you for making this happen."

"You're going to like it there. It's a very special place."

"I think you're right. I have something to share with you. When we boarded the flight, the pilot gave me a bag with snacks. There was a package of Ritz peanut butter crackers. When I saw them, I remembered that was the name of Dexter's new partner."

"His partner's name is Peanut Butter?"

"No, just Butter."

"So it's a street name."

"That's right. I asked Dexter what it meant, and he said Butter was real slippery. I think they met in prison. Hopefully it will help your investigation."

He made a fist bump and let out a silent *Hooyah.*

"It does help. Thank you," he said.

"It was the least I could do."

"I have a favor to ask. A video was posted on YouTube of me shooting the tires of the bikers at your apartment complex. You and your baby are in it as well. More than likely, there will be a criminal investigation into what happened."

"Are you going to get in trouble?"

"That's what I'm trying to avoid. If a police officer comes to the farm, and asks you about the video, I want you to tell him that it was a stranger who helped you, and that you don't know the stranger's name. Will you do that for me?"

"Of course. You saved our lives."

"Thank you. Send photos after you get settled in."

"I will. Goodbye, Jon."

He ended the call and let out another yell. When he'd first become a cop, knowing a suspect's nickname had been a useless piece of information. Now, because of the information superhighway, it was a powerful tool to tracking down a suspect.

He got on the internet. Because he was a member of Team Adam, he had access to many law enforcement agencies' criminal databases, including those housed in the Florida Department of Law Enforcement's headquarters in Tallahassee. The FDLE databases were called specialty databases, and included nicknames, descriptions of tattoos, and other identifying features of the 1.7 million citizens who'd been incarcerated in Florida's prisons.

The nickname database was a powerful tool. Many criminals used aliases, and as a result, made it difficult for the police to track them down, especially if the police only had the criminal's real name to work with. Nicknames were different. Once a criminal was given a nickname, it usually stayed with him for the rest of his life.

The nickname site had been updated, the colors in patriotic red, white, and blue. He entered the name *Butter* into the search engine, and hit "Enter." A second later a mug shot appeared, along with a physical description, criminal history, and last known address.

Devin "Butter" Highnote, five foot eight, 170 pounds, mud-brown eyes, brown hair, a native of Saint Petersburg, Florida, with a rap sheet dating back twenty years, including arrests for armed robbery and attempted murder.

He leaned back in his chair and shut his eyes. The pieces of the puzzle were starting to come together. Dexter Hudson and Devin Highnote were in Saint Petersburg, preparing to abduct another victim. Highnote was also a native of Saint Petersburg, which wasn't a coincidence. The next victim was connected to Butter through one of his crimes.

He needed help, and called Nicki. She got to school early for band practice, and he hoped to catch her before classes began. Voice mail picked up, and he left a message.

Nicki was as passionate about catching criminals as her aunt, and sixty seconds later, she called back. "Hey, Jon! I saw the YouTube video. You took those bikers to school!"

"It wasn't me," he said solemnly.

"Right," she said, laughing.

"I'm serious, Nicki. It wasn't me, even though you and I know otherwise. If any of your classmates bring it up, you need to tell them that. Understood?"

"You bet."

"I have an assignment for your CSI class. If you pull this off, you'll help me break this case wide open. Think you can talk your teacher into it?"

"Sure. What do you want us to do?"

"I need you to run a background check on an ex-convict named Devin Highnote from Saint Petersburg. Devin was an inmate in Raiford Prison not that long ago. I need your class to find out why he was sent there."

"That shouldn't be too hard. Is he one of the kidnappers?"

"I believe he is. Call me once you find something."

He said goodbye. Having a class of bright high school kids helping him was a real bonus, and he made a mental note to do something special for them once the investigation was over. He put his laptop under his arm and headed for the door.

Going downstairs, he entered the hotel's business center, and connected the laptop wirelessly to the laser printer that guests could use free of charge. Moments later, two copies of Devin Highnote's information spit out of the printer. One copy for him, the second for Beth. His cell phone rang, and he saw that it was her.

"I was just thinking of you," he answered.

"I'm ten minutes from your hotel. Are you still there?"

"I'm in the lobby."

"Stay there. We need to talk. You're back on the case."

"I thought I was persona non grata."

"Not anymore. My boss had a stroke this morning, and is in the hospital. He never put the order to stay away from you in writing, so I'm home free."

"Let me return the favor. Dexter Hudson's new partner is an ex-con named Devin Highnote, and he's from Saint Petersburg. I'm close to figuring out who their next victim will be. If we get lucky, we might catch them in the act."

"How can you know who their next victim is?"

"She's a witness from one of Highnote's previous crimes. I'll explain when you get here."

"Meet me in the valet area in front of the hotel. I need coffee."

He trotted up the stairwell to his room, and deposited his laptop in the wall safe. Then he ran back downstairs and went outside to wait. His heart was racing, and not just from the exertion. He was about to break the case open. Very soon, the victims he'd seen on the video in Echo's apartment would be free, and home with their loved ones.

He knew of no greater feeling in the world.

CHAPTER 29

The tables were taken at the Starbucks near his hotel, so they sat in Daniels's vehicle and sipped their steaming brews. He'd handed her the sheet of information about Highnote when he'd gotten into the car, and she still hadn't looked at it. That wasn't like Beth, and he sensed that something was amiss.

"Am I on the case again, or not?" he asked.

"You are, but first we need some ground rules," she said.

"And why is that?"

"My team mutinied over my decision to bring you on board the first time. They think you're a walking time bomb, and that your behavior puts their careers in jeopardy. I can't let that happen again."

He sipped his brew and said nothing. Daniels and her team had been spinning their wheels for a month while innocent women were getting snatched all over Florida. So what if he broke the rules every once in a while? When it came to saving people's lives, the only report card that mattered was getting the victim back alive.

"From now on, I want you talk to me before you make a move," she said. "You have to be totally transparent. Think you can do that?"

He nearly said no. He'd bent the rules in the navy, as a cop, and as a private investigator, and didn't see himself changing at this stage in the game. But he needed Beth's help if he was going to break this open, so he told a lie.

"Of course," he said.

"Glad to hear it." The sheet on Highnote lay on the seat between them. She picked it up and started to read. "Tell me how this guy fits in."

"Devin Highnote is one of Dexter's recruits from Raiford Prison. The next victim will be connected to him."

"Connected how?"

"If my theory is correct, the next victim will be someone who testified against Highnote at his trial. That's the thread that connects the victims. They all witnessed crimes, and testified against the men who committed them. You've heard the expression, 'No good deed goes unpunished'? Well, being abducted is their punishment."

"So the victims are being punished for being Good Samaritans."

"That's right."

"If your theory is correct, then one of the victims helped send your brother in prison. Do you know which one it was?"

He nodded solemnly. "I do. It was Elsie Tanner. She was visiting Fort Lauderdale and witnessed the robbery Logan was involved in, and she later testified at his trial. I didn't make the connection at first because her name is actually Lisa Catherine, not Elsie."

The memory was painful, and she let a moment pass before speaking again.

"Was that Dexter's recruitment pitch?" she asked. "Join my gang, and I'll help you get revenge on the person that put you away?"

"That's part of the pitch."

"What's the rest?"

"The gang's ringleader, Cano, is a drug dealer. Cano's original gang got arrested, and sent back to Colombia. Cano wants to start peddling drugs again from inside prison and needs to communicate with his suppliers using cell phones and laptops. But he needs a new gang to push the product for him."

"So they're being recruited to be drug dealers," Daniels said. "How does Dexter Hudson fit in?"

"Dexter is Cano's lieutenant. His job is to recruit inmates who are ready to be released, which he did with my brother. He dangles a carrot in their faces to get them on board."

"The carrot being revenge and a job."

"That's only part of the offer. There's a third incentive."

"Which is what?"

"A big chunk of money. Dexter bragged to his biker buddies about the house he was going to buy. My brother, Logan, also was looking to buy a house. Where were they going to get the money? Not from banks."

Her coffee cup was empty. She squeezed it so hard that it was crushed in her hand. Her light-brown eyes were burning a hole into his soul. "They were going to sell the victims into slavery, and give each of the gang members a portion of the proceeds."

"That's what I'm thinking," he said. "The victims were going to pay for those houses. That was the third incentive, and it was big enough to get Logan and many other inmates to join."

She tossed her cup to the floor and cursed under her breath. She was kicking herself for not recognizing these clues, and solving the puzzle herself. It happened to the best investigators, but telling her that wasn't going to change how she felt.

"Are you sure about this, Jon?" she said.

"One hundred percent sure. The video I saw in Echo's apartment was the clincher," he said.

"Why was that?"

"The victims looked well cared for. Their clothes were clean, and none of them were sporting visible bruises. They were preparing food in a large kitchen, with each having a different assignment. Their captors were preparing them for slavery." He paused, then said, "You've busted human traffickers. How much is a woman worth?"

"There's a scale that traffickers use," she said. "You would think that pretty young girls fetch the most money, but that's not the case. Pretty girls are good for sex, and not much else. They usually don't have any skills, so they sit around all day.

"A middle-aged woman gets more money, especially if she's educated. Educated women know how to cook, how to clean, and plenty of other useful things."

"How much would an educated woman go for?"

"The going rate is between three and four hundred thousand dollars. They're in high demand in Central and South America, which is where most of them end up."

"Who are the buyers?"

"Wealthy people."

They fell silent. The conversation had upset her, and he went into the building and purchased a chocolate chunk muffin from the bakery and brought it to her. Sweets were her weakness, and she tore off a piece of muffin and popped it into her mouth.

"Did you get anything for yourself?" she asked.

"I was hoping we could share," he said.

"Better eat fast. I'm hungry."

They finished off the muffin in silence. Then he said, "I have another theory for your consideration."

"Go ahead," she said.

"I've never had experience dealing with human traffickers. Based upon what I've read, they're fairly sophisticated."

"That would be an understatement. There are several rings that the FBI has been chasing with no success. They use burner phones and always pay in cash. They're masters at flying under the radar."

"They sound like real pros."

"They are. We usually only catch them when they screw up. They don't make many mistakes."

"So they're well trained."

"Very well trained. So what's your point?"

"Cano is a drug dealer who got into the kidnapping business in order to lure recruits into his gang. He's a neophyte when it comes to human trafficking, yet his gang has managed to abduct thirteen women and not get caught. Does that sound right to you?"

There was a spark in Daniels's eyes that hadn't been there before. She popped the last crumb into her mouth and stared at him with a burning intensity.

"Finish your thought," she said.

"Cano isn't masterminding the abductions. Dexter Hudson is. He got his education when he was running with the Outlaws before he got sent to prison."

"So you think the Outlaws are the actual traffickers. Can you prove it?"

"I think so. The Outlaws are kidnapping women who dance in strips clubs, and selling them into slavery. A dancer named Lexi is one of their recent victims. I saw her on the YouTube video in Echo's apartment. Echo told me that other dancers have also disappeared. None of them have families, so people forget about them."

"So Dexter is the real mastermind."

"That's right. It makes sense, when you think about it."

"How so?"

"It bothered me that Cano used Dexter to recruit for him. Cano is from South America, so it would have made more sense if he asked a Latino. But Cano asked Dexter, who's a white southern boy. There had to be a reason, don't you think?"

"You're saying that Cano asked Dexter because the Outlaws were already running a trafficking ring, and Dexter would know how to hide the victims, and later move them."

"Yes. The apparatus was already in place. The Outlaws own a building that has sleeping quarters and a large kitchen. The victims are brought there one at a time, then they're shipped out and sold into slavery. I'm guessing the building is in the Tampa Bay area, because that's where the gang is."

"So Cano doesn't have anything to do with the kidnappings."

"No. He's just a low-life drug dealer."

His cell phone rang. He took it out of his pocket and saw that it was Nicki calling. Daniels saw the screen as well and said, "Is my niece helping you again?"

"She is, indeed." He hit the answer button. "Hi, Nicki. I'm sitting here with your aunt Beth. Tell me that you have good news."

"Try great news," the teenager said excitedly.

CHAPTER 30

When it came to sleuthing, there was strength in numbers.

Nicki's CSI class had twenty-two enthusiastic students, each of whom had a laptop computer with high-speed internet access. To find the name of the person who'd testified against Devin Highnote at his trial, the class had visited a website called RapSheets.org.

Lancaster had told the class about this site during his visit. RapSheets.org was the largest crime statistic website in the world, and contained millions of arrest records, along with a local jail inmate search, which he often utilized to see if a suspect was already behind bars.

The site's arrest records were broken out by state and county. Nicki's class had gone to the Florida section, and chosen Pinellas County, where Saint Petersburg was located. They'd entered Devin Highnote's name and done a search that produced his rap sheet. Highnote was not a common last name, and only one felon matched in the database.

Seven years ago, Highnote had been arrested for rape, prosecuted, found guilty, and sent away to prison. The mug shot showed an unshaven brute with soulless eyes and a lump on his temple, which he'd probably gotten during his arrest.

The site had not contained any details from his trial. To get those transcripts would have required a trip to the Pinellas County courthouse, where a formal records request would have to be submitted to a records clerk. If the transcripts were not digitalized, it might take the clerk several days to produce them.

Undaunted, Nicki's class had gone onto Google and entered the words *Devin Highnote rapist Saint Petersburg FL* into the search engine. This had produced a short newspaper article from the *Saint Petersburg Times* that had focused on the officers who'd tracked Highnote down. There was no mention of any witnesses at the trial.

The class had hit a dead end. The teacher, whose name was Ms. Edie Bachman, had gone around the room, and posed a question to each student: "If this was your case, how would you move it forward, knowing that time is of the essence?"

One student had suggested hiring a private plane and flying to Saint Petersburg. Several others had taken a pass. Then a student named Sasha Clarke served up an idea. Her uncle Albert was a reporter for the *Tampa Bay Times*, which was what the newspaper was now called. Sasha offered to call her uncle, and ask him if he knew the reporter who'd written the Highnote article.

Ms. Bachman liked the idea, and told Sasha to do it. Sasha made the call, and spoke to her uncle. Her uncle knew the reporter quite well, their cubicles being a few feet apart. Sasha's call was transferred to the reporter, whose name was Ernie Ross.

Ernie Ross had no trouble recalling the details of the Highnote trial. He'd called Devin Highnote a monster, and said that the woman who'd testified against him deserved a medal for bravery. Her name was Rachel Baye, and she lived in Saint Pete Beach.

Had Lancaster been in the same room with Nicki, he would have given her a hug. Instead, he promised to return to her school and give another talk. He thanked her and ended the call.

"She's a natural," he said.

"It drives my sister crazy that she's so into police work," Daniels said.

"Think she'll grow out of it?"

"I sure hope so. Can't have two of us in the family."

"Maybe she'll join the FBI, and you'll report to her someday."

"That's not funny."

They were still parked at the Starbucks with the engine running. Daniels retrieved her briefcase off the back seat and took out her laptop. The FBI was famous for tracking down suspects, and had access to driver's license information in every state, as well as access to the databases of every major credit card company. Using the two pieces of information that they had—the name Rachel Baye and the city of Saint Pete Beach—she was able to pull up an address in under a minute.

Using his cell phone, he pulled up Google Maps and entered the address. An automated voice said that Baye's home was forty minutes away by car in light traffic. The voice continued to give directions as Daniels weaved through traffic.

He did a background check on Baye without breaking his connection to Google. She was on Facebook with a profile photo that showed an athletic woman doing yoga on the beach. She was originally from Cleveland, and had studied holistic medicine at Ohio University. She listed her profession as yoga instructor.

He did a search of her address. A link to the real estate site Zillow appeared. Baye lived in a four-bedroom house a block from the ocean with an estimated value of $2.1 million, the property taxes more than thirty grand a year.

"You're way too quiet," Daniels said.

"Rachel Baye lives in a two-million-dollar house," he said.

"Is that a problem?"

"In my experience, wealthy people don't testify at criminal trials."

"Why do you think that is?"

"I think they're afraid of retribution."

"Maybe she isn't wealthy, and rents a room."

They made good time, and Daniels parked at the curb. They got out and had a look around. Not that long ago, Saint Pete Beach had been a wasteland of flophouses and the homeless, the area barely scraping by. The area had gone through a renaissance, with new construction on every block. The place looked alive again.

They walked up the front path. The house was a McMansion and dwarfed the other homes around it. Daniels pinned her badge to her jacket and rang the bell. The door opened, and a well-dressed older woman stuck her head out, scowling.

"Did you see the sign when you drove down the street? No solicitors." Her eyes fell on the badge. "Oh! My mistake. May I help you?"

"I'm Special Agent Daniels with the FBI," Daniels said. "This gentleman is Jon Lancaster. Are you Rachel Baye?"

The woman brought her hand to her mouth. "No, I'm not. Has something happened to poor Rachel?"

"Please let me ask the questions. What is your name?"

"Harriet Ward. I told Rachel she needed to move away, for her safety."

"May we please come in?"

"I don't know. Do you like dogs?"

"So long as they don't bite."

"My babies won't bite you."

Ward ushered them inside. The interior reeked of money. The lobby had a checkered marble floor and a glistening chandelier, and that was just the entranceway. A pack of well-groomed dogs stood at rapt attention a few feet inside. They ranged in size from teacup to small pony, and had the alertness of circus animals.

"My husband passed away several years ago, and I went to the pound to get a new friend. This is what I came home with," Ward said with a smile.

"I own two rescues myself," Daniels said. "Now, I need to ask you some questions. Does Rachel Baye currently live here?"

Ward knelt down. The pooches surrounded her, and she petted them while they licked her face. "Not anymore. Rachel rented the apartment above the garage. She was a wonderful tenant, used to help me walk the dogs. A few months back, she started being threatened by that horrible man. He sent her emails, then called her. She went to the police for help, but there wasn't much they could do."

"Do you know his name?"

"He never said who he was. Rachel was sure that it was a man she'd helped send to prison. I believe his name was Devin. Rachel was running on the beach one night years ago, and saw this monster raping a teenager. She called the police, and they arrested him. She was the only witness at his trial."

"Was his name Devin Highnote?"

"That sounds right."

"Do you know where she moved to? We need to get in contact with her. Her life may be in danger."

"Rachel didn't give me a forwarding address. I think she's still living near the beach. She's having her mail sent to a post office box."

"Do you have her cell phone number?"

"It's in the contacts in my cell phone. Let me go get it. May I offer you and your friend something cold to drink?"

"We're fine," Daniels said.

Ward retreated into the back of the house. The pack followed her, except for a Saint Bernard that tipped the scales at two hundred pounds. He parked himself in front of them and lay down. Resting his head on his paws, he gave them a hostile stare.

"He doesn't like you," Daniels said.

"He's looking at you, not me," Lancaster said.

Ward returned with her cell phone and two bottled waters, which she handed to them. "You both look thirsty. I have two numbers for Rachel, work and personal. Would you like both?"

"Please." Daniels wrote down the numbers on a small notepad. Flipping it shut, she said, "Would you mind giving Rachel a call? I'm afraid she won't answer my call, since it's a strange number. But she might answer yours."

"I'd be more than happy to," Ward said.

Ward called the personal number, and got voice mail. Then she called the yoga studio where Rachel worked. She got a live person this time, and asked for Rachel. A moment later, her face crashed. She thanked the other person, and ended the call.

"Rachel called the owner this morning, said she was stopping at the mall before she got to work," Ward said. "She asked the owner if he wanted a smoothie, and he told her to bring him one. She never came in. I hope to God nothing has happened to her."

"Is Rachel a responsible person?" Daniels asked.

"She is. She house-sat for me many times, and was very conscientious."

Daniels looked at Lancaster and frowned. They were thinking the same thought: Baye had been abducted by Dexter Hudson and Devin Highnote while at the mall. Unless her abductors had left telltale clues—which so far, they hadn't done—their chances of finding her weren't great. But that didn't mean they weren't going to try.

"Which mall would Rachel have gone to?" Daniels asked.

"Tyrone Square," Ward said. "It's not far."

"Any idea where she might have bought her smoothies?"

"She liked the Smoothie King," Ward said. "It's on the main level."

CHAPTER 31

Retail malls were dying, and Tyrone Square was no exception, the parking lot so empty that it felt like the entrance to a ghost town.

Daniels parked by the main entrance, and they went inside. A directory showed Smoothie King on the other end of the mall, and they started walking. Being inside a mall, looking for clues to a kidnapping, felt like déjà vu all over again.

Dexter Hudson had tailed Elsie Tanner at the Citrus Park Mall before following her home. He'd never figured out how Dexter had tracked Elsie to the mall, or known which stores she'd be shopping in. And now Dexter had done it again, tracking down Rachel Baye, who was trying to keep her whereabouts unknown.

A wall plaque that said PROPERTY SERVICES/SECURITY caught his eye. He stopped walking, and Daniels halted as well. She shot him a questioning look.

"We're not going to learn anything new in the smoothie store," he said. "But we might catch a break watching the mall's surveillance videos."

"What are you expecting to find?"

"Dexter is hunting his victims in shopping malls. How does he know they're there? Maybe the mall videos will tell us. It's worth a quick look."

"I think we should speak to the manager at Smoothie King. Want to split up?"

"Not really. Mall security won't do what I ask them. But they will do what *you* ask them."

"All right, we'll do mall security first."

The security office was a cavern with a wall of ancient video monitors. Daniels introduced herself and asked to see the videos taken outside the Smoothie King earlier that morning. The videos were retrieved and played. A line of at least twenty customers stood outside the Smoothie King, which had yet to open. The time stamp said that the video had been taken at 8:35 that morning.

"The mall doesn't open until nine, but management started opening the south entrance early because the owner of the Smoothie King was complaining he was losing business," the security guard in charge said.

"What time does the Smoothie King open?" Daniels asked.

"Eight thirty. A lot of people place their orders online. Is there someone in particular you're looking for?"

Lancaster retrieved Baye's Facebook page and showed it to the guard. "Her name's Rachel, and she works in a yoga studio. She's blonde and athletic."

The guard enlarged the images on the screen. They both leaned in.

"I see her. She's the thirteenth person in line," Lancaster said.

"How unlucky for her," Daniels said under her breath.

The minutes slipped by. At 8:40 a.m., a man wearing a black Stetson appeared on the video. The man was not in line, but seemed preoccupied with looking at the customers who were. The man stepped backward and disappeared.

"That looked like Dexter." To the guard, he said, "Where do you think the guy wearing the cowboy hat went?"

"Probably to the south parking lot," the guard said. "Should I pull up the videos?"

"Yes," they both said.

A video of the south parking lot appeared. It was shaded, the vehicles easy to make out. A man wearing a black Stetson hustled out of the mall and made a straight line to a parked car. The car was caked in dirt and missing a hub cap.

The driver's window came down, and a man stuck his head out.

"Please freeze the frame," Daniels said.

The guard froze the frame.

"Now, blow it up," she said.

The guard enlarged the frame so the man's face became visible. The brutish features were easily identifiable, even sporting a scruffy beard. It was Highnote.

"Okay, start the video again," she said.

The video resumed playing. Dexter knelt down, and Highnote passed him a pack of smokes and a lighter. He lit up, and the two men began to talk. The conversation became heated, the disagreement almost palpable.

"What's this about?" Daniels asked.

"It looks like Highnote wanted to bail, only Dexter wouldn't let him," Lancaster said.

"Do you think Highnote got cold feet?"

"Uh-huh. He's fresh out of prison, and doesn't want to go back."

The two men came to an agreement, and Highnote rolled up his window. Dexter came around the car and climbed into the passenger seat.

"Looks like Dexter won the argument," Daniels said.

She asked him to advance the video sixty seconds. The guard did as told, then hit play. They watched Baye exit the mall holding a cardboard tray with four smoothies, which she balanced on one hand, her cell phone and car keys in the other. She hopped into a pink Toyota Prius and drove away. She was talking on her cell phone without a care in the world. Highnote and Dexter followed her out of the lot.

"Those guys look like trouble," the guard said.

"They are trouble," Daniels said. "I need a copy of the two videos we just watched. Can you email them to me?"

Daniels gave him a business card, and the guard agreed to send her the videos. Taking out her notepad, she took down the guard's name, title, and email address.

Lancaster stared into space. Based upon what he'd seen, Highnote had gotten cold feet and tried to bail on Dexter, which meant he still had a conscience. Most criminals didn't have consciences, but there were exceptions. But Highnote was weak, and had let Dexter talk him into staying.

It made him think of Logan. His brother and Highnote were alike in several ways. Logan had also been weak, and had let some guys talk him into driving the getaway car for a botched heist. Then, in prison, he'd let Dexter talk him into joining his gang. Both were bad decisions that had cost his brother dearly.

But Logan still had a conscience, and had saved his life at the Jayhawk Motel. Logan had been talked into the bad things that he'd done, while the goods things had come from the heart. Logan had been corrupted, the same as Highnote. Neither would have gone down these roads had Dexter not talked them into it. Lancaster told himself that he was going to pay the bastard back if it was the last thing he did.

"Jon? You coming?"

Daniels stood at the door, ready to depart. He followed her out.

Daniels's car was baking, and she rolled down the windows to let the bubble of hot air escape. She started the engine and said, "Put your seat belt on."

"Not yet," he said. "We need to talk about this."

She threw the car into park and waited.

"Echo told me that Dexter could track anyone by knowing their email address. I'm starting to believe there's some validity to this," he said.

"How does it work?"

"It's somehow connected to the victim's cell phone. Just about everyone has a smartphone, and can send and receive emails. Dexter is sending his victims an email and then tracking their location from their cell phone."

"That technology doesn't exist. Try again."

He blew out his cheeks. "We know that two of the victims were out shopping before they were abducted. Baye was also at a mall. All she had in her possession were her car keys, and a cell phone. Dexter used the signal on Baye's phone to track her down. It's the only logical explanation."

"And he did this by sending Baye an email."

"I know it's flimsy, but how else could he know her location?"

"I don't know. Now, put on your seat belt."

Instead of complying, he continued talking. "Yesterday you told me about a company in Tampa called Phantom Communications that manufactured the encrypted cell phone that my brother had. You said that they might be connected to this. Maybe they've developed a technology to track cell phones using emails."

"Maybe they have. But right now, they're off limits."

"I thought you were getting a search warrant and were going to raid the place."

"The judge turned us down. We didn't show sufficient probable cause."

"But they're connected to this. They have to be."

"I'm sorry, Jon, but we lost in court. Now, would you put your seat belt on?"

Without a word, he opened his door and climbed out. He walked back toward the entrance of the mall and got in the shade before pulling up an app on his cell phone. Daniels pulled the car around to the entrance and rolled down her window.

"What are you doing?" she said angrily.

"Calling an Uber," he said. "You and I need to part ways."

The words stung, and for a moment she couldn't reply.

"You're ditching me?" she said.

"Afraid so," he replied.

"And exactly why are you doing that?"

"Because I'm not going to let a stupid judge stop me from visiting Phantom Communications and finding out how Dexter is doing this. And since this involves breaking the law, I assumed you won't want to come."

"What are you going to do, shove a gun in someone's face?"

"What do I look like, a thug?"

"Then what?"

"Let's just say that I'm going to pull a ruse that I've used before. It's a great way to get people to open up, and talk."

"What if your ruse backfires? You could get arrested and go to jail."

"It hasn't failed me so far." He looked at the screen on his cell phone. "My ride is two minutes away. I'll let you know how things turn out."

She threw the vehicle into drive and pulled out with a squeal of rubber. Her journey lasted less than a hundred yards. Hitting the brakes hard, she went into reverse, and returned to her original spot, glaring at him through her open window.

"Get in the car. I'm going with you," she said.

"But I'm going to break the law."

"I heard you the first time. Get in the damn car, before I change my mind."

She nearly hit his Uber driver on the way out of the parking lot.

CHAPTER 32

Daniels made record time to his hotel. Going to his car, he popped the trunk, and from a metal strongbox removed two phony search warrants, each of which had the words United States District Court/ Central District of Florida printed across the top, along with an official seal.

He'd first read about the use of fake documentation in a newspaper article. The New Orleans DA's office had been caught issuing fake subpoenas to a witness in a murder trial in an effort to subvert his testimony. The article had gotten him thinking what a great tool this would be when dealing with a witness who refused to cooperate.

He got back into Daniels's vehicle and, using his cell phone, found the address for Phantom Communications. He placed one of the search warrants on the dashboard and filled it out with a ballpoint pen.

"For the love of Christ, where did you get those?" Daniels asked.

"Off the internet," he said.

"Be serious."

"I am being serious. There are online companies that generate fake documents for a fee. You can buy search warrants, subpoenas, even deportation notices. For a few extra bucks, they'll customize them. They're a great negotiating tool."

"Sounds like you've used them before."

"Only once. A twelve-year-old girl went missing. Her neighbor was the last to see her, but he wouldn't talk to me. I decided to gamble, and went to his place with a fake search warrant. He let me in, and there was a marijuana tree growing in the living room. I made a deal with him. I'd give him a pass on the tree if he opened up about the girl."

"Did he?"

"Yes. The neighbor said that he thought the stepfather was molesting the girl. I tipped off the police, and they searched the property. They found the girl locked up in a toolshed."

"You broke all sorts of laws doing that."

"Her family sent me a crystal paperweight with a thank-you note. It sits on the desk in my study. I'll show it to you the next time you come over."

"It was still wrong."

"You can pull out, I won't hold it against you."

"Not on your life. Get me directions off your phone."

Soon they were on familiar roads, heading to Tampa. When he was finished with the warrant, he checked his spelling, and caught a mistake. The company was on North Rocky Point Drive, only he'd spelled it Pinte. He tore up the document and started over.

"Is that why you brought two? In case you made a mistake?" Daniels asked.

"Yeah. When I was a SEAL, we sometimes used fake documents inside foreign countries. One time in Libya, our commanding officer made a mistake on a form, and had to abort the mission."

"So now you always bring two."

"Always."

- - -

Phantom Communications was located in a sleek office building called The Pointe. True to its name, the building jutted out on a narrow landfill that overlooked the Gulf of Mexico's sparkling waters. The guard at the reception desk was reading a section of the paper that contained the day's races at Tampa Bay Downs.

"What can I do for you?" the guard asked.

Daniels placed her wallet on the desk. The guard took his job seriously, and studied her badge and photo ID. Satisfied, he slid the wallet back to her.

"Sorry, but I've never met an FBI agent before," he said.

"No need to apologize," she said. "We're here to see a company called Phantom Communications. I need to know which floor they're on."

The guard flipped through the three-ring binder on his desk. "Phantom is on the eighth floor, suite #812C. I need to let them know you're coming."

"I'd prefer that you not do that."

"Our insurance company requires it. Otherwise, I'll get in trouble."

She took the search warrant out of Lancaster's hand and waved it in the guard's face. "We need to search their offices. If you tell them we're here, they may destroy important information. There are lives at stake here. Am I making myself clear?"

The guard's face reddened, and he nodded.

"I didn't hear you," Daniels said.

"Crystal clear. I won't call them."

"Good answer. Do you know how many people work there? I'd like to know what I'm dealing with before we serve them."

"I honestly don't," the guard replied. "The C suites are pretty small. I can't imagine there are more than a couple of people working there."

Daniels rapped the counter in appreciation. They took an elevator to the eighth floor and walked down a carpeted hallway to the very last door.

"Let me do the talking," she said.

"You're starting to sound like a willing coconspirator," he said.

"Shut up."

She twisted the knob, and they entered. Suite 812 was broken into three offices distinguished by the letters *A*, *B*, and *C*. A and B were vacant, and hadn't been used in a while. C had a lone occupant, a skinny guy with shoulder-length hair and a ring in his nose. He was listening to music on a pair of headphones while staring at his computer screen. The music owned him, and he acted like he was on another planet.

He looked up as they approached, then pointed at his incredibly messy desk.

"Just leave it there," he said.

Daniels stuck her badge in his face. It brought him back to earth, and he ripped off his headphones and tried to speak. She cut him off.

"Back away from the computer, and keep your hands where I can see them."

His face turned white, and he rose from his desk. It was almost comical how scared he looked. Like he knew he'd been breaking the law, and had been worried that it might catch up with him. Judgment day had arrived, and he didn't look the least bit ready.

"What's your name, and what do you do?" Daniels said.

"Garret Oldham. My friends call me Gar. I'm a programmer."

"Does anyone else work here?"

"There was a girl named Wendy, but she quit last week."

Lancaster was standing to Daniels's right. He wanted to see what was on Gar's computer, and he stepped between them, using his hand to swivel the PC so the screen was facing him. Gar tried to object, and Lancaster showed him the fake warrant.

"Do you know what this is?" he asked.

The remaining blood in Gar's face drained away, and he sank back into his chair and shut his eyes. Daniels grabbed his wrist and checked his pulse.

"He's passed out. You really scared him."

"Take a look at this."

Daniels turned her attention to the PC. On its screen was an aerial map of the Tampa area with dozens of pulsating dots of light. The dots were different colors and expanded and collapsed like heartbeats. Suddenly, one of the dots darted across the map like a player in a video game, and left the picture.

"What are we looking at?" Daniels asked.

"I think he's following people," he said.

"On their cell phones?"

"That would be my guess."

The program's operating system was Microsoft Windows, and there were multiple open folders displayed on the bottom of the screen. He dragged the mouse over the first folder and clicked on it. An aerial map of Saint Petersburg appeared, also with pulsating dots of lights. Examination of the other folders showed maps of several cities in Florida.

Gar's desk was cluttered with papers, and Lancaster sifted through them, hoping they might shed some light on the images. They turned out to be overdraft statements from Gar's bank and dunning notices from creditors, and they painted a picture of a man up to his eyeballs in debt. Gar began to stir, and mumbled under his breath.

"He's coming to. What do you want to do?" Daniels asked.

"I want to grill him. You okay with that?"

"Sure, but no rough stuff."

"I just want to scare him."

He went to the door and locked it. Returning, he borrowed Daniels's handcuffs, and slapped one of the cuffs onto Gar's wrist, then locked the other to the arm of his chair. Daniels shot him a disapproving look, but said nothing.

A bottled water sat on the desk. He unscrewed it, and poured the contents onto Gar's head, soaking his neck and shirt. The programmer awoke with a start, and tried to stand. Seeing that he was a prisoner of the chair, he howled. "Let me go!"

"You're in lots of trouble. Don't make it worse," Lancaster said.

Gar rattled the handcuff. "Is this necessary?"

"That's entirely up to you. Are you going to cooperate?"

He blinked, thinking hard. "Define *cooperate*."

"We want you to explain the work that you do."

"I do lots of different work. Which campaign are you talking about?"

"Tell us how you're tracking people's cell phones."

"I want a lawyer."

"You sure about that?"

Gar smiled, thinking he had the upper hand. "Damn straight."

Gar was being cute, believing that a lawyer would bail him out of jail, and that he'd walk away unscathed. His eyes needed to be opened, and Lancaster decided to play his hand. "The company you work for is in trouble. They willingly sold encrypted cell phones to a drug dealer, which is a third-degree felony, and could get you sent to prison. You got any priors?"

"What?"

"Prior arrests."

Gar swallowed hard. "I got busted for pot once."

"You'll do five years. You'll make a lot of new friends."

"I didn't have anything to do with those phones," the programmer protested.

"Good luck proving that in court. Meanwhile, Special Agent Daniels will tell the judge you're a flight risk, and ask him to post a high bail, which you won't be able to meet. You'll have to plot your defense behind bars, which isn't easy. Think about it."

Gar fell back in his chair. "They'll kill me if they find out I squealed," he said.

"Who's going to kill you?" Daniels asked.

"My employer, the bikers," he said.

"You mean the Outlaws," Lancaster said.

"That's right, the Outlaws. They'd cut my heart out if they found out I betrayed them. I'll take my chances in prison, thank you very much."

It wasn't the response Lancaster was expecting. He shot Daniels a glance, needing her help. She took his cue, and placed her hand on Gar's sleeve.

"If you help us, I'll get you put into the government's witness protection program," she said. "You'll get a new identity, and a new life. We'll relocate you to another part of the country where the Outlaws don't have a presence. You'll be home free."

"You're not screwing with me, are you?"

"I'll put it in writing, if you want me to."

"What about my girlfriend?" he asked.

"What about her?"

"Can she come with me?"

"I don't see why not."

Gar wasn't sold. His eyes fell on the stack of unfriendly mail littering his desk. Were those obligations going to follow him as well? Daniels picked up on his vibe.

"I can take care of those as well," she said.

"You've got yourself a deal," the programmer said.

CHAPTER 33

Once he was uncuffed, Gar's attitude changed for the better. He grabbed a soda from a small fridge and offered them drinks as well. He wasn't a bad guy, just a guy who'd gotten himself caught up in a bad situation. If given a second chance, he would probably walk the straight and narrow for the rest of his life.

"How did you come to work for the Outlaws?" Daniels asked.

"It didn't start out that way," Gar said. "When I went to work for Phantom, they were a legitimate marketing company who specialized in mobile advertising campaigns. Our motto was, Data won't change the world without the right people to understand it. We did ten million in sales our first year."

"Out of this office?" Daniels asked.

"I wish. The company started in Miami, then branched out, and opened satellite offices in Orlando and Tampa, which is when I joined. We used to have thirty employees, with four working here."

"Did you sell encrypted cell phones?" Daniels asked.

"No, I did not," he said emphatically. "That was a side business out of Miami that I wasn't involved with."

"What exactly did you do in this office?"

"We did three things for our clients: mobile advertising campaigns, location measurement—which is analyzing GPS location data of a client's customers through their smartphones—and business intelligence, which is a fancy name for statistical analysis."

"Sounds like a good business model," Daniels said. "What happened?"

"Google happened," he said. "They offered the same services for less money, and wiped us off the map. The company shrank down to six employees, with just me and Wendy in Tampa. One day the owner called me, and said he was having cash flow problems. He asked me to start paying the office bills on my credit cards."

"Did you?"

"Yeah. He promised to pay me back once things got worked out."

Something dropped in the pit of Lancaster's stomach, and he pointed at the letters on the desk. "Is that where those came from?"

"Afraid so," Gar said.

"Why did you go along with this?" Daniels asked him.

"Maybe this sounds naive, but I believed him when he said he'd get things worked out. This is the best job I've ever had, and I didn't want it to end."

"When did the Outlaws enter the picture?" Daniels asked.

"Three months ago. The owner said he had a new backer, and he'd be coming by with a check. That was music to my ears, because I was about to get thrown out of my apartment. That afternoon, a biker appeared in the lobby. The guard refused to let him in, and called me. I called the owner, and was told this was our new partner."

"So you let him upstairs," Daniels said.

"I didn't have much choice," Gar said.

"Describe him," Lancaster said.

"He was a mean hombre, and wore all black," Gar said. "He said his name was Dexter. I never got his last name."

"What happened then?" Daniels asked.

"Dexter gave me a money order for five grand, which he called an installment," Gar said. "He had a job for me, and said that he'd give me five grand every two weeks until it was done. I was fifty grand in debt, so I couldn't say no."

"So you had reservations about working for him," Lancaster said.

"You bet. He made my skin crawl."

"What was the job?" Daniels asked.

Gar took a swallow of his soda and wiped his mouth on his sleeve. A guilty look spread across his face, and he spent a moment gathering his thoughts.

"He wanted me to track people," the programmer confessed.

"On their cell phones?" Lancaster said.

"That's right. You know about this?"

"We don't know how it works. Explain it to us," Daniels said.

"In mobile advertising, there's a metric called location measurement, which lets retailers track cross-channel advertising campaigns to see if the ads are influencing foot traffic in stores. All the major brands do this."

"What's a cross-channel campaign?" Daniels asked.

"It's a campaign that runs on three channels," he said. "Personal computer is the first channel. The second channel is tablets, like iPads. The third channel is mobile phones. That's cross-channel."

"Got it. How does location measurement work?"

"Okay. Let's say you're Nike, and you want to promote a new line of sneakers. Your goal is to drive customers into your stores, which are located inside shopping malls. So you run a cross-channel video campaign that is targeted against consumers who meet your profile and live in zip codes that are located within a ten-mile radius of your stores."

"You can do that?" Daniels asked.

"Piece of cake. Nikes sends us a video, and we wrap it with a tag. When a viewer watches the video, the tag recognizes the viewer's IP address, and stores it. We then use a software program to find the mobile phone tied to your IP address."

"Let me be sure I've got this straight," Daniels said. "If I watch a Nike video on my laptop, your company can determine where my mobile phone is?"

"That's right. The software program is called a device graph, and it lets us determine the mobile phones tied to the IP address the campaign is delivered to. We then partner with hundreds of apps that track your location, which lets us know where your mobile phone is. It's fairly easy to find you, once we've served you an ad."

"That can't be legal."

"It's perfectly legal. Have you downloaded an app recently? Before it becomes functional, you're asked to accept the terms of use. No one reads what those terms are. If they did, they'd see that they're permitting the app's designer to track their location, and sell that information. The industry has a name for this. We call it terms of abuse."

"How long does it take your technology to do this?"

"Nanoseconds."

He shook his head. Corporations were monitoring his movements every day, and he hadn't known it. He glanced at Daniels, hoping she'd take over.

"Okay, so Dexter paid you a visit, and said he had a job for you," she said. "What exactly did he want you to do?"

"Dexter wanted me to track a specific person using location measurement," Gar said. "The idea was that we'd bombard this person with a tagged video ad, and start monitoring her location when she went shopping."

"Can you track specific people?"

"I didn't think we could," Gar admitted. "But Dexter said that the Miami and Orlando offices had done it, so I was wrong."

"Your other offices tracked people for Dexter," Daniels said.

"Yeah. Tracking is supposed to be anonymous, meaning we don't know the identities of the people we're tracking. But it isn't hard to attach a name to an IP address, and track a specific person."

"And you did this for him."

"Yes, regrettably."

"You knew it was wrong."

"I did. But I also knew that if I didn't go along, I'd be living out of my car. So I agreed to do what Dexter wanted."

Something wasn't adding up, and Lancaster jumped in. "Dexter's full name is Dexter Hudson, and he spent the last fifteen years in prison. How did he suddenly get tech savvy, and know about location measurement?"

"That bothered me too," Gar said. "How does a guy who rides in a biker gang know about mobile device tracking? The second time Dexter visited my office, I asked him. He said that one of his biker buddies was on the FBI's Most Wanted list, and got run down and arrested. His buddy's lawyer made the prosecutor reveal how his client was found. There's some legal name for this."

"Discovery," Daniels said.

"That's it, discovery. So the FBI had to reveal how they found Dexter's buddy. It turned out that they used location measurement."

Lancaster shook his head in disbelief. If a criminal defense attorney had asked him how he'd tracked down a client, he would have invented an answer and not tipped his hand, knowing that criminal attorneys were sometimes in cahoots with their clients. But the FBI did things by the book, and had given the Outlaws a valuable tool.

"So you tracked specific people for Dexter, and sent their whereabouts to him," Lancaster said.

"Not exactly," Gar said. "The Miami office created video ads, which they emailed to me. I wrapped the ads in tags, and bombarded the people Dexter wanted to find. Then I let Dexter do the tracking. I wanted no part of that."

"How did Dexter track them?"

"He used an app on his mobile phone that I gave him," Gar said. "I told him that wasn't the app's purpose, but he didn't care. I told him that it was wrong, but he didn't care."

Daniels started to ask a question, but was drowned out by a roar of motorcycles coming from outside. Gar said, "That doesn't sound good." They rose from their chairs and went to the window. Down in the parking lot, four leather-clad bikers had parked by the entrance. They were banged up, leading Lancaster to believe they'd been part of the gang at Echo's complex the night before. Dexter Hudson was not among them, which was a shame, because he was looking forward to confronting him.

"What's this about?" Lancaster asked.

"Must be payback time," Gar said.

"You did something to the Outlaws that warranted payback?"

"The last time Dexter was here, he threatened to beat me up if I talked to anyone about this," Gar said. "It bothered me, so I decided to file a police report. Since I didn't know Dexter's last name, I filed the report against his company, which is called One Percent Solutions. Those guys must be his partners."

"We need to get out of here," Daniels said. "You're not coming back, so grab whatever belongings you want to keep."

Gar scooped his laptop off the desk. From a desk drawer he grabbed several personal belongings and shoved them in his pockets.

"Ready when you are," the programmer said.

- - -

They took the stairwell to the floor directly below, went into the hallway, and stood by the elevators. The LED display showed that one of the cars was coming up.

Lancaster drew his SIG and aimed at the door, in case the bikers decided to stop at this floor for some reason. Daniels drew her sidearm as well.

"Jesus Christ," Gar said. "Are you going to shoot them?"

Lancaster nearly said, *Yes, I'm going to put a bullet into each one of their hearts as payback for the pain and suffering they've caused,* but bit his lip instead.

"Let's hope it doesn't come down to that," Daniels said.

The elevator didn't stop, but instead went to the next floor. After a few moments, Daniels pressed the down button, and the car descended to their level. It was empty, and they put their weapons away. Reaching the lobby, they got out.

"We need to blow out of here," Daniels said. "Once your friends see that you're gone, they'll come downstairs. We don't want to be here when that happens."

"One second," Gar said. "I want to ask the guard why he let those guys come up. He's supposed to call with every visitor."

The guard was not at his post. A quick search revealed him inside a storage room with a bump on his forehead. The guard was awake, and in the act of dialing 911.

"Those goons attacked me," the guard said.

"Sorry to hear that," Daniels said. "We need to get this gentleman to a safe place. Lock this door behind you when we leave, and don't come out until the police arrive."

"I'll do that," the guard said.

The door clicked behind them. Crossing the lobby, Lancaster glanced at the elevators, and saw that a car was descending and would soon be in the lobby. Drawing his SIG, he backed out of the building with Daniels and Gar by his side. He didn't want the bikers running them down, and he went to where their motorcycles were parked and gave the one on the end a good kick, toppling it over, and taking the others down with it.

"Aren't we clever," Daniels said.

CHAPTER 34

They drove to Gar's apartment so he could pack a suitcase and then drove to the Marriott on State Road 54, where Daniels arranged for Gar to be put into a room on the same floor that her team was staying on. The hotel was nearly sold out, and the manager had to shuffle some reservations to see if he could accommodate her.

Gar was looking pale as the reality of his situation sank in, and Lancaster asked if he wanted a drink. His offer was received with an enthusiastic yes, and Lancaster told Daniels that he was going to take Gar across the street and buy him a beer.

"Make sure nothing happens to him," she said.

"Not on my watch," he said.

There were several options to get a drink, and he picked Glory Days because of its dark interior. It was quiet, and he chose a booth near the bar.

"What's your pleasure?" Lancaster asked.

"I'd like an IPA on draft, and a glass of water," Gar said. "That scene at work was scary. I'm glad you guys showed up."

"So am I. I'll be right back."

Happy hour ran all afternoon, and Lancaster delivered four pints of beer to their table, along with two tall glasses of water, which required three trips to the bar. When he was done, he slid into the booth, and they clinked glasses. Gar polished off his beer and went to work on his second pint. It relaxed him, and when he spoke, his voice was subdued. "Do you know what the most difficult part of being a programmer is?"

Lancaster had not expected this to become a confession. He sipped his beer and said, "I have no idea. Staying up to date on new technology?"

"The most difficult part is not breaking the law. The ability to monitor people is so refined that there isn't any privacy anymore. None. Zero. Zip."

"But people can turn off their devices if they want to," he said. "No one's forcing them to leave them on."

"You're right, no one is forcing them. Yet the average cell phone user keeps their phone within five feet of their body, twenty-four hours a day. And that allows people like me to monitor their behavior and location all the time."

Lancaster thought about his own cell phone habits. He didn't have a landline where he lived, and relied on his cell phone for business and personal calls. He kept the phone powered up all day, and carried it in his pocket. At night, his cell phone sat on his night table getting charged and wasn't turned off. He didn't think of his behavior as being predictable, yet obviously it was.

"It sounds like an addiction," he said.

"It is an addiction. And you can blame the designers. They created phones that used intermittent reinforcement to keep their users hooked. Just like slot machines."

"My cell phone isn't a slot machine. There's no payout."

"Yes, there is. Your cell phone can receive emails, texts, and voice messages. If it rings, you look at the screen. If it makes a doorbell sound, you check your email. If it vibrates, you look to see who texted you."

"But I don't have to do any of those things. I can just leave it in my pocket."

"But you don't. If your phone makes a noise, you look, because you're hoping that the caller or message is important, or a person you care about. That's the payout."

Lancaster wasn't sure that he bought into what Gar was saying. Then his cell phone rang. He wanted to leave it in his pocket, just to prove Gar wrong, but there was a chance that it was Beth calling with some piece of news.

It was her. He said, "Hey. We're across the street at Glory Days."

"And I'm still trying to get our friend a room on the same floor with my team," she said. "I had no idea this was going to take an Act of Congress to get done."

"Want me to come over, and straighten them out?"

"Very funny. I'll join you once I'm done."

He put his cell phone away. Gar had polished off his second pint and was smiling. IPAs were popular because of their unique taste and high alçohol content, and it took only a couple to get a buzz. Lancaster sensed that Gar had something he wanted to get off his chest, and he slid one of his beers across the table.

"Drink up," he said.

"Thanks. I'm telling you this stuff for a reason," Gar said. "You may not believe this, but I have ethics. Violating a person's privacy is wrong, and I've never intentionally done that."

"Then what were all those dots on your computer screen?"

"They were just that—dots. There weren't names attached to them. Those people were served a tagged video ad, and I tracked them when they entered a store that sold the product in that ad."

"And since it was anonymous, you weren't invading their privacy."

"That's right. All the campaigns I worked on were anonymous. I wouldn't have had it any other way. That's not true for other programmers I know."

The confession was starting to feel more like an apology. He didn't like that, and said, "But what about the work you did for One Percent

Solutions? That sure as hell wasn't anonymous. You were tracking individual people."

"All I did was serve those people video ads, and then Dexter tracked them on his cell phone with an app I gave him."

"That's a cop-out."

"No, it's not."

"You're complicit."

"To a certain degree, I am. Like I told you before, I needed the money to live. But I told Dexter what the rules were, and that he'd get in trouble if he broke them."

"Afraid it didn't work."

"Let me finish. I also told Dexter that if I found out he broke the law, I'd turn him over to the police. That's why he threatened me."

"So you covered your ass. Big deal."

"I meant what I said. If Dexter broke the law using the technology I gave him, I'd turn him over, which I'm still prepared to do. If not to the police, then to you and Special Agent Daniels."

Gar was offering up Dexter, which sounded like a bunch of nonsense, considering that the programmer hadn't even known Dexter's last name.

"How do you plan to turn him over? Do you know where he lives?"

"Afraid not."

"Then how are you going to do it?"

"Before I answer that, will you answer my question?"

"Which is what?"

"What laws has Dexter broken, besides threatening me?"

He counted them off on the fingers of his hand. "He's responsible for multiple kidnappings and two murders. He's also running a human trafficking ring with his biker buddies, and selling his victims into slavery. Now, how do you plan to do this?"

Gar opened an app on his cell phone and gave it to him. On the screen was an aerial map of the Tampa Bay area that covered from

Saint Petersburg to New Port Richey. In the area between Dunedin and Tarpon Springs pulsated a single purple dot. The dot was moving in a southerly direction in a straight line.

"Use your finger to enlarge the screen," Gar said.

He did as told and zoomed in. Major roads appeared on the map, and he saw that the dot was traveling south on Alternate US 19.

"That's Dexter," Gar said proudly. "The app that he's using to track his victims sends out a signal every few seconds, which lets me track him by GPS. It's a special feature I built, in case I needed to turn him in."

His opinion of Gar changed. This was the right thing to do.

"Could Dexter know that you're tracking him?" he asked.

"I can't see how. The signal eats up the battery, but that's true for most apps."

"I want one of these."

"You got it. It's stored in my laptop. I'll send one to you, and walk you through the installation. Special Agent Daniels can have one too."

"I'm sure she'll appreciate that."

The purple dot turned off Alternate US 19 and drove down an unmarked road that ended at the gulf, then came to a stop. He guessed it was either private or a dirt road. The nearest landmark was the Sherwood Forest RV Resort, which was due south.

Daniels entered the restaurant, got an iced tea at the bar, and slid into the booth. He mumbled hello without looking up from Gar's phone. The purple dot had stopped moving, and he wondered if that was Dexter's hideout.

"What are you looking at?" she asked.

"Our killer," he said.

CHAPTER 35

Lancaster had always despised people who walked around in public staring like zombies at their cell phones. These people were everywhere—in movie theaters, malls, and especially restaurants. Instead of engaging in normal conversations with their friends, they chose to be slaves to their iPhones and Droids.

And now, he was one of them.

His cell phone clutched in his hand, he rode shotgun while Daniels burned down State Road 54 toward Tarpon Springs. She drove like a hot-rodding teenager, and jockeyed between cars without slowing down. Behind them, four members of Daniels's team were packed in an SUV, armed to the teeth. On his phone, the purple dot that was Dexter Hudson had not moved in the past twenty minutes.

"Why do you think he did it?" Daniels asked.

Lancaster shook his head, not understanding.

"Why did Gar give Dexter an app that could be traced?"

They had just left Gar at the Marriott with the remaining two members of the team. Before leaving, Gar had gone on his laptop, and sent each of them an app that would allow them to track Dexter. That app now resided on both their cell phones.

"I guess he wanted to go to heaven," he said.

"You're saying Gar has a conscience," she said.

"I think so. Gar sensed that Dexter was up to no good, so he made the app traceable, in case Dexter broke the law."

"How noble."

"You're not impressed."

"I think Gar is complicit in Dexter's crimes."

"In what way was Gar complicit? He didn't know that Dexter planned to abduct the people he was tracing, and sell them into slavery. For all Gar knew, Dexter was a private investigator trying to track someone down. Nothing illegal there."

"I think you're being way too nice here."

He laughed under his breath. He couldn't remember anyone ever accusing him of being nice, and he said, "Cyber technology is the Wild West, and there aren't many rules. Most programmers know that cell phone technology is dangerous in the wrong hands. Give Gar some credit for hedging his bets."

"I still think he's a snake."

"A snake who just helped us."

"That doesn't change a damn thing."

State Road 54 ended at US 19. Daniels took a left on a yellow traffic light, forcing her team to run the light when it was red. Lancaster looked over his shoulder to see if there was a police cruiser lurking about, fearing they might get pulled over.

"Stop being so paranoid," she said.

"You drive too fast. You're going to cause an accident."

She laughed. "Says the man who shoots out the tires of motorcycles and sends people to hospitals, that's funny."

He didn't have an answer for that, and said nothing. US 19 was a collection of ragtag strip shopping centers and failed restaurants, which in a few years would be torn down and replaced by new strip centers and restaurants. A road sign announced Tampa Road ahead, and he told Daniels to put on her indicator, so her team wouldn't be caught by surprise when she turned.

"You really have issues with my driving, don't you?" she said.

"It could be improved," he suggested.

"Coming from you, that's absurd."

"I'm not going to apologize for what I did to those bikers last night. But I didn't put anyone else's safety at risk. The way you drive, everyone on the road is in danger."

"I have a clean driving record."

"So far."

Tampa Road bisected neighborhoods with upscale homes and plushly landscaped yards. As Daniels raced down it, the purple dot on his cell phone disappeared.

"Shit," he swore. "Dexter just went dark."

"Meaning what?"

"The app on his phone has stopped transmitting."

"Why would that happen?"

"Gar said the app on Dexter's phone would stop sending a signal if Dexter turned his cell phone off, or if the battery died."

"So what do we do? Drive around, hoping we spot him?"

"That's like looking for a needle in a haystack. Dexter turned down an unmarked road north of the Sherwood Forest RV park, and stayed there for forty-five minutes. Let's see if we can find where he was."

"You think it's his hideout?"

"Could be. We won't know until we look."

"He might still be there. Just because his phone died, doesn't mean he left."

"From your lips to God's ears," he said.

Reaching Alternate US 19, Daniels turned right and crawled down the highway, allowing Lancaster to visually inspect each turn and gravel path wide enough to accommodate a car. A quarter mile later, he spotted a dirt road with a blue sign that said RichJo Lane. The road was privately owned, which was why it hadn't shown up on Google Maps. Daniels made the turn, as did her team's SUV.

The road was filled with potholes that made for a rocky drive. Lining the sides were cinder block structures best described as shacks. Residents had dumped sofas and rusted barbecues in their front yards, as if expecting some invisible force to cart them away. It gave the place an air of desperation and lost hope.

At the road's end was a single-story building with a thatched roof and a gravel parking area. It had been a business once, either a bar or snack shop. The grounds were overgrown and filled with junk.

Daniels hit her brakes. "What do you think?"

"I think it warrants a closer look."

She parked in the lot, as did the SUV. Her team got out with weapons drawn and did a sweep of the property. Lancaster hopped out of the car, drew his SIG, and took a quick look around. There were picnic tables and a garbage can overflowing with beer bottles. On the side of the building hung a faded sign that said EARL's BBQ.

He went to a window and stuck his face to the glass. The interior was clean and filled with Formica-topped tables and chairs. Running along a wall was a bar with stools and a TV set mounted to the ceiling. Movement caught his eye, and he spied a cigarette butt in an ashtray on a table, a curl of smoke rising off its tip. Next to it was the stub of a cigar, also still lit. He'd just missed Dexter, and he silently cursed.

He twisted the knob to the front door. It was locked, and he contemplated kicking it in, and having a look around. That would draw Beth's wrath, and he returned to the lot, where he found her inspecting fresh tire tracks.

"We just missed them," she said. "You think this is his hideout?"

"I think it's more of a hangout. There are tables and chairs inside, and they look pretty clean. I'm guessing the Outlaws use this place as a gathering spot. It's off the beaten path, and I don't think the neighbors are going to call 911 when they get too rowdy. We need to find out who owns the place."

"Want me to do a records search?"

"That would be a good start."

The team reappeared and announced the grounds were clear. It was early afternoon, and Daniels wondered aloud if Dexter had gone to get something to eat. If that was the case, he would be returning soon. She told the team to park on the other side of Alternate 19, and to call her if they saw a vehicle pull down the road. Her team got into the SUV and left.

While they sat in her vehicle, Daniels did a search on her laptop of Earl's BBQ in Palm Harbor. She found an old listing on Yelp with reviews that raved about the great baby back ribs and homemade potato salad. The reviews were several years old, and a note on the page said that Earl's was no longer in business.

"That didn't get me anywhere," she said.

"Try Manta.com. It's a business site for companies," he suggested. "Maybe the corporate name is something different."

She gave it a shot and used her credit card to pull up the information. "Good call. The site says Earl's BBQ was owned by a limited liability corporation called Down Home Cooking in Safety Harbor. Is that near here?"

"It's right around the corner."

She did a search of Down Home Cooking and discovered that it was owned by a man named Earl Casselberry, that the company's annual revenues were $250,000, and that it had four employees.

"This is a dead end," she said.

"Go back to Yelp, and see if there's an address listed for Earl's BBQ," he said.

"What good is that going to do?"

"I think Earl Casselberry sold his restaurant to the Outlaws, and they use it for meetings that they don't want to have at their clubhouse."

"You think the Outlaws own this place?"

He nodded. "I think Dexter has a key to the front door. People that have keys are usually owners."

"Your reasoning is a little weak."

"If you've got any better ideas, fire away."

She found the restaurant's address on Yelp and typed it into Google, and a listing came up on Zillow that showed the property's history and estimated value. Earl's BBQ had been sold two years ago. The current owner was listed as One Percent Solutions.

"You're right. The Outlaws own this place," she said.

"You sound surprised."

"Call it professional jealousy. You said that the Outlaws are holding secret meetings here. Why would they do that?"

"We know they sell speed to truckers, and are involved in human trafficking," he said. "My guess is, they come here to pay off their people. They don't want to engage in that activity at their clubhouse, because too many cars parked in the street would draw suspicion. This is a much better meeting place."

"That makes sense. Dexter and his boys have done their job, and now they want to be compensated."

As a cop, he had busted pimps and pushers, and learned the business side of drug dealing and prostitution. In those operations, the criminals got their money as the services were rendered. He'd never heard of criminals being paid up front.

"Traffickers get paid in advance? How does that work?" he asked.

"It's similar to adoptions. A couple wants a baby, so they hire an adoption attorney. The attorney acts like a broker, and gets his money up front before he delivers the child. People involved in human trafficking work the same way. Brokers advertise on the dark web, and negotiate deals to secure slaves for wealthy buyers. The buyer specifies the type of slave they want, and the broker contacts his sources, and asks for bids. Once the broker has a bid, he contacts the buyer, and a deal is worked out. The buyer is required to put the money up front, just like an adoption."

"How does the broker know the trafficker won't take the money and disappear?"

"The trafficker has to submit proof to the broker that he has the slave. This is usually done with a videotape, or a live conference call. Brokers that deal in volume often send reps to check out the slaves before the money is handed over."

"Check out how?"

"The reps give the slaves medical exams to make sure they're in good health. They also make sure the slaves haven't been physically harmed."

"Do you think there's a rep involved here?"

"Based upon my experience, I'd say yes. There are now fourteen victims when you add in Rachel Baye, which is a big number. The broker probably sent a rep to inspect the merchandise."

He thought back to the cigarette and cigar stubs in the ashtray. Had Dexter met the rep in the restaurant, and taken him to inspect the merchandise? If that was the case, there would soon be a large amount of cash changing hands, and fourteen innocent women would be whisked away, never to be seen again.

Daniels took a call on her cell phone. Hanging up, she said, "That was my team. A delivery truck just turned down RichJo Lane, and is heading our way."

"Should we leave?"

"Let's stay put, and see what they want."

A truck backed into the lot and parked next to the restaurant. It was painted blue and said, Crystal Ice, Serving Pinellas County for 50 Years. Two uniformed men worked with admirable efficiency unloading and transferring bags of ice by dollies to a large ice machine on the side of the building. One of the men opened the padlock on the machine with a combination, then relocked it when they were done.

His partner came over to Daniels's vehicle holding a receipt in his hand.

"He must think we're the owners," she said.

"Let's not disappoint him," he said.

He hopped out and engaged the man. He was handed a pen, and scribbled his name on the line acknowledging the order of ice had been received. The truck left, and he got back into the passenger seat and handed Daniels the receipt.

"Two hundred pounds of ice," he said. "Looks like they're having a party."

- - -

Daniels burned down RichJo Lane and crossed the road to where her team was parked. They huddled up, and she explained to them what needed to be done. They were going to set up a surveillance of the area that would allow them to monitor every vehicle that went into, and pulled out of, RichJo Lane. This would include surveillance equipment mounted on vehicles and parked in strategic locations, plus satellite monitoring of the neighborhood. Then, she placed a call into the FBI's Tampa office, and requested a team of additional agents to help with the bust.

Lancaster stayed in the car, content to be a fly on the wall. This was Beth's show, and he did not want to give the perception of interfering. Beth's team didn't trust him, and the best thing he could do was keep a low profile.

He decided to open Gar's app to see if the blinking purple dot had returned. To his surprise, the dot was there, blinking away. It appeared to be fairly close. Was Dexter right around the corner, and they'd somehow missed him?

Staring at the cell phone's screen, he saw what the problem was. The dot was in the ocean, moving away from land.

CHAPTER 36

Holding his cell phone, he managed to pull Beth away from her team. The purple dot was continuing to cross the water, and she stared at it, then at him.

"He's in a boat," she said.

"If we're lucky, we might be able to spot him."

"I'll drive."

He used his cell phone to find the nearest marina. It was in a town due south of Palm Harbor called Ozona, and Beth ran two red lights getting there. The marina shared parking with a popular restaurant, and the lot was overflowing with vehicles. She parked on the shoulder of the road, and they got out.

"Let's find the manager," she said. "Maybe he has a boat we can use."

The ponytailed hippie who ran the marina was named Chuck. Chuck looked like he smoked his breakfast and drank his lunch. Seeing Daniels's badge, he sobered up in a hurry. "Sorry, but all of our rental boats are out right now," he said. "If you like, I can take you out on my fishing boat. I know the waters around here pretty well."

They accepted his offer and soon were racing across Saint Joseph Sound in a thirty-foot Boston Whaler. A mile from shore, the waters became crowded, with dozens of pleasure boats out for an enjoyable excursion. The purple dot on Lancaster's phone had stopped moving, and he realized that one of these rigs contained Dexter and his broker friend.

"Is it always this crowded?" Daniels shouted.

"This is nothing. You should see the weekends," Chuck shouted back.

"What happens on the weekends?"

Chuck killed the engine so they could talk. He came to the front of the boat, where Daniels was sitting, and pointed at the body of land to the west. It looked like a tropical paradise with sandy white beaches and towering palm trees. It appeared big enough to accommodate people, yet had only a handful of structures.

"See that little piece of heaven over there?" Chuck said. "It's called Honeymoon Island, and it's rated one of the top beaches in the world. Mankind hasn't ruined it yet, which is why tourists are so eager to see it."

Lancaster continued to stare at his phone. The dot was close to the shore of Honeymoon Island, but so were a lot of vessels, and it made him wonder if Dexter had brought his guest here to do some sightseeing.

Daniels was also studying Gar's app on her cell phone. Lancaster joined her at the front of the boat and said, "This is strange, don't you think?"

"They're doing business," she said.

"You think so? They could be fishing, for all we know."

"I've dealt with slave brokers before, and they're all business. They show up, pay for the merchandise, and leave. Dexter must be keeping the victims somewhere nearby." She called to Chuck, who stood on the other side of the boat. "Does Honeymoon Island have houses for rent?"

"Afraid not," Chuck replied. "It's a state park, and stuff like that isn't allowed. The only buildings are the gift shop and a snack bar."

"So much for that idea," she said.

She had Chuck drive the boat around, hoping to get lucky. They made visual contact with people in several boats, but none of them resembled Dexter.

"We're just getting a sunburn," Beth said. "Let's go back to the marina. I need to coordinate with the FBI agents that are being sent by the Tampa office."

It wasn't Lancaster's show, so he said nothing. Chuck pulled the boat into the marina twenty minutes later and tied up. When Daniels offered to compensate him for his time, the marine manager politely declined.

"I don't know what this is all about, but I'm sure it's for a good cause," he said. "Good luck with whomever you're trying to find."

- - -

There was a science to conducting a surveillance operation that required law enforcement to keep its presence a secret or risk having the operation blow up in its face. The Bureau of Alcohol, Tobacco, and Firearms had found this out the hard way after a resident in the town of Waco had alerted the leader of the Branch Davidians that their compound was about to be raided. This had resulted in the deaths of four government agents, and the eventual deaths of eighty-two members of the cult.

The director of the FBI's Tampa office did not want something similar happening to his agents when they raided the Outlaws' hideout, so he had set up headquarters in a spacious suite at the Beso Del Sol Resort in Dunedin, a ten-minute drive away.

Lancaster counted twelve agents as he entered the suite. Daniels's entire team was present, the rest Tampa based. An aerial map of Palm Harbor was pinned to the wall, and they were deciding the best way to conduct their raid.

The Tampa director stood by the window on his cell phone. His name was Special Agent Christopher Baldini, and he had ex-military written all over him: short haircut, ramrod-straight posture, steely gaze. He folded his phone and came toward them.

"Special Agent Daniels," he said. "Chris Baldini."

They briskly shook hands. As Daniels started to introduce Lancaster, Baldini cut her short. "I know who your friend is," he said.

"You know each other?" Daniels said.

"I didn't say that." He shot Lancaster a disapproving look. "You're the crazy bastard that likes to shoot out motorcycle tires and cause accidents."

"Jon Lancaster. Nice to meet you," he said.

"Are you trying to be funny? Because you're not. It's people like you that give law enforcement a bad name," Baldini said, seething.

"I don't know what you're talking about."

"You're not the guy in the YouTube video that was posted last night?"

"What guy?"

"The guy wearing the Yankees baseball cap that shot up a biker gang."

"Not me. I hate the Yankees."

Baldini made a noise that sounded like a growl. The other agents had their backs to them and were pretending not to be eavesdropping, only it was obvious they were hanging on every word. Had one of Daniels's team told Baldini about him?

"I already don't like you," Baldini said.

"I'm an acquired taste," Lancaster said.

"Jon is a retired detective who works for Team Adam," Daniels said, jumping in. "He's been incredibly helpful with this investigation, and I'd like you to treat him with respect."

Baldini was having none of it and glared at Lancaster. "Would you mind stepping outside? I need to have a private conversation with Special Agent Daniels," he said.

Lancaster knew when he wasn't wanted, and moved to the door. "I'll be in the car if you need me," he said.

- - -

The truth be known, he actually liked the Yankees. It hadn't started out that way. Having been raised in the south, he'd grown up believing that the Yankees were nothing more than a team from the Northeast with an arrogant owner who was willing to buy his way to a championship. They were the team to root against, not for.

One day, he'd driven to Port Saint Lucie to watch a spring training game pitting the Mets against the Yankees. His reason for going was to see if Tim Tebow—the greatest college football player that Florida had ever produced—could play baseball. Tebow had signed a minor league contract with the Mets, and was scheduled to start.

Tebow's outing that day had been regrettable, with three strikeouts and a fielding error. Worse, he'd gotten into a heated argument with the umpire over a called strike, and had to be pulled back to the dugout by his teammates. It was not Tim's finest hour.

But the trip hadn't been a waste. He'd gotten to see the Yankees play, and learn about their history. The Yankees had won more championships than any other team, and made their players adhere to a strict set of rules, including short haircuts, no beards, and uniforms that didn't have the players' names stitched across the back. The emphasis was on the team, and not the individual, and he'd liked that.

Daniels appeared and got into the car. He plumbed her face and saw sadness.

"Are you kicking me off the investigation?" he asked.

"Not me. Baldini."

"Same difference."

"I'm sorry, Jon."

"Did one of your team tell that asshole I was a liability?"

"Actually, it was my boss. J. T. is supposed to be resting, but he won't stop doing his job. He emailed Baldini, and told him all about you."

He held up his cell phone and pointed at the purple dot. It was moving south, probably preparing to dock at the marina that it had disembarked from. "Did you explain to Baldini that if it wasn't for me, you wouldn't have gotten a bead on Dexter?"

"I most certainly did."

"What did he say?"

"Baldini asked me to thank you for your contribution to the investigation. He also told me to tell you that if he sees you snooping around, he'll personally handcuff you, and take you down to the nearest police station. He wasn't kidding, Jon."

"He's ex-military, isn't he?"

"He was in the marines. Is it that easy to tell?"

He pulled up the Uber app on his phone and booked a ride back to the Holiday Inn in Oldsmar where he was staying. The app informed him that his ride would be arriving in five minutes. He hoped that was enough time for him to say what needed to be said.

"I want to give you some advice," he said. "Under no circumstances should you let this idiot take over this case. He's a bull in a china shop, and will only screw things up. Am I making myself clear, Beth?"

"Baldini is a veteran agent. He—"

"I don't care if he's the second coming of Christ," he interrupted. "That guy has no emotional investment in the victims. That's the only thing that's important here—the victims. They are somewhere close by, and you need to bring them home. Those women, and their families, are counting on you."

"Damn it, Jon, don't you think I know that?"

"I'm sure you do. But Baldini doesn't, or if he does, he doesn't care. His first priority is busting Dexter and his gang, and claiming the scalp. Rescuing Dexter's victims is his second priority."

"How can you know that, meeting him just once?"

"If Baldini cared about the victims, he would have sat me down, and pulled every piece of information out of me that he could. Then he would have given me the boot. Instead, he called me an asshole, and had you fire me."

Daniels processed his argument, and could not come up with a response.

"When I was in the military, my team's missions were in hostile countries," he said. "The kidnappers hated us, and would execute their hostages before letting them be saved. We took that into account on every mission."

"You think Dexter will kill his victims to spite us?" she said.

"Absolutely. He's a one percenter, and hates authority. If he thinks the FBI is going to bust him, he'll give the order for the victims to be killed."

"You need to come back inside, and tell Baldini this."

"Fuck Baldini."

"Jon, please. Do this, for me."

"You heard me. You couldn't have picked a worse person to help you."

He got a call from the Uber driver. His ride was right around the corner, and he started to get out of the car. Daniels stopped him.

"God damn it, Jon. Why are you acting like this?"

"That little bastard threatened to handcuff me," he said. "What if I walk in there, and he makes good on his promise? I'm not going to risk that, Beth."

"Risk what?"

His driver's ride was a silver Prius. A vehicle matching that description pulled into the parking lot. He gave her a look and opened his door.

"You're going to continue working the case, aren't you?" she said.

"Whatever gave you that idea?" he said.

CHAPTER 37

His room hadn't been cleaned, and he hung the Do Not Disturb sign before going in. He'd never been kicked off an investigation before, and didn't like the way it made him feel. He decided to take a hot shower and wash the feeling away.

He emptied his pockets while undressing. Today's plunder was relatively light—some loose change, and the receipt from the ice delivery to Earl's BBQ. He started to crumble it into a ball, but his eye caught something he hadn't seen earlier. One Percent Solutions, the Outlaws' shell company, was called OPS LLC on the receipt.

The shower could wait. He opened his laptop and did a search of OPS on a website called Manta, which compiled information about small businesses and charged a fee to download the reports.

He typed his credit card information into the checkout, and soon was reading the report on OPS. It had been formed as a limited liability corporation in 2010, and listed the Outlaws' clubhouse in Saint Petersburg as its main address. It also did business under the names Rebel Soul, West Coast Renegades, and Hurry Sunrise.

He stared into space. Criminals often hid their financial activities through shell companies, and he guessed that was the case here. He'd been working off the assumption that the gang's victims were being kept in a building the gang owned. If that was true, then there would be a record of the building's purchase, perhaps under one of these company names.

The three companies needed to be checked out. If he could find the listing of a sale, it might lead him to where the victims were being held. If it did pan out, he'd go rescue them with the help of the local police, and keep the FBI out of the picture. It would piss Beth off, but at this point, he didn't care.

He needed a jolt of caffeine. As he fixed a cup, he got a call from Lauren Gamble, and he answered hoping she had a lead for him.

"Hey, Lauren. What have you got for me?" he greeted her.

"Nothing, I'm afraid. But I need to talk to you," she said.

"I'm up to my eyeballs right now. Can it wait?"

"I don't think that's a good idea. I'm finishing my piece on you, and I found something in your past that I wanted to discuss."

Your past. She made it sound ominous. He didn't want to hear what it was, and tried to sidestep her. "No one wants to read about me. I'm retired, remember?"

"I think our readers would be interested to know why you chose to cancel a vacation to the Keys, and came to Tampa to help with the investigation."

"I came because I was asked to by Team Adam," he said. "Focus on that, and skip the rest."

"You told me you volunteered for the job," she said.

"What difference does it make?"

"There's a difference between being asked to do a job and volunteering to do a job. You volunteered to come to Tampa, and I think I know why."

He didn't like where the conversation was headed, and took a deep breath before replying. "Is that so. Okay, fire away. Why did I come to Tampa?"

"Because you're obsessed with helping others."

"That's news to me."

"Admit it, you are."

"I like helping people. I also like Jimmy Buffett music. Neither of those things make me OCD."

"You interrupted your vacation for a job that didn't pay anything. That's not normal."

"I disagree. I need to run."

"I know what happened."

The breath caught in his throat. "Come again?"

"In the Macy's department store when you were a kid. I know what happened."

He sat on the edge of the bed, and tried not to panic. "How did you find out?"

"Our intern did. Since you were once a Broward County detective, I had him dig through old newspaper articles about you. The Fort Lauderdale *Sun-Sentinel* recently digitalized their back copies going back to the 1970s, and I was hoping there might be a story that filled in the blanks. He found one that was written before you were a cop. It was published in September 1981, and your mother was quoted extensively in it."

He touched his brow, and his hand came away covered in sweat. He'd known Gamble was trouble when he'd met her, but he had gone against his better judgment and brought her into his confidence. Stupid him.

"Do you have any idea how painful this is?" he asked. "Do you?"

"I'm sorry, Jon."

"Really? Then make it go away."

"It's too late for that. The intern showed my boss and me the story at the same time, and my boss told me to include it."

"Tell your boss you won't do it."

"He'll just give my piece to another reporter to finish. I'm afraid there's no going back on this. I've already finished a rough draft. I need to ask you some questions. It shouldn't take very long."

He had run out of arguments, and shook his head in defeat.

"Can I see what you've written?" he asked.

"I don't see why not. I'll send it after we hang up. Call me after you read it."

"Thank you. I'll do that."

He ended the call and threw his cell phone across the room. His past was not an open book for strangers to read and analyze. Nor did he want his friends to see what had happened to him, and the resulting trauma it had caused. If the past couldn't be buried, how could a person heal?

He got on his laptop. Gamble's email arrived with an attachment, and he read the story twice. It was factual, yet still wrong. She had made assumptions that she had no earthly right to make. He spent a few minutes calming down before calling her back. They arranged to meet in thirty minutes.

Ending the call, he again threw his cell phone across the room.

CHAPTER 38

Their meeting spot was a watering hole on the northern tip of Old Tampa Bay called Jack Willie's Bar, Grill, and Tiki. The building had a thatched roof and outdoor seating overlooking the water, and a live band was blasting out the oldies.

Pulling into the parking lot, he had an idea. The Outlaws' three shell companies needed to be checked out, and he couldn't be on his computer while talking to Gamble. He decided to call Nicki, knowing she'd be willing to help. Only this time, the terms were going to be different.

"Hi, Nicki. You doing homework?"

"All done for the day," the teenager said. "I just read a story on the news about a woman named Rachel Baye disappearing in Saint Petersburg. The police think it may be linked to the other cases. Is it?"

"Afraid so. Would you be interested in doing some cyber sleuthing for me?"

"You bet! Can I ask my classmates to pitch in as well?"

"No, you can't. This is very sensitive. If one of your friends posted it on social media, innocent people might get hurt. You have to run solo on this one. And you have to promise me you won't speak to anyone about it."

"Sure. I won't speak to anyone about this, so help me God."

"Do you have something to write with?"

"I've got a pen right here."

"Great. Write down the names of the following companies. Rebel Soul, West Coast Renegades, and Hurry Sunrise. I'm interested in seeing if they've purchased any real estate in the past ten years. The two places that are of most interest are Pinellas and Pasco Counties. If you find a sale, get as much information about it as you can."

"I'll get to work on it right away. Do you and Aunt Beth know why these women are being targeted? We talked about it in class today, and no one can figure it out."

He considered telling her the truth. The victims had been targeted because they'd chosen to fight evil instead of hiding from it, and had been punished for their good deeds. Life wasn't fair, and sometimes, it was downright cruel. But Nicki was young and impressionable, and perhaps that message wasn't the right one for him to be delivering.

"We're not certain what the motivation is," he said. "Call me if you find anything."

"Will do. Say hi to Aunt Beth for me."

- - -

Many restaurants in Florida pretended to be yesteryear, and hung sepia-toned photos on the walls and wrote fake histories on their menus. Jack Willie's was the real deal, and had a weather-beaten ambiance that came with age. He found Gamble at the bar nursing a club soda, and ordered a coke and a bowl of pretzels. Drinks in hand, they took an empty table in the back of the restaurant. Although the bandstand was outside, the loud music made conversation impossible.

"They'll be taking a break in a few minutes," she said, nearly shouting.

It was an odd choice for a meeting place, and he wondered if Gamble had picked it because she was afraid that their conversation might turn ugly, and wanted the protection of a large crowd if he got out of line.

He ate pretzels while staring at his cell phone. The purple dot had remained stopped near the tip of Honeymoon Island, and he guessed Dexter and his guest had decided to do some fishing. Outside, the band wrapped up their last number to smattering applause. The lead singer announced a short break, and asked everyone to be kind to their waitresses.

"What are the chances I can convince your boss to kill this story?" he asked.

"Zero and none," she said.

"Then let's get it over with."

"You read my story. Were there any mistakes you'd like me to correct?"

"The tone was wrong."

She stiffened. "How so?"

"You didn't capture the pain my family went through. It was a different time back then. We were all a lot more innocent."

"I'm sorry."

"How old are you, anyway?"

"I'll be twenty-eight next month."

He watched the carbonated bubbles rise to the top of his drink. The things Gamble had written about had happened before she'd been born, and it probably wasn't fair of him to criticize her writing style, or lack of understanding. If he told her his side of things, maybe she'd do a rewrite, and capture what had really happened.

"Back in high school, my English teacher had us read a poem by Dylan Thomas about a girl dying in a fire in London," he said. "The last line has always stayed with me. 'After the first death, there is no other.'"

"The loss of innocence," Gamble said.

"That's right. The first time you experience death is a life-altering experience. It happened young for me. I was five. The world was different then. We left our doors unlocked, and kids played outside without supervision. There were no AMBER Alerts, or kids on milk boxes, or national databases of missing children. None of that existed. There was no need.

"That changed in the summer of 1981. My family had finished dinner, and we were in the den watching TV when the program got interrupted by a news alert. A kid named Adam Walsh was missing, and his parents were offering a reward.

"I remember how scared my mom and dad got after that. They started locking up the house, and forbade my brother and I to play anywhere but in the backyard, which was fenced in. We became prisoners in our own home, and so did our friends.

"Reward posters started appearing on phone poles and billboards. We went to the airport to pick up a relative, and volunteers were handing out flyers. At church, the pastor said a prayer for Adam's safety. Everyone had an emotional stake in his return."

"I had no idea it was that intense," Gamble said.

"It was the only thing on people's minds," he said. "Two weeks later, my mom was in the kitchen, when I heard her crying. I ran in, and my dad was holding her. She had the radio on, and it was saying that a fisherman had found a kid's head floating in a canal in Vero Beach. The medical examiner had used dental records to confirm that it was Adam Walsh."

His throat had gone dry, and he took a swallow of his drink before continuing. "I ran into my brother's room, and told him. Logan had a portable radio, and we sat on his bed, and listened to a local station. It was all they talked about. One of the newscasters said that Adam had been abducted from the Sears in Hollywood, and that freaked us out. A few weeks before, we'd been at the Macy's in Pembroke Pines, which was a few miles away. A weirdo had tried to lure me into his car, and my brother kicked him in the balls, and I got away. We hadn't told anyone about it, but decided we'd better tell our parents, considering what had happened."

"Wait. The newspaper article said you *had* told your parents."

"The article was wrong. We were afraid of being punished, so we didn't tell them. Please change that in your piece."

"I will."

"Thank you." He finished his drink and took a deep breath.

"What made you think he was a weirdo?" Gamble asked.

"While he was trying to get me into his car, my brother kicked him in the groin, and his shirt came out of his pants. He was wearing a purple dress underneath."

"So he was a cross-dresser."

"Among other things."

"How did he lure you out of the store?"

"With candy. Let me finish my story, okay?"

"Sorry, I didn't mean to interrupt."

"We went into the kitchen and told my parents," he said. "My mother cried her eyes out, she got so upset. Then we drove to the police station, and my brother and I told the detectives what had happened. The next day, a police sketch artist came to the house, and drew a composite based upon our description. That should have been the end of it, only somehow it got leaked to the newspaper. A reporter called the house, and wanted to know why we hadn't come forward earlier. My mother told him that we'd been traumatized, and she didn't want us hurt any more."

"So your mother covered for you."

"That's right, she covered for her boys. It wasn't pretty."

"How so?"

"We got harassing phone calls. People wanted someone to blame, so they took their anger out on my mom. It got so bad that we had our number changed."

His glass was empty, and he went to the bar to get a refill and more pretzels. When he came back, he saw Gamble fumbling with her cell phone, and he guessed that she was recording their conversation. He'd dealt with reporters enough to know that this was part of their job, and he took no offense.

"Have some pretzels," he said.

"No, thank you," she said. "When did your family learn that it was Ottis Toole who'd tried to abduct you?"

"That happened two years later. A drifter named Henry Lee Lucas had gotten arrested in Texas for murder and was facing the electric chair. The police cut a deal with him, and Lucas confessed to killing over two hundred women, which made him the worst serial killer in history. Lucas also said he had a partner."

"Ottis Toole."

"The one and only. Toole was in prison in Florida for setting fires, so the police had a chat with him. Toole admitted to killing women with Lucas. Then, he got really emotional, and he confessed to killing Adam Walsh."

"Why do you think he got emotional?"

"It must have bothered him. I guess even monsters have souls. Soon after that, the police came to our house, and showed us Toole's photograph. Logan made a positive identification. All I did was cry."

"Toole was horrible looking, wasn't he?"

"His eyes weren't normal. He looked like he was sleepwalking."

"How did it make you feel, knowing it was him?"

"Horrible. I knew that it could have been me, and not poor Adam. Let's wrap this up."

"Just one more question."

He braced himself. He knew what her question was, and wanted to answer her in such a manner that there would be no doubt in her mind that he was telling the truth about the course that his life had taken as an adult, and the decisions he'd made.

"You became a member of Team Adam after retiring from the police department," Gamble said. "Did you know at the time that it had been named after Adam Walsh, and that his parents were responsible for it being started?"

"Believe it or not, I didn't," he said.

"How is that possible?"

"You don't believe me?"

"I didn't say that. It just seems unlikely that you wouldn't know."

"I knew who John Walsh was through *America's Most Wanted*. But I wasn't aware of the other things he and his wife had done, like establishing the National Center for Missing and Exploited Children and helping start the AMBER Alert program."

"But you did make the connection."

"Not right away. When I was asked to join Team Adam, I assumed the name had a biblical connotation. At my first orientation, I was given a handbook with the Team Adam guidelines. Adam's photo was on the cover. That's when I knew."

"Did it give you goose bumps?"

Certain things in life were meant to be, and when they happened, their occurrence almost felt preordained. At that moment, he'd known what he was going to do with the rest of his life, and it had made him feel whole.

"I guess," he said. "I need to go."

"One more question."

"You've run out of those."

"This is a simple one. How did your brother feel when he learned that you'd become a member of Team Adam, and had dedicated yourself to finding missing kids?"

"My brother never found out."

"Why's that?"

"He died before I had a chance to tell him."

"That's sad. I'm sorry."

She'd wanted a happy ending, but those were in short supply these days. Her question made him wonder how Logan would have reacted to the news that he was working for the organization founded by the parents of Adam Walsh. His brother would have seen the irony of it, but would Logan have appreciated the rest? Most people spent their lives not knowing why they'd been put on this earth, but a lucky few did, and he was one of those lucky few.

He walked her outside to where her car was parked. She gave him back the handgun he'd given her for protection a few days ago. He said goodbye and started to walk away.

"I'm sure he would have been proud of you," he heard her say.

CHAPTER 39

He drove back to his hotel with his phone resting on his leg, the purple dot still parked in the waters north of Honeymoon Island. Dexter and the broker appeared to be bunked down for the night, and he assumed their boat had sleeping quarters.

As he entered his hotel room, he got a call from his favorite teenage sleuth. He wanted her news to be good, and wash away his conversation with Gamble. He kicked off his shoes and sat on the room's solitary chair before taking her call.

"Hey, Nicki, what's up?" he asked.

"I got a hit," the teenager said excitedly. "The Outlaws have another business they're running on the side, and I found out what it is."

There was no greater pleasure than cracking a case wide open, the surge of adrenaline better than any drug.

"Are you near your laptop? I just sent you a link," she said.

He scooted his chair up to the desk and booted up his laptop. It had gone into sleep mode, and was slow coming to life. "Which of the companies was it?"

"Hurry Sunrise," she said. "The other two were duds."

Going into his inbox, he opened Nicki's email, and clicked on the link. Hurry Sunrise was a charter fishing outfit that operated out of the marina that he and Daniels had visited that day. The company had been in business for thirty years, and specialized in taking large groups on three- and four-day excursions. There were photographs of sunburned clients holding trophy fish up to the camera, along with testimonials saying how great the staff were.

He found himself shaking his head. He knew guys who ran charter fishing companies in the Keys, and they barely scraped by. It didn't seem like the type of business the Outlaws would be involved with, and he wondered if there was something below the surface that he wasn't seeing.

"Are you sure this is the right Hurry Sunrise?" he asked.

"I'm positive," Nicki said. "The company has a charter fishing license, which I traced to a Saint Petersburg address that is also the Outlaws' clubhouse."

"Huh," he said in frustration.

"What's wrong?"

"It just doesn't sound like a business they'd be involved with."

"Well, that's the strange thing, I'm not sure they really are running a business. During one of the talks you gave to my class, you said that a good investigator would run down every lead, and see where it took her. So I took your advice, and called the contact number on their site."

"You called them? That was nervy."

"Actually, it was fun. I got an answering machine that said the company wasn't taking any bookings, and that I should leave a message. When I tried to do that, a recording said the mailbox was full."

"That's strange."

"That's what I thought. For the heck of it, I called two other charter fishing companies that operate out of the same marina, and told them I was looking to hire a boat for my father's birthday party. They were more than happy to take my business. I asked them what dates were best, and both companies said their calendars were wide open."

"So business is slow, except for Hurry Sunrise."

"I don't think Hurry Sunrise has any business. You told my class that crooks use legitimate businesses to hide illegal activity. What was the expression you used?"

"A front."

"That's right. I think Hurry Sunrise is a front."

It felt like a dead end. He had hoped that one of the Outlaws' shell companies had purchased a building to house the gang's victims, and that Nicki would turn up the real estate transaction, and that would lead him to breaking this open. Instead, she'd found a charter fishing company that had stopped doing business for reasons that weren't entirely clear.

"Good job," he said, not wanting to burst her bubble.

"Thanks. What do you think it means?"

"I have no idea. Why would a gang of crooks run a business, but not take any customers? It doesn't add up."

"It bothered me too. I wanted to call the previous owner, and ask him, but I didn't think he'd talk to me."

"What previous owner?"

"His name is Captain Peyton Lynch. He's mentioned in the company's reviews on Yelp. I found his address and phone number on Whitepages.com. He lives in Dunedin, which isn't far from the marina."

"How do you know this guy sold the company?"

"A reviewer on Yelp mentioned it, and said he really missed him."

If Peyton Lynch was local, perhaps he'd know why the Outlaws had decided to stop taking customers after purchasing his business. He needed to call the guy, and see if he could get him talking.

"That's some excellent detective work. Good job," he said.

"Thanks. Do you want Captain Lynch's phone number?"

"Please."

- - -

Dunedin refused to bend to corporate America. Lining Main Street were eclectic shops and restaurants and several microbreweries. The locals had somehow managed to keep out franchise restaurants and chain retail stores, and it gave the place a special feel.

Sea Sea Riders restaurant was housed in a Key West–style cottage just off the main drag. He found Lynch at the bar drinking a rum and coke and chatting with a pretty bartender half his age. A border collie sat by his feet, licking its paws.

"Captain Lynch? My name is Jon Lancaster, and I work with a law enforcement agency called Team Adam," he introduced himself. "I spoke to your roommate, and he said I might find you here. May I have a few minutes of your time?"

Lynch spent a moment reading his Team Adam business card. His face was a burgundy color, his mop of hair snow white. His hands were the size of small dinner plates, and were scarred from countless cuts and scrapes.

"What's this about?" Lynch asked.

"I'd like to talk to you about the Outlaws," he said.

His eyes flickered. "What about them?"

"You sold your charter fishing company to them, is that correct?"

Lynch tossed the card on the bar and frowned. "Yes, I did. I knew something was wrong with those guys, I just couldn't put a finger on what it was. Sure, I'll talk. You want something to drink?"

"A club soda would be good."

"Hey, Amber, get me a refill and my friend here a club soda."

They went outside for some privacy. The patio was empty, and they took a table beneath a large oak. The border collie dutifully followed, and parked himself at Lynch's feet. He was rewarded with a dog biscuit, which he happily chewed.

"What's your pup's name?" Lancaster asked.

"Ruddy. He's a rescue. They're the best kind," Lynch said.

"I've heard people say that. The things I need to ask you must stay confidential."

"This sounds like trouble."

He let the comment pass and took a sip of his drink.

"Will my name be kept out of this?" Lynch asked, sounding anxious.

"Of course. I won't include your name on any of my reports."

"Fair enough. What do you want to know?"

"How did you come to sell your business to the Outlaws?"

"In the beginning, they were customers," Lynch said. "They booked a charter trip, and four of them showed up at the marina on their Harleys, so I took them out. We've got a lot of bikers around here, most of them lawyers and stockbrokers who ride on the weekends, so I didn't pay it much attention.

"Everything went fine at first. We threw lines in the water, and my first mate served them beers. I tried to strike up a conversation, but they weren't in the mood. A lot of my customers are celebrating a birthday or a reunion, but that wasn't the case here. I thought it was strange, but what was I going to do?

"An hour into the trip, one of them asked for a tour of the boat, so I showed him around. He asked a lot of questions, and I started wondering if he was going into the charter business himself."

"What kind of questions?"

"He asked about maintenance cost, cost of gas, the licenses I needed, that sort of stuff. He asked if the coast guard ever bothered us, which I found sort of strange."

"Had they?"

"Nope. The coast guard didn't hassle us, and had never come on board. I told him I'd been in business a long time, and had a clean reputation."

"Do other charter captains have bad reputations?"

"Some of them do, sure. They let the partying get out of hand, if you know what I mean. I never let that happen."

"Did he offer to buy your business then?"

"That happened a few days later. I came to the marina one morning, and the guy was waiting for me. His name was Hawk. He offered to buy my boats, and he also wanted the business name, which is incorporated."

"So he wanted to buy your reputation."

Lynch rubbed his chin. "I suppose he did. Never thought of it that way."

"And you agreed."

"Not at first, I didn't. It was obvious that Hawk and his friends didn't know squat about fishing or running a charter business, so I asked him to his face if he was planning to use my boats to run drugs. Hawk said he'd swear on a stack of Bibles that he wouldn't use my boats for that, which I found funny as hell."

"Why's that?"

"Because that guy hadn't been near a Bible in his life. Anyway, I was still on the fence, but then he made his offer. The number blew me away."

"He offered you a lot."

"That's right. The recession hit me hard, and I was drowning in debt. I couldn't say no, even though I had reservations about the guy. We closed the deal a week later, which was another eye-opener."

"Why was that?"

"Hawk came to the closing with two duffel bags filled with cash. I'd never seen that much money in my life."

"Would you mind telling me how much money?"

"I'd rather not. I didn't report all of it on my taxes."

"This won't go into my report. I'm just curious."

"It was over seven figures."

One of the worst mistakes an investigator could make was to make assumptions, because it often led to false conclusions. He'd assumed Lynch was a small-time operator, which Lynch had just shattered by admitting that he'd made a killing selling his business to the Outlaws. There were boats, and then there were *boats*, and the vessels that Lynch had sold to the bikers had fetched over $1 million. That was a huge investment, and it made him wonder how big the boats really were.

Lynch had gone back to petting his friend, who'd rolled over on his back. He looked up at his guest and said, "It was a deal with the devil, wasn't it?"

"You couldn't have known what they were up to," he said.

"But I felt it in my gut. They were bad news."

"If they hadn't bought your business, they would have bought someone else's."

"So I should stop flogging myself, is that what you're saying?"

"You did nothing wrong. Would you by chance have photographs of the boats you sold to them? It would help in my investigation."

"I've got a few photos on my phone. I look at them sometimes when I get nostalgic. Give me your email, and I'll send them to you."

- - -

He waited until he was in his car before looking at the photographs. It confirmed his suspicion about why the Outlaws had spent so much money for a business that they hadn't intended to run, and he spun his wheels leaving the lot.

CHAPTER 40

Back at his hotel, he killed the engine, and then sipped the double espresso he'd bought from the Starbucks down the road. It snapped back his eyelids, and he became wide awake. That was good, because he didn't intend to go to bed anytime soon.

Two plans had been forming in his head, each independent of the other. First and foremost, he needed to rescue the gang's victims. He could let the FBI handle that, but had decided it would be best to do so himself. Rescue missions had been his forte in the military, and the odds of the mission being successful were greater if he was in charge.

The second plan was to pay back Dexter for murdering his brother. Sending Dexter back to prison would not bring him any satisfaction. Dexter needed a bullet put in him, and he had to figure out a way to accomplish that, without being thrown in jail.

Behind the hotel was a courtyard where a fountain spewed colored water. He took an empty bench and sent a text to a dependable ex-SEAL named Carlo, who, along with his partners Mike and Karl, had done jobs for him before. Carlo quickly replied, saying the team was on a hush-hush assignment overseas, and wouldn't be home for a month.

He decided to take another route. The Navy SEAL program had started in Florida during World War II, and today there was a museum that celebrated this. Located in Fort Pierce, it was called the Navy SEAL

Museum, and it resided on the training grounds of the original navy frogmen.

The museum's mission was to preserve the legacy of a group of soldiers whose missions would forever remain secret. It did this by displaying the amazing seacraft and weaponry that had been developed for the SEALs. This included special boats designed to evade radar and submersibles used to insert soldiers behind enemy lines.

The museum also served another purpose. Its directors, all navy veterans, had established a network of ex-SEALs who were available for hire. This resource was called ETHOS, and while its services didn't come cheap, its members were in constant demand. Saving pennies was not the objective when human lives were at stake.

An automated service picked up. He punched in an extension, and was routed to the voice mail of Lieutenant Mark Starkweather, a cover for the ETHOS network. He identified himself, and asked for a call back. Sixty seconds later, he got one.

"This is Jon Lancaster, and I need some help," he said.

"First things first. What are the passwords?" the operator asked.

"Forged by adversity."

"Who do you help?"

"Those that cannot help themselves."

"That works. What are you looking for?"

He explained the mission and the number of men needed to accomplish it. The operator did a quick check of her database, and said that there was a four-man scuba team in the Saint Petersburg area that was available for hire. The ingenuity of the Outlaws operation was that their victims were being held captive in open waters, in plain sight. A group of SEALs wearing scuba equipment could approach in a boat, dive into the water, and stage their mission. The Outlaws would never see them coming.

The operator quoted him a price, which he agreed to. It wasn't cheap. He would ask Daniels to have the FBI reimburse him, and if they turned him down, he'd ask Team Adam. If they said no, he'd foot the bill himself.

"Where would you like to meet to discuss your mission?" the operator asked.

He gave the operator the name of the marina in Ozona.

"What time would you like to meet?" she asked.

"As soon as possible," he said.

- - -

The restaurant next to the marina was still serving food, and he ate raw oysters at the bar while watching a muted TV. Most of the diners had cleared out, and the bartender was making noises like he wanted to go home.

At 10:25 p.m. he got a text from the scuba team. They had reached the marina, and were about to pull in. He tossed a handful of bills onto the bar to cover his food.

"Keep the change," he said.

He hustled over to the marina. The main office was locked up, but there was plenty of activity on the boats, with people holding loud parties and carrying on, and his presence didn't cause any concern. He walked out onto the end of a long dock, and leaned against a piling to wait. The wind had died, and the water reflected the flickering lights of the restaurant and of the full moon. A puttering sound snapped his head. Using his cell phone like a beacon, he watched a vessel motor toward him.

He helped them tie up. Their boat was called a bowrider. The bow had a unique construction, with a swim platform for wakeboarders that was also ideal for scuba divers to get in and out of the water.

The scuba team consisted of four men, ranging in age from late thirties to early fifties. Each wore shorts and a long-sleeve athletic shirt.

They shared an easy camaraderie, and looked no different from any other group who'd spent the day fishing.

One of the group was taller than the others, and wore his hair slicked back. He joined Lancaster on the dock and offered his hand.

"I'm Trent," he said. "Sorry it took us so long to get here. We had to fill up several of the tanks with air, and it took a while."

"No need to apologize. I appreciate you taking the job on short notice."

"Anything to help a brother SEAL."

Lancaster had not put his cell phone away. He pulled up the photograph of the charter fishing vessel that Peyton Lynch had sent him, and passed the cell phone to Trent. Trent studied the photograph before passing the cell phone to his team.

"This is your target," Lancaster said. "It was being used as a charter fishing vessel before the Outlaws motorcycle gang bought it. I don't know how you approached the marina, but you may have passed it on your way in."

"We came in from the north. The south is too shallow," Trent said.

"I saw this boat," one of the team said. "It was huge. There was a guy on the stern with a gun strapped to his side. I waved, but he didn't wave back."

"They running drugs?" Trent asked.

"Not drugs," he said.

Trent stared at him, as did the others. They wanted to know not just because they were curious but also because it was important for them to understand the nature of the mission. In the heart of every SEAL was an unmatched personal ethic. SEALs weren't just great soldiers, they were also great people, and they lived their lives without compromise or regret. If he had told them that this mission was a personal vendetta, they would have bolted. So he left that part out, and focused on what was truly important.

"They're slave traders," he said. "They kidnap women, and ferry them onto the boat, where the women are held as prisoners. When the boat's full, they set sail."

"Who in God's name buys slaves?" Trent said.

"There are brokers who sell slaves to wealthy people in Central and South America. One of those brokers is on the boat right now, inspecting the merchandise."

"That's sick."

"I felt the same way when it was explained to me. This operation has been going on for several years, so it's safe to say there have been many victims."

Trent looked away, and Lancaster sensed that he was trying to control his anger. Every one of those victims had a family whose lives had been ruined by the Outlaws. They needed to be stopped, and in the process, shown no remorse.

"How do you want us to handle it?" Trent asked.

"The broker will come back to shore so he can attend a meeting to pay some ex-convicts who assisted in the abductions," he said. "With him will be a biker named Dexter Hudson. Those guys are not your concern."

"Who's dealing with them?"

"The FBI is. They've got a team that's staked out the meeting place. When the broker and Dexter meet the ex-cons, the FBI will swoop in, and make the bust. Once that happens, you will incapacitate the men on the boat who are guarding the victims. Then you'll call me, and I'll send the FBI out to bring the victims ashore."

"Should we greet the FBI when they come out?"

"No. You'll need to disappear. Unless you want your names put in a report."

"I think we'd like to avoid that. Okay, guys, any questions?"

The man who'd mentioned seeing the armed guard spoke up. "What if the people on the boat engage us? How should we handle that?"

"The only important people on that boat are the victims," Lancaster said. "If one of the bikers acts up, put a bullet in his head."

"That's murder."

"Take the body with you, and dump it in the ocean. Anything else?"

The men shook their heads. Trent jumped back in the boat, and they prepared to leave. Lancaster felt like he'd left something out. On every mission he'd ever gone on, the commanding officer had given the team a short bio of the person they were about to rescue. It had given the mission a gravitas that otherwise wouldn't have been there.

"There's one more thing you should know," he said. "These victims all share something in common. Each one of them helped put a bad person in prison. They did a good deed, and got repaid with a bad deed."

"They're heroes," Trent said.

"That's right. The ex-cons that the FBI are going to arrest tomorrow are the guys these women helped put in prison. It will be fitting when those guys find out that their victims are going home, and they're heading back to the joint."

"Sounds like a happy ending to me," Trent said.

Lancaster untied the boat and tossed Trent the rope. He waited until it had disappeared into the night before departing.

CHAPTER 41

As a cop, he'd never liked it when civilians took the law into their own hands. It was vigilantism, and often led to innocent people getting hurt.

But there were exceptions to this, and he left the marina believing the victims on the charter fishing boat would be safer if Trent's team rescued them, as opposed to the FBI. Rescue operations were tricky, and people with military training were better at doing them. He didn't care if the FBI got their noses bent out of shape because he'd invaded their turf. All he cared about was the victims, and their families.

Traffic was light as he drove north on Alternate US 19. Reaching Palm Harbor, he spotted the street sign for RichJo Lane, and he slowed down. He assumed that the FBI had posted a stakeout in anticipation of conducting a raid when Dexter and the ex-cons met up, and he wanted to see if he could spot them.

Across the street from the entrance to RichJo Lane was a tire store. Parked in the lot was a large camper with multiple antennae on the roof. The camper hadn't been there earlier in the day, and he assumed it was filled with FBI agents.

He crawled past RichJo Lane. He didn't spot any other FBI vehicles, but that didn't mean they weren't here. When making busts, the

FBI liked to use overwhelming force, and he assumed that more agents were nearby.

A pair of headlights appeared in his mirror. A car had pulled out of RichJo Lane, and was also heading north. Earlier that day, he'd seen a number of residences on the street, and guessed it got a fair amount of traffic.

The car gave him an idea.

He had resigned himself to the fact that he probably wasn't going to pay Dexter back for killing his brother. If he put a bullet into Dexter, he would not only end up in jail but also endanger the bust, as well as put the victims' lives in jeopardy.

So he couldn't put Dexter out of his misery. But maybe he could get someone else to do it. It was the next best option, and would taste just as sweet.

A mile down the road he spotted a second camper parked in front of a storage facility. It was identical to the camper up the street, with multiple antennae on the roof. To conduct the raid, the FBI would use armored vehicles, which was standard operating procedure. The storage facility was the right size to hold a pair of such vehicles.

The FBI had the area covered. If he put his plan into action, they might spot him, and that would be bad. Did he want to risk his freedom to pay Dexter back?

He decided he needed a second opinion.

- - -

He kept driving until he reached Dunedin. The first business he saw was a craft brewery. It was housed in a snug little building that could have been a concession stand on the beach. There were bike racks in front, and he guessed their brews had such a high alcohol content that locals didn't risk driving for fear of getting pulled over.

The tasting room had five empty stools. A chalkboard behind the bar announced that day's selections. The beers had exotic names like Ale of Two Cities, Imaginary Friends, and Control Freak. A female bartender asked his pleasure, and he picked a farmhouse ale called Evil Urges. She placed a pint in front of him.

"Do you want to run a tab?"

He gave her a credit card. There were no TVs or jukeboxes, the only noise the sounds that came out of people's mouths.

"What's your name?" he asked.

"Elizabeth. My friends call me Liz," she said.

She had a kind face and soulful eyes, and impressed him as the honest type. "My name is Jon. Do you mind if I ask you a question? It's nothing personal, I'm just a little torn."

Liz crossed her arms in front of her chest. She'd had guys bend her ear before, and didn't act as if his request were anything out of the ordinary.

"You break up with your girlfriend?" she asked.

"I wish it was that simple," he said.

"When is breaking up with your lady simple?"

"Sorry, that didn't come out right." He took a sip of his beer, and tried again. "When I was a teenager, my older brother got arrested for being part of a convenience store robbery where the owner got shot and later died. My brother and his partners got arrested, and were put on trial."

"This is heavy," she said.

"I can stop if you want," he said.

Liz put her elbows on the bar, and looked him in the eye. "How long ago was this?"

"Twenty-five years ago."

"Wow. And it's still eating you up?"

"Afraid so."

"Were you part of the robbery?"

"No, I was at home, doing my homework."

She took a can of soda out of the cooler, popped the top, and clinked it against his glass. "Okay, you've hooked me. So what's your question?"

"My brother wanted me to testify at the trial, and say that he was at home with me during the robbery. The problem was, a witness picked my brother out of a lineup, and there was also a videotape. My brother was guilty, and nothing I was going to say would have changed that."

"So you didn't do it."

He shook his head, and took a long swallow of his beer.

"Did they put him away?"

"Yeah. He got out two months ago. I saw him, and he still held it against me. I've been thinking about it ever since. I did the right thing, but also the wrong thing."

"How so?"

"I spoke the truth when I got up on the stand. That was the right thing. But I didn't stand up for him, and that was wrong."

"You couldn't have done both. So what's your question?"

"If you were in my shoes, what would you have done?"

The question caught her by surprise. She finished her soda and crushed the empty can between her palms. He had made her feel uncomfortable, which had not been his purpose for coming in. He threw money down for his drink, and told her to keep the change. She retrieved his credit card and slid it toward him.

"Good night. Thanks for listening," he said.

"You don't have to leave," she said.

"Yes, I do. I shouldn't have bothered you."

"You're not bothering me, really."

It didn't feel that way. He said good night, and made for the door.

"You really want to know what I would have done?" she said.

He turned around and slowly nodded.

"If it had been me, I would have lied, and said he was home," she said.

"But lying wouldn't have changed things," he said.

"Doesn't matter. He's still your brother."

Not just his brother, but also his hero. And he hadn't stuck up for him. There was always time to make amends, and he said, "Is there an all-night grocery nearby?"

CHAPTER 42

Daniels thought she was going to have a heart attack.

She was staked out across the street from RichJo Lane. On the camper's roof were three high-resolution, infrared digital cameras that allowed her to not only capture the license plate on a car at night but also peer into the car, and get a good look at the driver. These images were sent to a computer whose screen she now stared at. A man that could have been Jon's twin had just turned down RichJo Lane. The images were being recorded, and she played them back, just to be sure.

The resemblance was uncanny. Same round face and stubble of beard. And the trademark baseball cap, this time one bearing the logo of the Miami Marlins.

She told herself that it couldn't be him. Baldini had threatened to arrest Jon and throw him in jail if he showed his face, and she couldn't imagine Jon taking that risk.

She replayed the video. On the passenger seat was a bag of groceries with a loaf of bread sticking out. She remembered Jon once saying how he liked to put groceries in the passenger seat when tailing a suspect. If the suspect happened to look in the mirror, he'd see the groceries, and think it wasn't a cop on his ass.

She told herself it was a coincidence. Jon wasn't that dumb.

"Find something?" a voice asked.

She glanced over her shoulder. Three other agents shared the camper, and were drinking coffee. Baldini was with them, and was facing her.

"Just a car," she said.

"A car," he repeated.

"Yes, a car. It turned down RichJo Lane. It was nothing."

His eyes were cold and unfriendly. Baldini hadn't let her out of his sight, and she felt like she was being stalked. He returned to his conversation.

She switched screens. A satellite shot of RichJo Lane appeared, taken through an infrared lens. The local police used satellite surveillance to catch burglars, and had given the FBI permission to use the satellite for their bust.

The car pulled in front of the building that had once housed Earl's BBQ. A dark figure got out and disappeared in the building's shadows. She had convinced herself that it wasn't Jon. But if it wasn't Jon, then who was he, and what interest did he have at Earl's BBQ at this time of night? Out of the corner of her eye, she spied Baldini coming toward her. She touched her mouse, and the screen returned to real time.

Baldini touched her shoulder. He'd done that before, and she'd told him to not do it again. It obviously hadn't sunk in, and she slid her chair back, catching him in the thigh. He yelped.

"Stop sneaking up on me," she said.

"Sorry," he said, rubbing his leg. "What are you looking at?"

"Like I just said, it was nothing."

"Why do I think you're hiding something from me?"

"Why would I do that?"

"Because you don't like me."

The other agents feigned conversation among themselves. She slid out of her chair and moved toward the door. "Let's take this outside. One of you guys needs to take over for me."

She left the camper before Baldini could reply.

- - -

Daniels walked around to the front of the camper, and waited to see if the car came out of RichJo Lane. Baldini edged up beside her. He was breathing on her neck, and it was all she could do not to tell him off.

"You must be looking at *something*," he said.

"A car pulled down the street a minute ago, and pulled into the BBQ joint. I think the guy is taking a leak," she said.

"Should we go check?"

"And blow our cover? That's a bad idea. If the guy stays too long, I'll call the sheriff, and have him send a cruiser."

"That works. So what's the problem?"

"Who said there was a problem?"

"I did. You're seething. Are you angry because I yanked Lancaster off the investigation and you guys are in a relationship?"

"Leave our relationship out of this. Jon was conducting an independent investigation, and knows things. You should have interviewed him."

"My mistake. I assumed he told you everything he knew."

"Why did you assume that?"

"I assumed you were sleeping with him."

"Did you now?"

"You're not?"

It wasn't easy being a female agent with the FBI. The ratio was one to five, with men getting most of the top jobs. When a female did get promoted, there were the inevitable rumblings about the agent having slept with her boss.

Daniels had gotten ahead, and she hadn't done it on her back. Instead, she'd outperformed her peers, and earned it. She'd also made it a point to mute her looks, and hadn't worn a lot of makeup on the job. It was the only way to keep the rumors away.

Baldini would have known this about her, had he asked around. Instead, he'd made an assumption about her, and demeaned her at the same time. It was worse than a stab in the back; it was a stab in the front, and she decided to make him pay for it.

Her right hand went up to the side of his head and pushed, while her left hand grabbed his wrist and pulled. At the same time, the bottom of her right foot swept his leg out from under him.

Push, pull, sweep.

He hit the pavement hard, and banged his head. Groaning, he struggled to rise. She put her foot on his chest, and kept him down.

"Let me up. Someone might come out," he pleaded.

"Afraid they'll see you lying on the ground?" she asked.

"I'm sorry. It was a stupid thing to say."

"Is that what you and the other guys were talking about? How you thought I was screwing Lancaster, and that it was clouding my judgment?"

"It was nothing like that."

"But you were talking about me, weren't you?"

"So what? No harm, no foul."

She dug her heel into his chest and watched him squirm. It shouldn't have brought her pleasure, but it did. "Let's be clear about something. I work at headquarters, and see your bosses every day. If I put in a bad word, your career will be over."

"What kind of bad word?"

"I'll say that you're drinking on the job."

"But that isn't true!"

"And I'm not sleeping with Jon Lancaster. But you assumed that I was, and told the others. That hurts me, and my reputation. It also hurts my career. Do you see my point?"

A knowing look spread across his face, and he nodded.

"I'll tell them I was wrong," he said.

Not an apology, but an admission of guilt. She liked that.

"Is that a promise, Special Agent Baldini?"

"Yes, Special Agent Daniels, it's a promise."

She removed her foot from his chest and stepped back. He slowly climbed off the pavement, and dusted himself off. His clothes weren't torn, and there were no visible bruises or scrapes. It could have been worse, a fact that he seemed to appreciate.

"Was that a judo move you used to take me down?" he asked.

"Muay Thai," she said. Baldini went inside the camper. As he did, a pair of headlights came down RichJo Lane. She hid behind the front of the camper, and watched the vehicle turn onto Alternate 19 and head south. It was the car with the driver who resembled Jon.

She glanced at her watch. The car had been back there for ten minutes. It could have been a guy having a cigarette and drinking a beer. Or it could have been Jon, up to no good. She needed to find out, and went inside the camper.

The agent warming her chair gave it up. Baldini was not present, and she guessed he was in the bathroom, checking himself out in the mirror. The stupid bastard had no idea how close she'd come to kicking out his front teeth.

"Anything going on?" she asked.

"Nothing much," the seat warmer said. "I need more coffee. Want some?"

"No, but thanks for asking."

The agent went into the kitchen in the back of the camper. Now alone, she replayed the tape of the car turning down RichJo Lane. Freezing the frame, she memorized the letters and numbers on the license plate. Then, she made a call. The FBI was wired into the DMV databases in every state, and could run down license plates at warp speed.

Within a minute she had her answer. The vehicle belonged to National Car Rental. The bureau had agreements with the rental car companies, and she made a second call. This time, it took a little longer for her to get an answer.

The car was a 2018 Ford Fusion, and had been rented out of the Tampa International location earlier in the evening. The renter's name was Jon Lancaster.

PART FOUR

Smoke and Mirrors

CHAPTER 43

If Lancaster had learned anything during his time on the police force, it was that the world was a better place with certain people dead.

It was true. Some people had evil in their hearts, and the harm they wreaked upon society was incalculable. Lost lives, shattered families, psychological scars that never healed—their mark on the world a bloodied footprint.

Dexter Hudson was such a person. In the short time he'd been out of prison, he'd murdered two people and orchestrated the kidnappings of fourteen more. Sending him back to prison wouldn't change him—he'd just find new ways to cause harm. The only way to stop a person like Dexter was to remove him from this earth.

If he had one regret, it was that he wouldn't be the one to do it.

- - -

Sleep wasn't an option. That would come later, when the mission was over.

He dropped the rental off and retrieved his car from short-term parking. Back at his hotel, he showered and put on fresh clothes. Then, he drank a cup of coffee and thought about how he was going to handle

Daniels when she found out what he'd done. She wasn't going to be happy with him, and he told himself she'd have to get over it.

He drove to Tampa Road and headed west, then headed south on Alternate US 19, and pulled off into a fast-food joint so he was directly situated between the Ozona marina and RichJo Lane in Palm Harbor. He didn't want to be accidentally spotted by the FBI, and he parked on the side of the building. It was three a.m., and the streets were bare.

He opened the Arlo app on his cell phone. Arlo was a security company whose products could be purchased in any Best Buy or off the internet, a supply of which he kept in the trunk of his car. Their gadgets weren't expensive, which was part of their appeal. Many times, he'd left them behind after a job, as he was planning to do now.

A few hours ago, he'd gone to Earl's BBQ, and mounted four wireless security cameras to the gutters. Each camera had a crystal-clear picture, and allowed him to monitor the parking lot, as well as the road that led to the restaurant. No one was going to come onto that property without him seeing it. The system also had audio, and he now listened to the noisy frogs and crickets that lived in the bushes by the restaurant.

There was a drawback. The cameras had to be connected to a router to send their signal to the cloud. To solve that problem, he'd placed a Wi-Fi hotspot into an oak tree. Leaving the hotspot behind was a risk, since he paid a monthly fee to use it, and it could be traced back to him. Hopefully, the FBI wouldn't do any climbing after the bust.

He switched apps, and stared at the purple dot. It was still out in the gulf. Dexter and the broker had spent a night on the boat. When the sun came up, they'd return to land, and drive down to Earl's to pay off the gang. Once that happened, he'd put his plan into motion, and put Dexter out of his misery.

A tapping sound awakened her. Early-morning sunlight streamed through the camper window, and Daniels hopped out of bed, fearing she'd overslept. Opening the door, she found Baldini on the other side.

"What's up?" she asked.

"The purple dot is moving. Dexter is coming ashore," he said.

"Has there been any activity outside the BBQ joint?"

"No, it's been quiet."

"Give me a minute."

Sixty seconds later, she came out of the bedroom, and went straight to the bank of computers where the other agents had gathered. Each screen showed a map of the gulf with the purple dot moving in a southeasterly direction. The dot came to shore, and stopped at a spot on the map that said Ozona. Dexter and the broker were about to tie up at the marina that she'd visited the day before. She considered sending a team to arrest them as they disembarked, but decided it was a bad idea. If Dexter alerted his gang with his cell phone, they'd vanish in the wind.

She couldn't let anyone escape. It was her moral duty to bust every member of the gang, and to put them away. Men who trafficked were just as bad as murderers, and ruined just as many lives. The dot did not stay long at the marina, and soon was traveling north on Alternate US 19, the two men now in a car.

"They're going to be here soon," she said. "If they don't turn down RichJo Lane, we'll have to run them down."

"We're prepared for that," Baldini said.

Baldini was keeping his distance. He would be nice to her from now on, but would he change? In her experience, guys like him never learned their lesson.

She went outside, and stood in the camper's shadow, where she had a clear view of Alternate US 19, and could see every vehicle driving past. Baldini soon joined her. In his hand was a pack of smokes. He banged two out, and gave her one.

"Stick this in your mouth," he said.

"No thanks," she said.

"People come outside to smoke cigarettes. It will make you look normal."

"I don't look normal?"

"Come on, you know what I mean."

He was playing nice, and she let him light her cigarette. A black pickup came into view, slowed, and put its blinker on. It had two passengers, both male. As it turned down RichJo Lane, she spotted the driver. Pushing fifty, with a droopy mustache and sideburns. Dexter and the broker had arrived.

"They're here," she said.

"I think we should nail them," he said. "Just to be safe."

"We need to wait. His friends will be arriving soon."

"How can you be so certain his friends will come?"

A deafening roar interrupted her thoughts. A pair of Harleys driven by two guys decked out in black leather came down Alternate US 19 and turned down RichJo Lane. They were immediately followed by a line of cars and another motorbike, all of which made the turn. She gave Baldini a look.

"Need any more convincing?" she asked.

"You were right. Sorry," he said.

"Let's go put our body armor on, shall we?"

Fifteen minutes earlier, Lancaster had gotten a call from Trent.

"We've got some activity," Trent said. "There's a dinghy tied up to the boat with the victims. Two men just got on, and are heading north toward the marina."

"Did you get a look at them?" he asked.

"You bet. The first guy was dressed all in black. His buddy was Hispanic, and wore shades and a lot of gold jewelry. He looked like a pimp."

Dexter and the broker were heading to shore. It was time to put his plan into action, and he said, "Is your team ready to board the boat, and rescue the victims?"

"We're all suited up. Just say when."

"When."

"Gotcha. Just to reconfirm, if one of these jokers gives us trouble, you want us to dispose of him, correct?"

"That's right. My only regret is that I won't be there to see you do it."

"Well put. I'll fill you in on the details later."

The line went dead. He put the phone away, and stared at the oncoming traffic. Rush hour was underway, and traffic was picking up. A black pickup appeared. It was moving slow, the driver's window rolled down. Dexter was at the wheel, talking with the broker in the passenger seat. The vehicle was moving so slow that he could have run them down, and put a bullet in Dexter's head.

He fought off the urge, and watched them pass.

The pickup was followed by two Harleys, their drivers a pair of mean-looking hombres. A stream of cars then followed. Most were commuters, as evidenced by the Starbucks cups in their hands. But several drivers didn't fit that profile, and wore the chiseled features of men who'd spent a portion of their lives behind bars. A lone Harley brought up the rear, the driver's hair blowing in the breeze.

The meeting at Earl's was about to go down.

He opened the Arlo app on his cell phone. The four surveillance cameras were recording, and he watched Dexter and the broker pull in. The broker grabbed a briefcase off the back seat before following Dexter inside.

The Harleys appeared, and parked by the front door. The drivers hopped off their bikes, and also headed inside. Eleven cars followed, and their drivers shuffled into the building. Finally, the last Harley appeared.

Three Harleys and eleven cars equaled fourteen vehicles. There were fourteen victims including Rachel Baye and the stripper Lexi, and he realized that each of the kidnappers was accounted for, except for his brother, Logan, who couldn't be there to claim his money.

He switched feeds. One of the cameras had a clear shot of the road outside the restaurant. Soon, the FBI would drive their armored vehicles down that road, and make the bust. It would be a military-style operation, and every agent involved would have sweaty palms. He'd worked with the FBI before, and seen how they reacted to high-stress situations. They were not people you wanted to provoke. When backed into a corner, they had no reservations about opening fire on their suspects.

Predictable behavior was easily manipulated, and he leaned back in his seat to wait.

CHAPTER 44

The last time Daniels had ridden inside an armored vehicle was during a hostage rescue at Hogan's Alley, a fake town inside of Quantico. The FBI used the town, built by Hollywood set designers, to train agents in a variety of law enforcement techniques, including simulated rescues.

That was years ago, and she'd forgotten how hot the interiors were. There were five other agents crammed inside. Each wore a bulletproof vest and helmet, and carried an assault rifle. Like her, sweat poured off their bodies.

They braked, and she stuck her face to the bulletproof glass. The second armored vehicle had stopped to allow the agents inside to jump out, and bang on the front doors of the homes on RichJo Lane. They were clearing the neighborhood in case the Outlaws decided to shoot it out.

Homeowners emerged and fled down the street, clutching pets to their chests. When the last person had been evacuated, her vehicle resumed moving ahead.

Reaching Earl's, the driver blocked the entrance. She and her team got out, as did Baldini's team, and everyone took up positions behind the vehicles. Two sharpshooters scurried into the parking lot, and also took up positions.

It had been agreed that Baldini would use a bullhorn to tell the Outlaws they were under arrest, and to come outside with their hands in the air. When the announcement did not happen, she wondered if the bullhorn was malfunctioning.

To her surprise, the bullhorn was passed to her.

"What's going on?" she asked.

"Special Agent Baldini lost his voice," the agent beside her said.

"You're kidding me."

"Afraid not," the agent said.

Loss of motor skills was a result of panicking, and she wondered if Baldini had ever participated in a hostage rescue before. He was big on the talk, but he couldn't walk the walk. She turned the bullhorn on, and raised it to her lips.

"This is Special Agent Daniels with the FBI. You are under arrest. I am ordering you to come out single file, with your arms in the air." She paused, and saw a face in a window. She'd gotten their attention and continued. "You can make this hard, or you can make this easy. It's up to you."

She lowered the bullhorn to her side. The restaurant's front door swung open, and a large man all in black came out, and did a quick appraisal of the situation. He slipped back inside, and the door closed behind him.

"Who was that guy?" the agent beside her asked.

"Dexter Hudson, the ringleader."

"What do you think he's doing?"

"He's talking it over with his mates. He knows that running is futile, and so is shooting it out. He's going to convince them to surrender."

"You think so?"

"Yes. I've seen it before. Just give him a minute."

Time went fast when you were having fun, and it crawled when you weren't. Daniels counted the seconds on her watch, and when a minute had slipped away, she raised the bullhorn. "Time's up. Either come out, or we're coming in."

The door opened, and Dexter emerged holding his hands in the air. He appeared bemused by his predicament.

"What seems to be the problem here?" he said in a loud voice.

"You and your friends are under arrest," Daniels said through the bullhorn.

"Arrest? We're having breakfast, for Christ's sake. And this is private property. You and your friends are trespassing. Please leave."

"Keep your hands where I can see them, and start walking toward me."

He stubbornly shook his head. "I think you've got the wrong address, ma'am."

"I don't think so. Is your name Dexter Hudson?"

The bemused look vanished. "What if it is?"

"Then I have the right address. Start walking."

"Not until I know what the charges are."

"Kidnapping and human trafficking, fourteen counts, and two counts of murder. And violating the terms of your parole. Is that enough for you?"

The party was over, and his shoulders sagged.

"Promise you won't shoot me, or my friends," he said, sounding scared.

"You have my word. Just don't do anything stupid."

"I wouldn't dream of it."

Before Dexter could take his first step, there was a loud pop that sounded like a firecracker going off, followed by three more pops in rapid succession. Dexter doubled at the waist, then lifted his head, his eyes filled with rage.

"You fucking bitch!" he shouted.

Daniels froze. None of the agents had let off a round.

"Wait!" she said.

It was too late. Dexter dropped his hands and pulled up the front of his shirt. He drew a pistol with lightning speed, and got off a round. The bullet hit the roof of the armored vehicle Daniels was standing behind, the sound echoing around them.

The snipers cut Dexter down. The front of his shirt became filled with holes, and he fell backward through the open door and disappeared. The restaurant's front windows were broken out by the men inside, who'd decided to shoot it out.

Then all hell broke loose.

CHAPTER 45

Still in his car, Lancaster watched the shootout on his cell phone. It wasn't as good as being there, but it was close enough.

By jacking up the audio, he was able to hear the bullets tear into the restaurant, and rip apart the men inside. Because his driver's window was down, he could also hear the gunfight on a slight delay. It was like listening to stereo.

He had never done victory dances as a soldier or a cop, but he felt like doing one now. The world was a safer place with these men gone, and he was happy to have been a part of it. Because the surveillance cameras were pointed at the street, he could see Beth and the other FBI agents, and it did not appear they had suffered any casualties.

He alternated watching the four feeds on his phone. One by one, the FBI's bullets blew the cameras out, until he was down to a single feed. The camera was on a gutter on the south side of the restaurant, facing slightly down.

He saw smoke. At first, he didn't know where it was coming from. Then it dawned on him that the restaurant had caught on fire.

The sound of bullets diminished, until there were none. The gutter fell off the side of the building, and the feed went dark.

- - -

The fire engines came from the south and blew past him. He shut his eyes and imagined the burning restaurant filled with corpses. The only piece of evidence he was worried about was the hotspot in the tree. Even if an investigator discovered the device, it would be difficult to piece together what he'd done.

Trent called him ten minutes later.

"Mission accomplished."

"Any casualties?"

"No, sir. We caught them eating breakfast. They never heard us board."

"How many were there?"

"Four."

"Where did you leave them?"

"We tied them up to four fishing chairs on the stern. One of my guys stuffed bread in their shirt pockets. When we left, the gulls were harassing them."

It was a wonderful image, and he savored it.

"What about the victims? What condition are they in?" he asked.

"They were locked in their rooms down below. We spoke to them through the doors, and they sounded okay. I considered letting them out, but I was afraid they'd beat their captors to death with frying pans, and I didn't want that on my hands."

"Got it. Send me a routing number, and I'll wire your payment."

"I'll do that. It's been nice doing business with you."

"Same here."

- - -

He called Gamble while driving to the marina.

"I'm on another line. Let me call you right back," she answered.

"Hang up on them," he said. "You need to get in your car, and drive over to the marina in Ozona. There's a restaurant next door called

Ozona Blue. Park in their lot instead of the marina's. And bring a cameraman with you."

"What's going on?"

"I can't tell you that. Just get over here."

"My boss will want to know."

"Tell him you're following up on a hot lead."

"I'm not going to lie to him. You've got to tell me what the deal is."

Gamble had helped him move the investigation forward, and he considered her an asset. But she worked in a newsroom, and he didn't want to risk having her blurt out what he told her, and her boss deciding to send a more seasoned reporter. He needed to control the narrative, and to do that, he needed to control her.

"Never mind. I'll call my friend at CNN. Have a nice day."

He ended the call. He didn't have a friend at CNN, or any other media outlet. He was bluffing, and thirty seconds later, it paid off when Gamble called him back.

"I'm on my way, and I've got a cameraman with me," she said.

"What did you tell your boss?"

"False alarm. He's out of the office, so I didn't have to deal with him."

"Great. Remember, park by the restaurant, not the marina."

"I heard you the first time," she said.

- - -

Chuck was in his office doing paperwork when Lancaster arrived at the marina. He pulled a handful of hundred-dollar bills out of his wallet, and dropped them on the desk. Chuck fanned the money out and silently counted it.

"This must be my lucky day," he said.

"I need to rent two boats, and two people to captain them," Lancaster said.

"When?"

"Right now. I've got two parties arriving in the next thirty minutes, so the boats need to be ready. Can you make that happen?"

"Not so fast. Is that FBI agent lady that I took out yesterday one of those parties?"

"She is. Is that a problem?"

"Is there going to be trouble? Like, people shooting guns? I don't want to get myself or one of my people caught in a firefight."

"The suspects have been apprehended, and are waiting to be picked up. No one will be put in harm's way. You have my word."

Lancaster didn't have a pretty face, but he did have an honest one. Chuck gave him a hard look, then stuck out his hand.

"You have yourself a deal," he said.

- - -

Lancaster stood by his car to wait for Gamble. He'd muted his phone before going into Chuck's office, and saw that Beth had called him and also sent a text.

Call me! her text read.

If he called Beth, it would get ugly, and he wasn't ready to deal with her rage just yet, so he called Gamble instead.

"How close are you?" he asked.

"Google Maps is saying that I'm three minutes away," she said. "I just got a news flash on my phone. There was a shootout in Palm Harbor earlier, and a whole bunch of people are dead. Did you have something to do with that?"

"Not me," he lied.

Gamble sent gravel into the air as she pulled into the lot, and parked. As her cameraman pulled his equipment out of the trunk, Gamble came over to where Lancaster stood. Every conversation they'd had began with her asking a question. That was about to change.

"You are about to get the greatest story of your life," Lancaster said. "I've located the kidnapping victims, and they're all safe. They're being held hostage on a fishing boat out in the gulf. Very soon, a team of FBI agents will rescue them, and you and your cameraman will be there to capture it. Does that sound good to you?"

"How did you orchestrate this?" Gamble blurted out.

He put his finger to his lips. "You don't get to ask questions, at least not to me. But you can talk to the FBI later. They busted this wide open, and deserve the credit."

"Why do I feel like I'm being played?"

"Go wait in the restaurant. When the time is right, I'll come in and get you. I've already arranged for a boat to take you out, so you can film while the rescue goes down."

"Sounds like you've thought of everything. Let's get some coffee, Dylan."

After they were gone, he called Beth.

"I'm going to kill you," the FBI agent said.

CHAPTER 46

Daniels shook with anger. Jon had set them up, and she was ready to throw a pair of handcuffs on him, and march him off to the nearest jail.

Three members of her team shared the car. Their clothes smelled of smoke, and their hair was filled with particles of soot. A shift in wind had sent smoke from the fire over them, and made a bad situation even worse.

She was going to catch hell for leaving the scene. EMS was still pulling bodies out of the smoldering rubble, and it was her job to supervise the collection of evidence. Instead, she'd left Baldini in charge, and she hoped that he didn't screw it up.

She pulled into the marina and parked by the restaurant. Jon was nowhere to be seen, and that enraged her even more. She got out, as did her team.

"Over here," a voice called.

Jon was in the marina, standing at the end of a long dock. She told her team to stay put, then hurried out of the parking lot and into the marina. As she marched down the dock, her fingers instinctively brushed the pair of cuffs on her belt.

"I thought you were my friend," she said.

"I am your friend." Then he added, "And I always will be."

"Friends don't set up friends."

"What are you talking about?"

From her purse she removed the blasting cap she'd found near the restaurant. Made of aluminum and tube shaped, it had a six-inch wire tail encased in plastic along with a tiny transmitter. She held the device in front of his face, and waited for a reaction. When none was forthcoming, she exploded.

"Don't you dare tell me that you don't know what this is," she said.

"I don't know what it is," he said.

"Stop playing games."

"I'm not."

"Have it your way. It's a blasting cap with a wireless detonator. I thought that these had a limited range, but obviously I was wrong. Did one of your SEAL buddies turn you on to it?" He didn't respond, so she continued. "You planted five blasting caps at the restaurant. Four of them went off, and tricked Dexter into thinking he was being shot at, so he drew on us. Admit it, Jon."

"I have no idea how those blasting caps got there," he said.

"There were surveillance cameras attached to the gutters that weren't there yesterday," she said accusingly. "You were nearby, watching the whole thing, and when the time was right, you detonated the caps. You wanted to pay Dexter back, and got the FBI to be your proxy."

"Not me."

"Go ahead and play dumb. It won't get you anywhere."

"Were any of your agents hurt?"

"We're fine, no thanks to you. The bikers died, and so did the broker."

"How about Dexter?"

"Dexter cashed in his chips. Are you going to come clean, or not?"

He shook his head.

"I've had some experience with blasting caps," she said. "You buy them in bulk. When I search that tricked-up vehicle of yours, am I going to find more of these? Because if I do, I'm going to arrest you."

He let out a deep breath. She had him dead to rights.

"May I see that?" he asked.

Without thinking, she handed him the cap. He gave it a heave, and it flew through the air and landed in the water, never to be seen again.

"God damn you! You're under arrest. Put your hands out."

She reached for her cuffs. He again shook his head.

"Don't you dare resist," she said.

"Don't you want to rescue the victims? Or should we let Baldini do that?" he said.

The words were slow to sink in.

"You found them?" He nodded, and she said, "Where?"

He pulled up a photo on his cell phone and showed her. "They're being held on this fishing boat a few miles north of here, near the tip of Honeymoon Island. Their captors are tied up, and won't give you any problems. I rented a motorboat to take you there."

"You rented me a boat?"

"And a captain. All you have to do is board, and free them."

It was all too much, and she struggled for a response.

"You need to hurry before they untie themselves," he said.

She ran back to the restaurant, and grabbed her crew. Moments later, they boarded the rented motorboat. As it pulled away from the dock, Jon gave a little wave, and it was all she could do not to shake her fist at him.

- - -

Lancaster found Gamble and Dylan having coffee inside the restaurant. He told them to settle their tab, and meet him at the dock.

The second rented boat was being handled by Chuck. Dylan passed his video camera to the captain, and then boarded. Gamble hadn't spoken a word, and was eyeing him coolly. Instead of boarding, she made

Lancaster follow her down the dock, so that Dylan and Chuck would not be able to hear what she was about to say.

"You haven't told me what you want," she said.

"You know what I want," he said. "I want you to kill the piece about me."

"But it's the heart of my story."

"No, it's not."

"Really? Then what is?"

"The FBI agent running the show is the heart of your story. Her name is Special Agent Elizabeth Daniels. She's devoted her life to saving victims of human trafficking, and is a real hero. Focus your story on her, not me. You won't regret it."

"Why do you say that?"

"Because this story will be picked up by every paper in the country. Don't you want to get your ticket punched, and go to work for a big newspaper in New York or Washington? Or would you rather stay in Tampa, covering city council meetings?"

"Who told you that I wanted to move?"

"A little bird. Now, do we have a deal, or not?"

She bit her lower lip. "You're a sneaky bastard."

"Is that a yes?"

"I'll have to meet her first."

"Remember, her name is Elizabeth Daniels. If you do a search on Google, you'll find a lot of great stories about her."

"I just might do that."

He watched them depart on Chuck's boat. He had given her the sales pitch, but it would take meeting Beth to seal the deal. Beth was a force of nature, and hopefully Gamble would recognize this, and shift the focus of her story.

He went to the restaurant and ordered breakfast while sitting at an outside table overlooking the water. The mission had gone as well as he could have expected. Dexter and company were dead, and the women on the boat would soon be free. His scrambled eggs and bacon came. He tried to eat, but realized his appetite had faded, and he balled up his napkin and tossed it on his plate. Every mission had collateral damage, and this one was no different. He'd harmed his relationship with Beth, and he didn't know if it could be repaired. He'd manipulated her into doing his bidding, and that was wrong. He'd broken their trust, and without trust, there was nothing.

His waiter asked if his food was okay. He made a lame excuse about having an upset stomach, and accepted a refill of his coffee. As he drank, he realized that this wasn't going to be easy. He'd fallen for Beth, and losing her would be hard.

He told himself that he'd get over it. Not right away, but he would. They shared a passion for their work, but it was also their work that separated them. Beth believed in following a strict set of rules, even when those rules were being bent by the people she was trying to apprehend. In that regard, she was almost noble.

He was different that way. He didn't believe in following rules when innocent lives were at stake, and his opponents were openly skirting the law. Rules were the enemy in those situations, and often led to the worst possible outcomes.

These feelings hadn't come from being a cop, or from his time in the military. They dated back to when he was a teenager, after he'd read a lengthy newspaper article about the man who'd tried to kidnap him, Ottis Toole. The article had called Toole one of the most proficient serial killers who'd ever lived. Along with killing Adam Walsh, Toole and his friend Henry Lee Lucas had murdered two hundred people across the Southeast, and had managed to escape detection by jumping in their car and hauling ass each time they took another life.

The article also said that Toole was a habitual offender, and no stranger to the police. Dozens of law enforcement officers had dealt with him, and considered him a risk. Yet they hadn't been able to stop Toole's killing spree.

That had gotten him thinking. What if one of those cops had manufactured a reason to pull Toole over, and search his car? Toole was a trophy hunter, and there was a good chance the cop would have found a piece of a victim's clothing or jewelry. Then the cop could have arrested Toole, and a lot of lives would have been saved.

Cops weren't supposed to do stuff like that. Even as a teenager he'd known that. But the way he saw it, if a cop knew a person was causing harm, the cop needed to find a way to stop it. By doing nothing, the evil only grew.

CHAPTER 47

The day after the shootout and rescue at sea, Lancaster drank cold beer on the sprawling back porch of the Palm Pavilion on Clearwater Beach, content to soak up the sun and chill.

Keeping tabs on Beth wasn't hard. Every few hours he went inside to the bar, parked himself in front of a TV, and persuaded the bartender to turn on the local news. He watched a dramatic video of the victims being escorted off the fishing boat a dozen times, and later, one of Skye Tanner being tearfully reunited with her mother. Beth was in each video, the cameraman capturing her in nearly every frame.

He also bought a copy of the paper, and read Gamble's article. She'd taken his advice and painted the FBI as heroes who'd risked their lives to free the victims. It wasn't true, but that didn't matter. It was a good read with a happy ending, and there weren't a lot of those kind of stories these days.

Gamble had written a sidebar about Beth, and talked about her career. He'd been dealing with Hollywood for a while, and he knew what the folks on the Left Coast liked. Very soon, Beth would be hearing from a studio wanting to buy her life story, and he wondered if she'd take the bait. Knowing her, she'd probably say no.

In the afternoon, he called Echo to hear about her new life in Tennessee. She sounded happy, and said that life on the farm was agreeing with her. She'd seen the news about the shootout at Earl's, and asked him if Dexter had perished. When he said yes, she breathed a sigh of relief into the phone.

He also texted Gar, to make sure the FBI had made good on their promise to put the programmer and his girlfriend in witness protection. Gar responded that they were in a new location, and while it wasn't as warm as Tampa, it was much safer.

On his second day, while he ate conch fritters at the bar, the show on the TV was interrupted by a live news conference featuring Florida's governor. The governor was a rich guy who dressed like Joe Sixpack whenever he was in front of the cameras, and he stood at a podium flanked by a wall of men and women wearing navy FBI windbreakers. The agents included Beth, Baldini, and their respective teams. They were basking in the glow of a job well done, and smiled for the cameras like they were getting their yearbook pictures taken. The governor's praise ran across the screen in closed captions, and included words like *true heroes* and *America's finest.*

When the governor was finished, he walked the line, and pumped each agent's hand. Reaching Beth, he stopped and hugged her. He was a foot taller and had to lean way down. It was awkward as hell, but he did it anyway. Beth had saved the day, and the other agents broke into a round of applause.

Lancaster resumed eating. He'd gotten the outcome that he'd wanted, yet it didn't erase the feeling that he'd lost the war. He hadn't spoken with Beth since the confrontation at the marina, nor had she tried to contact him. The silence had been deafening.

But that didn't mean he was giving up on their relationship. To give up was to fail before you ever tried, and Beth was too important to him to do that. As the Irish poet Samuel Beckett once said: *Ever tried. Ever failed. No matter. Try again. Fail again. Fail better.* He spent twenty minutes composing a text message that was only a few sentences long.

Telling her how proud of her he was, and happy for her team. He sent it, then slipped his cell phone into his pocket, and did not look at it again for an hour.

No response.

That hurt. Even an emoji of a hand flipping him the bird would have been better than nothing. He told himself that she would get back to him later, when she had a few minutes to herself.

The hours slipped by. He hung around for the sunset before returning to his hotel. While he packed, he imagined how Beth was handling the aftermath of her triumph. She could have celebrated with her team, only that wasn't like her. Beth wasn't a party person, and would have preferred a quiet dinner, and a chance to reflect.

But with who? She rarely socialized with other agents, and he didn't see her going out with Baldini or her team. If she'd been back home, she would have gotten together with one of her girlfriends. Instead, she would settle for eating takeout at her hotel.

She deserved a victory meal. She never said no to sushi, and a search on the internet turned up a joint called Sushi Alive. The reviews were decent, and it wasn't terribly far. He called and made a reservation for two.

Then he sent her a text and suggested they have dinner. His message included a link to the restaurant's website. He waited fifteen minutes but got no response. A number of reasons came to mind. Maybe her cell phone was turned off, or the battery had run out of juice. Or maybe she never wanted to speak with him again. That was certainly a possibility, and it was starting to feel like the end.

He went downstairs and checked out. Outside in his car, he checked his phone again, and saw that she hadn't texted him back. Whether she liked it or not, the investigation had changed her life. The FBI needed all the heroes they could get, and there were more promotions in store, her career's trajectory ascending like a rocket. Who could she talk to about this but him? No one. Nobody else would ever know the truth. It was their secret, and theirs alone.

Pulling out of the lot, he sent her another text that said, My treat.

A block from the hotel, his cell phone vibrated. He'd placed it facedown on his leg, not wanting the distraction as he drove. Turning it over, he smiled.

You're on, her message read.

AUTHOR'S NOTE

The day before Ottis Toole abducted Adam Walsh, he attempted to abduct another child at a shopping mall in South Florida. The details of that failed abduction have been altered for this story.

ABOUT THE AUTHOR

Photo © 2007 Robert Allen Sergeant

James Swain is the national bestselling author of more than twenty mystery novels and has worked as a magazine editor, a screenwriter, and a novelist. His books have been translated into a dozen languages and have been selected as Mysteries of the Year by *Publishers Weekly* and *Kirkus Reviews*. The author of *The King Tides*, the first novel in the Lancaster & Daniels series, Swain has been nominated for four Barry Awards, has received a Florida Book Award for fiction, and was awarded France's prestigious Prix Calibre .38 for Best American Crime Writing. When he isn't writing, he enjoys performing close-up magic. Visit him at www.jamesswain.com.